Our

Wendy

Kathryn Rider

Emerson Ormond

Dedicated to Laura Rider,
who is waiting up in Neverland for us.

CONTENTS

Prologue

"You're teasing me!" she cried, throwing a playful punch to my arm with a mischievous gleam in her eye. I smiled back, spreading my hands as if I were helpless to the situation.

"Fine, *fine*. So it wasn't a trail of colored leaves, birds, or the fact that you forgot what a path looks like. And we've already listed out the talking shrew…" I let my voice trail off, checking off every option with a count of my fingers as she folded her arms and rolled her eyes in mock frustration.

"And you're sure your nose wasn't stuck in a book?"

"Peter!"

"Okay, okay!" I laughed, throwing my hands up as she couldn't help but giggle. I shook my head with a smile, enjoying the moment but wanting desperately to know the truth. "Then what did bring you here? I mean, you don't just wander *ten miles* by mistake."

She drifted her gaze to the trees with humorous eyes. "I don't know, I… I guess I just wanted something new." She sat on her hands and rolled her shoulders forward, then stood up, admiring our surroundings with a deep breath of fresh air.

And with the distant squeak of Albie's call back at camp, she smiled and was gone.

I watched her go, still unable to comprehend what she had meant. Something new? It was hard, quite impossible actually, for me to fathom that all this had come from her wanting *something new*. She had changed my life, all of our lives, completely twisted around my world, and took me down a path I had never thought I'd go down.

But if I had known the half of it, what had changed so far would seem oh so little.

If only I had known.

And yet, I didn't know. I had no clue what was next as I stood, fingering my bed of hair smooth and peering through the trees with a smile on my lips. The sky was a bright blue, a white sun shining on every corner, and the only clouds were milky and tumid. The trees bared natural green leaves, which contrasted with the colors of the changed leaves on the ground, holding the hidden animals who were enjoying the last of summer.

Everything was perfect. This forest, the boys, her, me. I was on top of my own world, and there wasn't a soul in the sphere left to bring me down.

Not that I could think of, at least.

But that, that unparalleled ending, was what made it so easy to forget that dark and stormy nights do come most often when things are so seemingly *perfect*.

And it most certainly was not an ending.

Chapter One

Peter

We didn't want her to leave, so we tied her to the tree.

That's how it all began, really, when she came wandering into our part of the woods, searching for something, maybe someone. There was something about her that we had never seen before, the look of compassion in her eyes, this hint that she wanted... more. None of us could shake it, none of us could let her go, so with glances to one another and nods of heads, we made our decision.

She was ours, at least for a little while longer.

...

I pushed past branches into the clearing, leaves crunching loudly under my feet, and looked around with a grin. The round dirt clearing was surrounded by tall trees that reached the evening sky, dim but colorful and peppered with bright stars; it was exactly as I had wanted it, same as always. The ashes of the burned out fire pit in the middle, an old battered couch pushed up against the bark of trunks, set in front of it a wooden coffee table. Hung on sturdy branches were blankets tied with rope that made hammocks, across from them an abandoned burrow we had dug out and turned into a pantry. The dirt floor was scattered with knick-knacks we had picked up over the years, tucked into the corners of each person's "space."

It wasn't much, to some it was nothing. But to me, it was home.

And the boys dispersed around the camp made it just that. Fourteen-year-old Will was carefully placing the kindling in the ash pit to start up another fire. His dirty brown hair was pushed out of his face, smudged with ash and sweat from the fire and a day's work. The ten-year-old twins Oliver and Thomas were playing cards, and Elliot, who was three years older, his blonde hair brown and in desperate need of a bath, was slumped down on the couch in a tired heap. Delighted six-year-old Albie was the first to notice my return. He perked his head up from the book, my book, he was struggling to read, and met my eyes, his round cheeks pushed up from the smile spreading across his face. "Peter you're back!" He jumped up with a cry, turning all the attention towards me.

I shook my head happily, nodding to Elliot, who had immediately risen to assist me with the bags I was carrying. Thanking him, I then got down into a crouched position to ready myself for the big hug Albie was running at me with. He squeezed me tight, and I stood, the little boy in my arms, looking at me with the most animated expression. "Can you read to me, Peter? I'm trying, but it's just so hard, and not at all as exciting as when you read it aloud. Please! I've been very good today!" He hopped down from my grip and turned to Elliot with expecting eyes.

"Haven't I, Elli?"

Elliot nodded.

"See, I told you!"

"I never said I didn't believe you," I laughed. His grin became meek, but his eyes still remained eager for an answer. He looked back to the book on the couch and squeezed my hand expectantly. "Buddy right now I'm starving, and I'm sure the same is with all of you, so let's get supper first, and read tonight."

Albie shook his head solemnly, but his disappointment soon turned to curiosity at the site of the bags I had brought. Thomas and Oliver had abandoned their game and were now pulling out apples, pears, plums, bread, and squash. "I tried to take as much as I could," I told them, "But the village markets were busy today, and I could tell one worker had their eye on me."

Thomas shrugged, looking over the round juicy plum in his palm. "I think you did alright." He snatched up the food and went back to the cards that were laid out in his corner, an action that had everyone suddenly taking their pick of fruit. I waited until they were satisfied, grabbed an apple from the bag and began packing the rest of it away in our pantry burrow. Will was at my side in moments, his plum only half-eaten, an agitated look across his face.

"What's wrong?" I asked, sitting down with my back to a tree and taking a bite out of the apple. He slumped down beside me, a twitch in his eye when he spoke.

"The weather's getting nicer. More tourists are coming through the woods and you know-"

"Will we picked a nice spot," I cut him off, unwilling to hear it again. "The trails aren't even ten miles from here."

"What's ten miles in this forest?" he interjected, wanting me to hear him.

I dropped my gaze to my meal, wondering if it was worth debating. "It's ten miles off the trails that London people won't be willing to walk." He eyed me, skeptical, taking my point into consideration before continuing.

"I know, but what if they find us? There are more people coming through than usual. If they hear or see us, someone could alert social securities, or - or that man-"

I silenced him with a sharp look. "Then we'll pack up and move again. But we can't dwell on things that *may* happen, now can we?"

"No," he muttered, and left my side, returning to the fire he was making. Soon there was a bright sunset spark that turned into a small flickering flame, which grew larger as it caught on to the dead leaves and twigs and eventually the firewood on top. The boys slowly gathered around, finishing their food, and I was handed a book by Albie. It was an old book, the pages yellowed and the ink fading, some torn and others bent, and it smelled of dust and forest. But it was mine. I had had it since I could remember, something I always clung to and still wouldn't let go of.

Peter & Wendy. It was the original tale of Peter Pan, written by James Matthew Barrie, and I thought it to be the truest and most exciting tale of all time.

Albie looked at me with round eyes that lit up from the reflection of the dancing flames. "Are we *really* the lost boys from the book, Peter? Isn't that kinda... impossible?" It was a question I had been asked over a hundred times. I nodded, looking up at the boys around the fire.

Sure, it *was* impossible for us to be the exact boys in the book, for we didn't live in Neverland and had never fought a one-handed crook. But it was something more than that - it was who we were as people, what we had gone through and where we were now. "I'd say we are. I mean look at us - no parents, living in the woods where we have no rules and we never have to grow up, go to school or get jobs and be adults. If there was ever meant to be a real-life version of this tale," I placed my hand on the fragile book, "I believe we are just that. And all it takes is belief. Isn't that right?!" I raised my voice in the last sentence, and it was followed by hollers and whoops from the boys around me. Because just as I did, they all believed what I said was true. We *were* the lost boys, we were always meant to be, and just because we didn't have magic or a pirate with a hook against us didn't mean our story wasn't just as epic.

And that made me, well, our tale's very own Peter Pan.

I opened the book to the bookmarked page and began to read aloud. Everything fell silent, even the crickets and birds seemed to stop chattering to listen contently to the sound of my voice. And as I read, I carried us all into a world that was our own. Some of the boys closed their eyes, others laid down and watched the fire as if imagining the images coming to life inside it. The story had never gotten old, no matter how many times we read it; each time all would fall silent and listen.

That silence was broken, the boys whisked back into reality, when the snapping of twigs and leaves interrupted the scene. Will jumped to his feet, advancing towards the direction of the sound in a cautious manner. "Come out." His voice was icy, making Albie cling to me in fear of what was hiding behind the trees. I squeezed the boy's hand reassuringly and stood.

Seconds after his words, a girl came stumbling out into the clearing, falling to her knees. I peered at her through the dim light of the moon and stars, watching as she got up and dusted herself off. She was wearing a periwinkle knee-length dress with quarter length sleeves that were covered in lace flowers and synched at the waist with a white ribbon. On her feet, she wore black flats that were simple, but charming and elegant in the same way. Her hair was a light chestnut brown, slightly wavy, with pieces from the front pulled back to create a half-up, half-down look. She was pretty, I couldn't help but note as I stared, and I wish it had been brighter at the time, for then I would have noticed the brilliant blue eyes that looked back at all of us.

"I-I'm sorry, I'm lost - I suppose I've been going the wrong way, c-could any of you point me in the direction of the walking trails?" She spoke with a heavy British accent, staring at all of us with an expectant, fearful look. None of us knew how to respond. Not only had this stranger, this captivating, soft-spoken stranger just acknowledged us, but she had found us. It was slowly dawning on us that if we were to tell her where the trails were and she was to find her way back, she could address our whereabouts to anyone she pleased.

No one said a word.

"Please, I-I can't find my way home and it's getting dark and-" She stopped her chattering and took a closer look at all of us, the moon's light now passing over our faces. "You're... dirty... and so thin! You poor things! How long have you boys been out here? Are you lost, too? Where are your homes?" She looked at all of us with such empathy, this sad, motherly look in her eyes, and I couldn't help but shake my head. I, for some reason, couldn't stomach lying to her, and I supposed the truth was going to come out in one way or another, so I figured I may as well tell her.

"No, no. We're not lost. Quite the opposite actually. *This* is home." I spread my arms, gesturing to the space around us. She gaped in disbelief, her expression daunted.

"You must be joking," she breathed, looking around the clearing at the old furniture and makeshift hammocks. I shook my head solemnly, my next words coming out without much thought put into them.

"But it's getting dark, and the trails are miles from here so how about you-"

"Miles?" she interrupted, her eyes growing rounder. "I've been going the wrong way for miles?" Something about her look seemed off to me, like for the most part she was terrified, but a small bit of her, so small it was barely visible, showed a hint of... relief, was it?

"How about you stay with us the night?" I continued, the words fumbling out. The boys turned to me, an excited look in their eyes, and all heads then stared back at her.

The query scared her, and I didn't blame her, for the more time that stood between the question and the silence it now bared, I realized that we could have come across as rather mad. Not knowing if we were going to hurt her, she backed up slowly, stuttering in speech.

"I-I don't think I can... I must b-be getting home, if-if you could just point me in the right direction..."

"No please," Elliot approached her slowly in his usual sweetness, taking her by the arm and starting to pull her back. "It will be light out before you find your way home. We can show you in the morning. Here we have a warm fire and -"

"Let go of me!" she shrieked, yanking her arm out of his grip and stumbling back. Frightened, tired, and not looking where she was going, she tripped over a fallen branch and went flying back, her head hitting the forest floor with a thud. Will and I met eyes for a brief second before running towards her and both kneeling beside the now unconscious girl.

We all stared for a long while before Albie asked the very question we were all asking ourselves. He looked to me, then to her, then back at me with the most hopeful and curious face.

"Peter is she... is she our Wendy?"

Could it be true? Could it have been more than just a coincidence that this kind looking blue-eyed girl wearing a light blue dress had stumbled upon our direction when she could have journeyed any other way in the hundreds of miles of the Kielder forest?

Thomas and Oliver exchanged excited glances. "Yeah, she is Peter! It all makes sense, doesn't it?" Oliver exclaimed.

"What do we do with her?"

"If we leave her here she'll wake up and leave us!"

"How do we make her stay, Peter?"

"Peter?"

Questions aroused as I stared at the girl, who was sleeping soundly on top of the leaves and dirt. She needed to stay, just long enough to at least hear us out. We could make her *want* to stay. But first, first, we needed to make sure she wouldn't run when she woke.

"Will, grab some rope."

Chapter Two

Ever

I rose to the splatters of droplets on my face. Yawning, I rolled my neck around and went to lift my fingers to my cheeks to wipe off the water, when I felt a coarse material scratch back at me, securing my hands to what felt like tree bark. My eyes flew open, and I looked around wildly. Surely enough I was sitting against a tree, my wrists tied around its thin structure with rope. I struggled against the binds hopelessly, lifting my gaze to take in my surroundings. My journey through the woods had not been a dream. The fight, me running off, meeting a group of dirty boys… was all real. I was in the camp I had come across the night before, only it was sprinkling rain now, the fire was out and the boys were slumbering in hammocks draped on branches of trees. They looked so innocent and peaceful sleeping, just a bunch of helpless boys, but I wouldn't let that deter me from escaping.

My breath came in short, staggered masses. Heart pounding, I considered my options. I could scream for help, but that would wake my attackers. No, I wouldn't do that. I needed to figure out how to get out of the ties holding me to the tree. My wrists squirmed around to try to break them, but I couldn't figure out how to undo the knot holding me down. I gasped with effort, growing more and more frustrated with every passing minute that I struggled, and ended up letting out a cry of rage.

"Shhh," came a voice from behind me. My heart started to beat faster as I heard the footsteps approaching. A boy, the one who had first spoken to me the night before, came around the tree and crouched down in front of me. He had short, wildly wavy light brown hair, and a pleasant face, only his cheeks and forehead were smudged with dirt and soot. He was wearing clothes that were ragged and soiled but would have made a nice outfit were they new and clean. He had boots and tan pants, and a worn tunic with a little cloth vest over it that would have been green had he washed it more often. Now it was more of a tainted brown. But nevertheless, I couldn't help but think he was rather handsome, and he would have been more charming had he *not* decided to tie me up.

"What do you want with me?" I huffed, glaring him down. He hesitated, looking a bit… nervous, was it?

"Nothing," he said quickly and quietly, and began to untie my wrists. "I only couldn't have you making the journey back to the trails alone. It's dangerous out there, you know."

My breathing slowed. "Well, you could have just said so!" I exclaimed, trying to sound agitated but ending up seeming overall relieved - which I was. "You didn't have to tie me up."

He bit his lip. "Sorry. I just didn't want you waking up and leaving. Anyways, we best be going. The boys will be up soon and then they'll all want to come," he smiled a bit. "And God knows Albie can't make it two miles."

He made his way across the camp over to a big tree with a little hole dug out before it and grabbed two things from inside: plums. "Here," the boy offered, tossing me one. I grabbed it gingerly and looked it over, my mouth watering. In all the excitement, I had just realized how hungry I was.

The boy strode over to me, leading me out of the camp as he took a bite of the plum. I smiled, taking a bite of mine and looking at him.

"What?"

"Nothing; just a second ago I thought you were going to kill me, and now here you are giving me your food and taking me home."

He nodded. "Sorry about the way we came across last night. The boys and I... we aren't exactly the best at talking to strangers." He held back a prickly bush for me to walk past, and we continued on our way. The forest was beautiful, its trees reaching sky high, birds flying up above, everything so green and lively. But I was more interested in the boy.

"You never told me your name."

"Peter."

"Peter," I repeated softly. "How lovely. So, Peter, you and the boys back at camp, you live in these woods?"

He nodded again. I stared at him, puzzled. "But why? Don't you have to go to school? And how do you get food and water? And where are your parents? Do they live with you here, too?"

He shook his head with a frown. "We don't have parents. And we don't have to go to school. We're lost boys."

I let out a slight chuckle. "Lost boys? As in the ones from the story of Peter Pan."

"Yep." His face remained calm, and my laughter died.

"You're not serious, are you?"

He turned to me like there was no reason for him not to be serious. Like it wasn't at all ridiculous that he thought him and his friends were storybook characters. "You mean, you actually think you're from the fairytale?"

"Not exactly, but we are a version of it, yes." His explanation ended there, and we walked in silence a little while longer. I couldn't think of the right words to say. He was joking, he had to be.

"And this is Neverland?" I said with a laugh, all in total disbelief. He turned to me, a twinkle in his eye, and stretched his hand through a bush of vines in the way.

"That's for you to decide for yourself." He pushed back the vines, revealing the most spectacular sight. A lake, shimmering the purest blue, stretched for miles, its waters splashing and playing in the sun. Surrounding it on all sides were deep green trees, land that formed little peninsulas around it, their banks full of the brightest sands. I stepped out through the vine wall and found myself along the bank, sand underneath my feet. A little ways down was an island in the middle of the lake, itself full of trees, birds and all things alive. The songs of the creatures filled the air, the sun shone down on the blue water, warming the earth and filling me from head to toe with delight.

"It's... it's magnificent," I breathed, looking around in awe, and then back at a smiling Peter. "I've never seen such a beautiful place in all my life." I understood then, why he could think this was Neverland, why he would want to live in such alluring woods. Suddenly I felt my eyes close and my instincts take over. No. I could not let myself fall into his delusions.

I opened my eyes and faced Peter, who was looking out to the waters. "So you really believe that you are a lost boy living in Neverland."

He laughed. "Of course not." And I laughed too. I laughed with relief and the bliss that my new acquaintance was not completely loony. And then came his explanation.

"I believe that fate brought us together, that every boy back at camp was lost until we found each other. I believe that there was a reason someone gave me this book when I was young, and that I found this forest and all of its beauty. There is a reason that every day we play out our lives as if we were the people in the book, and that makes us them. *Fate* makes us them. And there was definitely a reason that fate sent a pretty girl in a blue dress to us."

Pretty?

"Okay," I swallowed. "So you believe you're a lost boy by fate? I'm sorry if that is difficult to fully comprehend, Peter-" I stopped dead in my tracks. "Peter. Peter as in… no, no that cannot be your real name." We met eyes and curiosity got the best of me. "Is it?"

The ghost of a grin appeared on his face. "It may be, and then again it may not be. But it's what they call me and it's what I call myself."

I shook my head at the loss for words. His smile crept back into my thoughts, and I cocked my head slightly. "You're always playing games, aren't you?"

He winked. "Well, we are lost boys, Darling."

"My name is Ever," I snapped back, suddenly revolted by his word choice.

"Are you sure 'bout that?" he cocked an eyebrow and grinned.

"Um, yes," I replied, annoyed. "I think I know my own-" and then I understood, remembering him calling me *"a pretty girl in a blue dress."* When he called me darling, he didn't mean in that way... he was trying to hint at it the whole time.

"Wait, you don't think that I'm... that I'm..." I stuttered.

"I want to hear you say it," he simpered, confirming my suspicions. I gulped.

"You think I-I'm Wendy Darling. Like, in the fairy tale."

"No, I think you're the Wendy Darling of our story. Our Wendy."

"That's insane," I breathed. "No, no..." I took a step back. "You're mad."

"Just listen to me a second -"

I threw my hands up. "No. I'm leaving. You're not Peter Pan, and those boys back there may be lost, but they are *not* the lost boys. I'm going home!"

"Fine," he replied. "I get it. This might sound mad, Wendy-"

"Don't call me that!"

"Ever... sorry. Go home, if you must. But I'm starting to get the feeling that home isn't really all you've hoped for." I wheeled around on my heel, glaring at him. But he met my eyes with such sincere compassion, my gaze faltered.

"Y-you're wrong. I love my home, just as it is." I realized that I was telling myself that just as much as I was telling him. I think he realized it, too. I waited for him to say something, but he didn't. He just stared at me with expecting eyes, wanting me to tell him the truth. Aggravated, I turned back around and started to storm off.

"We found Albie, starved and alone on the streets when he was three." I froze. "His lips were stained with the dirt he had eaten because he was so hungry. He cried for nights on end because his stomach hurt so terribly. Elliot grew up in a run-down orphanage where he got little food and care. The twins, Thomas and Oliver, almost died in a fire that killed their parents when they were eight. Will's father abused his mother and she took it out on him. Don't you see, we are lost boys. I try to do what I can for them, but I can't give them everything they need. They need a mother, Ever. They need a Wendy."

I clenched my jaw, trying not to think about his words. Didn't he care about what happened to me? I couldn't stay in these woods, worry my mother like that. And it was insane, completely twisted, to *tie a girl up,* kidnapping her. He was being selfish, wasn't he? I shook my head, turning around and blinking the tears out of my eyes. "I can't stay here, Peter."

I started to walk away when I heard him mumble under his breath, "I was afraid you might say that."

Suddenly, a searing pain shot through my head, and the world went black.

Chapter Three

Peter

"Are you sure about this Peter?" Elliot questioned, his face scrunching. "Maybe you should have just let her go." I shut him down with a warning look, my focus quickly reverting to the passed out girl, once again tied to the tree.

"Believe me, soon she will come to like it here and will thank me for making her stay," I told them all, but as the words came out they seemed just as cruel and self-centered as the current situation. Honestly, who kidnaps an innocent girl and claims they're doing it for her own favor?

Nevertheless, I stuck with my word and told the boys to prepare supper. Will had caught a salmon and was working with the kindling Elliot had collected to make a fire. We would have fish and cooked squash for dinner. The boys scattered, and I sat down with a sigh beside the sleeping girl. Her hair had fallen over her face and was now flying up with each peaceful breath and landing back on her cheek. I tucked it back behind her ear, speaking softly. "I'm trying to do the right thing… for you, for them. You'll like it here, just give us a chance.

Give *me* a chance." I waited, as if expecting an answer, then slowly rose

to my feet. She would wake up by the time supper was ready.

"So what's the deal with our new friend?" Will asked, meanwhile

skinning the fish we were going to eat. It was an unpleasant task, but

one Will certainly had the stomach for. I tried not to look down too

much at the bloody fish as I took my place beside him, helping get the

fire started as we spoke.

"She's going to stay until she likes it here," I said bluntly, staring

into the flames.

"Well that seems a bit harsh, doesn't it?" He sliced the off the head

of the creature, his nose wrinkling.

"Yeah," I sighed. "Yeah, it does. I just think it will be good."

"For who?" he said dubiously.

"Everyone," I looked around the clearing. "They need a mother."

He nodded, not looking up from his work. "I agree. But that might

be too much to ask of her," he waved his knife over to Ever, who was

peacefully slumbering against the tree. "I mean she's only what, fifteen?

And what makes you think she's going to want to stay, anyway? She's

blind to a life like this, used to luxury by the look of her clothing."

"Yeah, so maybe this will be good for her as well," I said, hating how stuck up I sounded. I knew, from a feeling deep down, that this was in some way the right decision. But everything else was screaming otherwise.

"Even so," he sighed in return, "if she takes care of everyone else, who takes care of her?" He got up, leaving me to ponder over the question.

I will, I told myself, and vowed that if she stayed I would always be there for her.

...

Smoke billowed from the burned out fire and the smell of cooked fish hung in the air. Our stomachs were full and our mouths no longer watering as the sun slowly faded from view. I set down the plate of fish next to Ever, who was still asleep. Placing a gentle hand on her shoulder, I shook her slightly, whispering close to her ear for her to wake up. She yawned and stretched out her legs, her eyes fluttering open and her expression falling into distress.

"I made you supper," I said before she could open her mouth, picking up the plate of smoked salmon and squash. She lifted her chin defiantly, eyes averting me.

"I'm not hungry."

I sighed. "Please, just eat it. We won't have food until afternoon tomorrow, and no doubt you're going to be hungry on an already empty stomach." I pushed the plate closer to her, watching her gaze drop to it and the tempted look in her eyes. But again, she raised her head.

"I told you I'm *not* hungry. And even if I were, how can I eat with my hands tied behind me?" She shot me a devious glance. I rolled my eyes, my folded arms hitting my sides, unwilling to play her game for even a second.

"I guess you'll never know since you're *not* hungry." I scooped up the plate, marching away and handing it off to Thomas and Oliver, who could never have too much to eat. Ever watched them devour the fish with a longing look, so much so that I nearly felt sorry for her.

Nearly.

I moaned, grabbing the pillow and blanket off my hammock and carrying them over to Ever.

"What, are you deciding to be generous now?" she mocked, her lip curling.

"Do you really think I'm going to leave you tied up like that all night?" I asked, mimicking her tone. She stopped taunting me and dropped her gaze.

"I really don't know what to think of you right now."

I ignored her comment, going around to the back of the tree and loosening the knot, freeing her wrists from the rope. She almost immediately jumped up at her freedom, but I caught her wrist, pulling her back down to the ground. "Hey," I warned, then signaled for Will to come over. He held her down with unsettled aggression while I looped the rope around the tree and tied it in a constrictors knot around her ankle, something nearly impossible to untie. She pulled at the rope, but it only tightened more securely around her ankle, and made no progress to gain her freedom.

I laid the blanket and pillow down within her reach, went back over to the pantry and pulled out an apple, going back over to her and placing it in her palm.

"Please, eat."

"Or what?" She glared daggers at me. I rolled my eyes and shrugged.

"Or you'll go hungry. You already passed up the fish, so believe me when I tell you that's all you get until lunch tomorrow." She opened her mouth to protest, but then snapped it shut, and brought the fruit to her lips.

She finished the apple quickly and tossed the core deeper into the forest. I sat next to her in silence, staring up at the stars and waiting for her to speak. Finally, she prompted the question. "How long am I your prisoner?" She spoke no longer out of anger, but more of sorrow.

"Until you'd rather be one of us."

I let my words sit as Albie sauntered over, book in hand. He plopped down next to Ever, opening the book to the bookmarked page. "Read to me Wendy," he said in a small voice.

"I'm not -" She started, but stopped mid-sentence when she met my warning glare. She looked at me, then back to the little boy next to her.

"You heard him," I said sharply, unsure why I suddenly felt so heated. "Read."

Slightly frightened, she picked up the book and began to read aloud. Her voice was so soothing and gentle, it made all the boys creep closer, and everything fell silent to listen. I slumped into a more comfortable position, Elliot laid down on the couch, and Albie laid his head on his Wendy's shoulder as she read. She stopped, startled, but only smiled a little and continued.

"'Do you really think so, Peter?' 'Yes, I do.' 'I think it's perfectly sweet of you,' she declared, 'and I'll get up again,' and she sat with him on the side of the bed. She also said she would give him a kiss if he liked, but Peter did not know what she meant, and he held out his hand expectantly. 'Surely you know what a kiss it?' she asked, aghast. 'I shall know when you give it to me,' he replied stiffly, and not to hurt his feeling she gave him a thimble."

And as she read I imagined the scene as I had never pictured it before. Because instead of fairytale characters, in my mind it was her and I. And instead of a thimble she placed in my palm, it was a kiss she planted on my cheek. A kiss that made my face redden and heart soar. And suddenly I didn't only imagine the kiss, I wanted it. But I buried the feeling, because no one had ever loved me like that, and she surely wasn't about to be the first.

...

That night I slept restlessly. Turning over in my hammock with a moan, I looked around to all the other boys, every one of them sound asleep, dreaming peacefully without a care in the world. I slipped out of the hammock and down the rope attached to the tree, passing by two boys on my way down. In her own tucked away corner, Ever was sitting with her back to the tree, her knees tucked to her chest, wrapped up in a little ball. I strode over to her, slowly taking a seat beside her and watching her glance up towards me. "Hey," I spoke softly, just loud enough for her to hear.

She didn't respond.

"Can - can I do anything for you?" I offered helplessly, my mind a jumble.

"Yeah," she mumbled. "You can let me go."

I bit my lip. I wasn't going to do that - I couldn't do that. Or at least that's what I told myself. "I'm sorry," I whispered, only to be silenced by her sharp words.

"No, you're not. A selfish boy like yourself hasn't the capability of *sorry.*"

"I'm not selfish!" I retorted, only to her cutting response.

"If you weren't you'd think about more than just yourself and you would let me free."

"I want you to like us, I just -"

"I hate you." Her hair fell over her face, clouding her dark expression from my view. I scoffed, standing up in agitation.

"Fine. Hate me, hate all of us for all I care! Just don't," I lowered my voice, sincerity sharpening my tone when I looked over to the slumbering boy. "Don't show it to Albie. He likes you, and for the time you're here you will act like you like him too."

"Why should I?" she snapped back, whipping around at me.

"Because I saw the way he looked at you. Like a son looking at his mother. And Ever, that child needs a mother figure, if only for a short time. Surely you aren't as cruel as to deny a six-year-old that?"

She looked back down at the ground, not able to respond. I walked off, hoping she would listen to my words, that she would care. Maybe kidnapping her wasn't the best way to get to her, maybe I should have been more gentle to start with. The truth was that I didn't know how to get her to like me, or to stay even, but I did know that I was going to get her to like the others.

And if Albie, or the twins, Elliot, or even Will was what kept her, that was fine by me. She had something that I couldn't give them, no matter how hard I tried, and I wanted that for them so badly. They may have had a big brother in me, someone who believed in them and wouldn't doubt them for a second, but they didn't have a Wendy.

And I was going to make sure that was what they got. If even for a little while.

Chapter Four

Ever

The next morning I woke up to birds tweeting and the sun rising in the distance. I felt a wave of calmness and relaxation as if there wasn't a care in the world. Except, at the same time, I felt this nagging sensation, as if something was dreadfully wrong.

But I pushed it away. For I liked this warmth of tranquility. An unusual and strange feeling, yet pleasant at the same time. Making me feel free.

Immediately I wanted the feeling to make me fly, far from my problems and sorrows. And it felt right. Like if I reached out far enough, stretched just a little further... I could touch it. And so I reached. And stretched. And longed.

And then his voice woke me.

"Wen-Ever? Er- here's breakfast." Peter tossed me a pear, and I glared daggers straight through him.

His face hardened, and he quickly cleared his throat.

"Eat. And then I want you to read to Albie. He's been begging me since he woke up, but *I* have to go replenish our food supply. Most of the boys can't, and those who can aren't very well at doing it. You will read to him, I have your word, don't I?"

I continued to glare, but not as intensely. As much as I didn't like taking orders from Peter *one bit,* it would at least give me something to do.

I took a bite out of the pear and chewed slowly. Finally, I nodded.

"Good," he replied.

And then he was gone.

...

I watched nearby ants devour what was left of my meal as I thought about my mother. My home. Wanting so badly to get rid of it. Ironically, though, now that it was gone, I wanted it back. With a passion.

"Wendy?" The young boy, Albie, called, interrupting me from my thoughts. "Peter said you would read to me today." He held out the book eagerly. I glanced at the cover and wasn't that surprised to see that the book was *Peter & Wendy.*

"Please! I've been great all morning, and have been waiting so goodly."

I glared, and answered angrily, "My names not Wen-"

And then my eyes met his. And what I saw was so heartbreakingly despairing. Eyes full of pain and sadness, that people beyond his years shouldn't have to suffer. His body so thin and frail, proof that he hadn't had someone who loved or cared for him properly in quite a long time. And yet, there was that hope, that child's joy.

But there was still despair. Despair so hopeless, so gut-wrenchingly sad...

And then I saw myself reflected back to me. My own eyes, filled with sympathy and compassion.

"M-my real name, it's actually Ever. Not Wendy."

"My real name is actually Albert. But everyone calls me Albie. Just like everyone calls you Wendy." He smiled at me, and then looked down at the book he was still holding out, as if to say, *take it.*

And that's what started our friendship.

...

" *'And yet a third time he sighs,' said Smee. Then at last he spoke passionately. 'The games up,' he cried. 'Those boys have found a mother.' "*

"Yes, we have!" Albie agreed, interrupting an angry Captain Hook. "We've found you, Wendy!"

I thought of reinstating the rule that my name was *not* Wendy, but Albie seemed so happy right then, so I refrained.

I continued reading, and he continued listening. Some of the boys even stopped working and came over to listen too. Soon, fruit and chunks of bread were passed out.

Why, I hadn't even noticed it was lunchtime already!

Since I couldn't eat my food while reading, I carefully set it on my dress and continued.

I read about a mermaid lagoon, pixie dust, and fairies. And for a second, a very quick one, of course, I couldn't blame all of them for wanting to be lost boys living in Neverland. It certainly seemed easier than living in London.

"Alright, boys," Will said, breaking me from my thoughts. "Let's give our new mother," - I glared at him, because I knew he only used the title "mother" to annoy me, as that's just who Will was - "a break so she can eat her lunch. Back to work, boys!"

There was a small current of groans and moans until finally, everyone left.

At least, *almost* everyone.

"Albie, what's wrong?" He looked hungrily at my food.

"I like being a lost boy. Except, I *always* have to work. And then people think I'm too young to do any of the hard work." His stomach growled, and I wondered if work was his real problem.

"Can you please read just a little more to me?" He pinched his fingers together, to show me how little. "Just a teeny bit more?"

I smiled back at him but shook my head. "I'm sorry, but the boys need you."

He nodded, then slowly turned around. "Alright. Thanks anyways, Wendy."

"Mhm. Oh, and Albie?" He turned back to face me. With a mischievous grin, I held out my apple to him.

I've never seen a six-year-old so surprised and delighted.

Smiling a bit, I brought a finger up to my lips, as he joyfully took the apple from me.

...

After I had eaten every bit of my lunch, I started drawing in the dirt with a stick. I thought about the fact that if my mother were here, she would be so disgusted.

The thought brought a small smile to my lips.

"Wendy! Wendy!" Albie yelped, running into the camp.

I unsuccessfully tried to get up.

"What, Albie?! What's wrong?"

"Huh? Oh, nothing. I was just excited for you to read to me. That's all." He shrugged, as if it was totally normal to run, screaming someone's name. Sitting down beside me, he handed me the book. Shaking my head, I took it from him.

"You can't scare me like that, Albie."

"Sorry. I didn't mean too. But I did all my work, and have been waiting *forever.*"

"Alright, alright. But I'm only reading one more chapter. And then it's bedtime." I smiled and ruffled his hair playfully, as we made ourselves comfortable in our little reading cove.

"Oh, should we gather all the boys?" Albie asked suddenly, as I opened my mouth to read. "They would hate to miss your reading."

"Of course!" I said, way too quickly. I closed my mouth before I blurted any other ways of saying that I *liked* it here or something.

Because I didn't!

"Good," Albie continued. "Because I just noticed - Peter hasn't made it to story time all day! He's probably *dying* to hear even a little."

"Oh, who? What's the right term… maybe kidnapper?" I quieted my voice. "Oh, yeah, definitely. He certainly wants to hear the story he's probably read and heard about a hundred times."

Albie's big brown eyes looked up at me, confused.

"It might just be me, but you sound mad at Peter." He shook his head. "I didn't even know that was possible."

"Of course I'm mad at him! Have you never- I mean *ever*- gotten angry at him?" Albie looked up at me, all innocence. "Not even once?!"

The little boy looked so muddled and slightly frightened at my outburst, it made sympathy fill my heart to the brim.

"I mean, he did save me." He replied quietly. Thinking earnestly, he finally shook his head. "I don't think I've ever gotten mad at him." Pause. "Wait! If you're mad at him…"

Albie looked up at me, frightened.

"Does - does that mean your mad at me too?"

"Oh, oh no, Albie. Darling, come here." I held his small cute chin in my hands. "I could never get mad at you."

"Really?" he asked, hopeful. "Then why are you mad at Peter - and… not me?"

"Let's put it this way. Do you kidnap people?"

"No."

"Ruin their lives?"

He thought for a second, scared at the thought, as we so often scare ourselves, then shook his head.

"Well, that's why I don't like Peter. Because he does."

"He does?"

I nodded. "But you don't." Wrapping an arm around his shoulder, I playfully tugged him to the ground.

Grinning, I took Albie's chin in my palm and brushed his uncut hair out of his face. "And that's why I love you. Alright? Because you would never do that to people." He nodded. "Good. Okay, boys," I called to the rest of them. "It's reading time!"

Elli and Thomas looked up and were over in seconds, quickly followed by Oliver, looking a bit uneasy.

Most likely another prank his twin, Thomas, made him do.

This time, I wasn't surprised when Albie laid himself in my lap. Elli came over and gradually relaxed his head on my shoulder. And I read again.

My small smile slowly grew bigger as I continued to read aloud. It was such a peaceful night, and I felt so happy, like pixie dust was real, and I was flying!

And then I looked up and saw Peter. He smiled as if to say, "*I told you so.*" The only thing I hated more than his know-it-all grin, was the fact that I found it sort of handsome.

I glared at him fiercely, and his smile slowly melted. He returned the glare, but instead of anger, it was full of disappointment.

At *me*!

As he turned away, I too felt a sense of disappointment, for the oddest reason.

I quickly kept reading so the sleepy boys wouldn't notice anything. But I couldn't get rid of this startling and confusing feeling of dismay.

Chapter Five

Peter

The week flew by like a summer's moon, passing over and disappearing before we knew it. Each day Ever grew closer and closer to Albie, and to the other boys, too. Elliot taught her how to play our way of playing cards; the twins pulled pranks that would have driven anyone off the edge, except our dear Wendy, who only laughed and smiled at them sweetly until they walked away. She thoroughly enjoyed their company, and I saw more and more smiles with every passing hour.

Except for every time we met eyes. Then her expression would darken, her eyes would grow cold and icy, and she would glare at me for a few seconds. I would return her stare, then look away boldly. And for some reason, something I couldn't grasp, it hurt. I'd never imagined in all the years of living out in the woods as "Peter Pan" that my Wendy would hate me with such a seething passion. She blamed me for keeping her captive, *me*, as if all the other boys hadn't wanted her to stay as well. At this point I didn't care if she left and never came back;

the only thing that kept her tied down was how much the other boys loved her.

...

"Read chapter eleven! Read chapter eleven, *please!*" Albie cried, pushing the book back into her hands. "See, look - it's called *Wendy's Story!* It's a sign, we should read it!"

She laughed, pressing the book back in his lap. "No, no, there are no signs. It's your bedtime anyways. I'd tuck you in, but..." She flashed me a hateful glance from across the clearing, then whispered something in Albie's ear. I rolled my eyes and turned away, anger flushing my cheeks. Taking a deep breath, I wheeled around and marched over to the two of them.

"Come on Albie, time for bed. We're going to have a *big* day tomorrow!" I stressed the word 'big', picking him up and twirling him into his hammock, trying to wipe the disappointed frown from his face.

"But I wanted to read with Wendy," he complained with a pouted lip. Out of the corner of my eye, I could see Ever's little smirk, but I ignored it. I nodded solemnly, bopping him on the nose before throwing the blanket over him.

"We'll read in the morning," I promised, tucking the blanket around him and slipping away.

Ever was silently reading to herself in the dim light of the night sky. I stormed over, snatching the book from her as she threw her head up in protest.

"Hey, I was-"

"Don't ever throw shade at me again in front of Albie, you hear me?!" I threatened, my voice low and hoarse. She shook her head, aghast, and turned away from me.

"I'm tired of you and your sick ways of turning them against me. *I* brought them here! *I* saved them from their old lives. Not you!" I jabbed a finger in her face, my blood boiling at her ability to remain calm in this eerie, foiling way. She folded her arms.

"Then why'd you bring me here?" She cocked her head, her fingers now playing mindlessly in the dirt. I froze, calmed myself and crouched down beside her, trying to emanate some form of control over her. Sighing, I rubbed my nose bridge, sitting down in complete defeat.

"Because I was… afraid." I paused, fishing for the right words. Control wasn't working; I needed to be sincere. I took a deep breath and calmed myself, seeing the lift of her eyes. It was working. Kindness was working.

"Because I wanted the boys to be happy. I was scared they wouldn't like it here. I tried to give them everything, but - but it's not enough. They need a mother." I lowered my tone, my eyes cold; that kindness was gone. "And they don't need her constantly tearing up the group."

She folded the pleats of her dress nonchalantly, glancing up occasionally. "But maybe I'm not really the one tearing everyone apart. You... could be doing that yourself. Everyone else seems fine, except... well, *you*."

I growled, getting up and pacing away. "You know, I've tried to reason with you, I really have-"

"Reason?!" She exclaimed furiously. "You've got to be bloody kidding me, Peter! You've held me captured here for days now! It's *insane*!"

I ignored her comment and continued on, knowing that some part of her liked it here. Some part of her saw the blessing hidden under the curse.

"But it's almost like the devil himself is playing tricks on you. Don't think Albie hasn't come telling me of the little things you've said here and there about me." Her face fell. "Yeah. Just because he's so suddenly 'in love' with his new buddy, doesn't mean all those years that

I was there for him disappear at the drop of a hat. He cares about you, and just doesn't understand one thing: why dear miss Wendy Darling refuses to see the good in Peter Pan."

I again got closer to her, now more sure of myself. I decided to take a more gentle approach on what I knew was going to be a harsh punishment. "Listen, I know you enjoy Albie and the other boys and - no, don't deny it. I've seen the way you guys interact. So I want to give you a chance. The other boys aren't as gullible, but Albie is so open-minded and innocent - he'll believe nearly everything you'll tell him. I can't have you filling his head with lies about me. So, until you learn to control your tongue, I forbid him to speak with you. I will talk to him about it in the morning. Now get some sleep, I think we'll both feel better if we're well rested."

She opened her mouth, gaping, and then closed it. Her eyes started to sparkle with, were they tears? I couldn't quite make it out because she quickly turned her head, her long hair falling over her face. I sighed, turning away and climbing up the tree into my bunk, being careful of the stacked hammocks full of slumbering boys I was passing. Looking back one more time, I watched our Wendy slowly lay her head down on the pillow and pull the blanket up to her chin, her back towards me. I wondered if I had made the right decision. Not just about this new rule with Albie, but even keeping her here in the first place. I had seen how she had just lit up little Albie's world, and the impact she had on all the other boys. She was exactly what they needed.

Then what was making this all so hard?

I guess I hadn't taken the time to realize that, as much as I wanted to deny it, she was exactly what I needed too.

...

My lips stretched into a wide open yawn as my eyes fluttered open. A hand was shaking me awake, quite tense and urgent. I turned over onto my back to see Will, stressed and biting down hard on his lip, waking me from my quiet sleep. Daylight shone through the trees, bringing to life the scene around me, and certainly clearing the fog from my head.

"What's wrong?" I asked, concern growing the longer I looked at him.

"I got up this morning and - and I was going to catch game for the day, so I woke Elliot and went to grab my stuff and that's when he told me that Ever, or - or Wen-"

"Just spit it out," I groaned, rubbing my tired eyes.

"Wendy's gone."

I jolted up, a sickening feeling rising in my stomach. Had she really left? I had supposed she would, and even kind of hoped so at the time being, but now that she was gone I realized what a mess she'd left for me to clean up. Was I supposed to tell Albie and the other boys that Wendy had fled? They would blame me, for sure, and…

No. It wouldn't come to that. I threw myself out of the hammock, down the ladder on the tree and turned so I was able to see the hopeless rope, still tied in its useless knot.

"Should I wake the others?" Will wondered aloud. I shook my head.

"No, don't wake them. And when they do wake, tell them that I've gone with her because she wanted to bathe in the lake."

He nodded slowly, still confused. "I don't understand, where are you going?"

At this, I smiled. Because I finally knew something about our Wendy that no one else would. "The only place she knows where to get to from here."

I pushed past the brambles, bushes, and trees in the way of the overgrown path that so badly needed carving out again. She couldn't have gotten far, not with the blankets she had slept in the night before still warm rather than gone cold. At last, I pulled apart the long vines that severed my view from the waters and found Wendy at the edge of the shore. Her shoes were off and beside her, her feet dipped into the water that splashed over her toes and recoiled back into its body. Her periwinkle dress waved in the wind, along with her hair, still in neat waves.

"Wendy?" I spoke loud enough for her to hear. She jumped up, alarmed, and turned to me, her back to the crashing waves. I saw hate in her eyes, a mixture of hate and... fear. She was afraid, terribly afraid. But not of me. She backed up into the water, deeper and deeper, until now it lined her waist. I followed her slowly, my hands up, calling after her.

"Ever, don't go deeper in. Please, just come back and we can sort this out."

"No!" she screamed back, the wind muffling her speech. "No, I won't! I hate it there, I really, really do!"

"You can't swim," I noted, my voice more concerned than demanding. She glared at me, her hands shaking. The water was indeed freezing and made me shiver nearly as much as her.

"You don't know that!" She bellowed back, her teeth chattering. I nodded.

"Yes, I do. There's fear in your eyes, and not because of me. Come back, please." I tried to go further in after her, but that only made her pace backward more. The alarm in my tone grew, my eyes wider. "Wendy, Wendy don't-"

"*Don't* call me that!"

"Don't go any further, there's a -"

My words were cut off when suddenly her feet slipped out from under her and she plummeted into the water, spluttering and coughing as she tried to keep herself up. But with one crashing wave over her head, she was down, the only trace of her being the bubbles that floated to the surface.

"-dropoff," I muttered, taking in a deep breath and diving in after her. The lake, however blue, was foggy underneath, and I felt around with my hands, feeling the slimy, gritty floor at my fingertips. I blinked, my eyes adjusting to the water, and finally saw her, sinking into the deeper part of the lake. I dove after her, about to grab her hand when a faint feeling came over me. I was losing air. Struggling, I pushed myself to the top, coming up quick enough to gulp in air and plunge back down and grab her by the hand. I pulled her up, securing my arms around her waist and kicked the two of us to the top, her weight dragging me downwards. After a long grapple of kicking and propelling myself to ascend, I finally reached the top, inhaling heavily when my face hit the morning air.

Getting her to the shore was the easy part. The waves practically pushed us forward, so I worried only about keeping hold of the unconscious girl in my arms. I heaved her onto the damp sand, pulling myself out of the water. "Wendy? Wendy?" I slapped her cheek gently and repetitively. She didn't stir, so using both palms, I did multiple chest compressions, checking her pulse to find nothing. Fear rose in my chest as I held her nose shut, opening her mouth and blowing into it, repeating the step every five seconds and following it with more chest compressions. Will knew better of the process than I did, but regardless, I had to try.

"Come on Ever, wake up," I pleaded, pushing down on her chest one more time. She coughed, water spluttering out of her mouth as her eyes blinked open. Turning over, she spit out all the water, and continued coughing, rubbing her sore throat. It took awhile, but she soon came to realize I was there, sitting dumbly beside her.

"Peter?" she asked faintly, recalling what happened in the water. She sat up, her eyes widening, and inched away from me. I grabbed her hand, pulling her back with a gentle frown. "You - you saved my life."

"Well I wasn't exactly going to let you drown, now was I?" I told her, wanting to see her at ease. She wasn't, and only stood up anxiously.

"You aren't going to take me back there," she said, arms crossed. I heaved a sigh, hoping this could be easier.

"Come on Ev," she shot me a warning glare at the nickname. "You like it back at camp, I know you do. I've seen you with the boys; you guys have something really special."

"Yeah, something you took away," she snorted crossly.

I nodded. "And I'm sorry. But you can have it back, you can have it all back - if you just return with me."

"And be confined as your prisoner again? I think not."

I shook my head with a snicker. She furrowed her eyebrows as I looked up, more exasperated than desperate now. "You haven't been '*confined*'," I said with a half-suppressed laugh. "I re-tied the rope's knot and made it so that it was child's play to get out of. It's been like that for a week and you know it."

She opened her mouth in protest but snapped it shut. Her eyes watered with angered tears as she tried to fight back, but couldn't.

"So you did know," I concluded, a question arousing. I lowered my voice, showing earnesty. "But if you knew all along, what kept you?"

She froze, sighed, and sat down in the sand, wringing out the folds of her soaked dress. I made my way over and sat down beside her, noticing that she didn't pull away or even turn her head. "I don't know," she breathed sorely, meeting my eyes.

"I think you do," I responded, getting no reply. "Come back with me for one week. No prisons, no rope, you'll be free. Just one week and then I promise I'll bring you home to your mother. All I need is a week more to let the boys make peace with your leaving and say goodbye, and then you can be back in the comfort of your own home. I promise," I repeated. She didn't seem so sure. "What is it?"

Ever let out a soft moan, digging her fingers in the sand. "It's just that my mum, she doesn't love me like Albie does, like Elli and even Will do. Or you, Peter. Goodness, you've tried so hard to win my liking, it kills me. My mother doesn't even come close to caring that much! She says she does and pretends to, but I know she doesn't. The feeling I get when Albie lays his head in my lap or comes to talk to me for no reason at all, it's a feeling I've never had before. And I love it."

I suppressed a smile. "We could be your new family, Ever. Not just for a week, but forever. *I* could - that is, if you didn't hate me so much."

She simpered, shaking her head and throwing sand at the waves. "I don't *hate* you. I guess it was just easier to loathe you than to admit I was grateful for a change of scenery." She let out a loud breath. "I'll stay the week, but only if we - if *I* can have a fresh start."

I smiled. "Sure. Can I call you Wendy?"

She glared at me, but not like last time. This stare she used more with the boys.

"Don't push it."

Chapter Six

$\mathcal{P}_{eter}$

"Peter look!" Ever called, excitement in her voice. I followed the sweet sound around the corner of the woods, my gaze dropping to where she was looking. A massive cluster of wild blueberry bushes surrounded us on three sides, the blue from the berries overwhelming the green of the bush.

"How have I never noticed this was here?" I gaped, facing her. She laughed.

"Because you never had me." It was true. She had been here three days out of captivity and already made the most satisfying stew out of the simple ingredients we had, organized our pantry, and discovered many edible herbs and plants throughout the woods based on books she'd read. She certainly was a mother in her own way, to all of us.

"Good thing I brought the basket," she murmured, picking a blueberry off its plant and popping it in her mouth with a satisfying bite. I nodded enthusiastically and started picking and gathering them into the basket, being careful to only pluck the ripe ones; we could come back on later days.

After we had nearly overflowed the basket with berries blue as the deepest waters, I turned to go back, our task done.

"Wait," Ever called after me, a hand pulling me back towards her. She bit her lip playfully. "Let's take the long way home."

I let her lead me in the other direction, smiling because I knew where we were going. My special place, that, over the days had become her's as well. The lake, our little peninsula that I had claimed from the moment I laid eyes on this forest. Its waters still sparkled with a certain surety that all would be well, radiating light and warmth. The sun seemed to never cease to shine on the very spot; it was almost as if the clouds parted ways at its passing.

Ever set down the basket gleefully, kicking off her shoes and running into the shallow waves as they blanketed the shore. "Come on Peter!" she called, looking to me with a breathtaking smile. I nodded and ran after her, all the while thinking how happy I was that I had her, that she was here with me and all the other boys. And then how despondent we'd all be at her leaving. She hit the water with her palm, sprinkling me with a shower of the cool Adam's ale. I chuckled and splashed her back, feeling with satisfaction the cold earth underneath my sunken feet.

We laughed and played in the lake like children, hitting each other with wet waves again and again. She once struck the pool so forcefully that a ripple of the water swelled over me and came crashing down, soaking me through.

"Oops!" she giggled, Ever actually *giggled*, as I shook the water off me, pretending to be mad. "Why don't you fly away now, Peter?"

I snickered and shot her a wry smile, then plunged my arm into the lake and swung it with such effort that she was drenched to the bone when the water hit her. She shrieked and ran towards the dry shore, I only a few paces behind her. We collapsed onto the sand, rolling onto our backs and laughing hysterically. "Oh Peter," she exclaimed between breaths, "I've never had so much fun in all my life!"

I rolled over on my side, facing her. "Can't it be like this every day?" I said soberly, sitting up. She furrowed her eyebrows, tossing her long wet hair behind her, pulling herself up as well.

"What are you trying to say?" She inquired, twisting her hair to wring it out and meanwhile dampening the sands. I sighed, slumping into an innocent pose.

"That you could stay, be with us! We all love you being here, and correct me if I'm wrong, but I think you like it too." I cocked my head to one side, watching her face confirm my beliefs. It was as if she were fighting an internal battle with herself. Alas, she flopped down in defeat, her expression sad, and I realized I had just ruined the first moment he had let herself just simply have fun.

"I... can't," she sighed, her face paling. "My mum will be worried sick - she needs me - or at least I think she does. I'm surprised there haven't been search parties out here already."

I'm not, I thought silently, deciding not to say anything. But instead, I dropped the subject. I hated the pained look on her face, the sadness in her eyes at the thought of all of it. "Just answer me one question," I couldn't help but say.

"Mhm," she lifted her gaze.

"Your sadness... is it because you miss your mother or is it because you know you're going to miss us?"

She didn't answer. I knew, or at least I thought I knew - hoped I knew her answer, but I wanted to hear it from her. I wanted her to speak more of her home life, and not just because I was curious, but because I cared. And out of the blue, her lower lip started to quiver, her hands shaking in slight tremors, and she seemed so distressed all at once that I could hardly hold my gaze to watch. And then all of the sudden her eyes watered up, on the brink of tears that soon spilled over onto her flushed cheeks and she began to cry.

"I love it here, I really do, Peter. And it really is Neverland because you never have to grow up, do grown-up things, or worry about who will care for you tomorrow. All I've felt here from you and the boys is love," she sniffled, wiping her nose. "But at night when the sky is dark and only the stars give light, I can hear cries of the animals in the forest. They seem so desperate and neglected, and then I can't help but cry, too, not because I don't feel love, but because when I go home all I'll want, all I'll ever want, is to feel that love again. But I won't have it, because just as Wendy does in the book, I have to go home. And I don't feel that sort of love back in London."

"But why, Ever?" I breathed, taking in and calming her shaking hands. "Why must you go?"

"Because I may be the only person that can give my mum the love that I got from all of you. Don't you see, Peter? I need to make the grown-up decision, and do what's right. Staying here is the selfish thing to do, and if I go, I can give that love to someone else: my mother."

Her words were so tender and caring, and I wanted to believe them - I did, truly. But a different truth that kept nagging at me inside.

"Forget them, Wendy. Forget them all. Come with me where you'll never, never have to worry about grown-up things again. Never is an awfully long time."

She smiled sadly, sniffling again. "That's from the book."

I nodded. "Your mother has a whole world looking out for her. But the boys back at camp, they just have you and me. And I - I only have you."

She wiped her eyes. "You're not going to change my mind, Peter. But I know something we can do?"

I perked up in interest. "What?"

"We can bury a symbol here, like the thimble Wendy gave Peter in the book - it represented a kiss. And this symbol, it can represent my heart. So that wherever I go, part of me will always be back in my true home."

I nodded eagerly, just noticing the silver locket around her neck. It had been neatly tucked into the collar of her dress, but now it stuck out and gleamed in the sun's light. "But Ever, you already have left a piece of your heart here, so why don't I do you one better?" I offered, opening the locket with my fingers.

She looked down. "Oh, it's empty. My mother gave it to me a while ago, hoping I would find a 'certain someone' to put in it." She rolled her eyes, recalling the memory. "That wasn't going to happen, but I've kept it anyways. I haven't found anything special enough to fill it with yet," she sighed, snapping it back shut.

"Well, I just did," I spoke up cheerfully. "Come. I'll show you back at camp."

...

I took the little torn piece of paper gingerly in my hands, walking it over to Ever, who was sitting on the fallen log at the edge of the clearing. "Open your locket," I told her, holding a steady gaze as she pulled out the necklace from under her dress and clicked it open. It was a small, heart-shaped charm, but perfect for what I was fitting in it. I pressed the piece of paper into it, and showed it to her, a smile forming on her lips.

"It's a small piece of the storybook."

I nodded. "Now, where ever you go, we will always be with you. And there, Wendy Darling, is your kiss."

She laughed lightly, and I smiled with triumph at the thought that I had just successfully been able to call her Wendy without any objection. It really was a special day.

"Now, no more talk of this. Let's cherish the time we have before we lose it. How does a game around the fire sound?"

"Perfect. You gather the boys, I'll get the fire dancing."

She lifted her chin with a beam. "We make quite the team, don't we."

"Yeah, It seems we do."

Chapter Seven

*P*eter

The next day rolled by like a summer's stroll, and I felt myself in the pure glee of it all the while. Ever devoted most of her morning and afternoon to the other boys, and we ran around hiding and finding one another, trying to catch each other in games of tag.

It was especially delightful when I found a curved looking twig, much like a hook, and held it in my hand, playfully threatening Wendy with a wink.

"Argh, I am the mighty Captain Hook, here to face my rival Peter Pan! Come out, Peter, or I shall take your Wendy!" I snatched her wrist and shot her a "play along" look, watching her lips form up into the sweetest mischievous smile, and then held back laughter as she flaunted her free hand over her forehead, and draped back.

"Oh my, whatever shall I do?! Peter, Peter Pan please! Come and save me!" She met eyes with Albie, who, with the greatest of smiles, came running into the scene, a long stick in hand.

"Let her go!" he shouted defiantly, and I pushed Ever away. He bent his knees back and got into a stance, waving his stick at me. "Ready to lose your other hand?" he smirked and then lunged. I fought him playfully, only deflecting the aggressive swings and ended up on the ground, him standing over me as champion.

Ever ran and picked him up in a great big hug, exclaiming something about him being her savior. Then, with the cutest little, up-to-no-good smile, he looked at me, then back at her and asked her for a thimble.

And with a knowing grin, she kissed him on the cheek.

All was well, but the best of times was when we were able to get away, just the two of us. We took a walk through an "undiscovered" place in the woods, and I let her lead the way.

Of course, these parts had already been combed through countless times, as there wasn't an inch of this forest in a radius of fifteen miles each way that hadn't been, but she didn't know that. So when we walked, talking and laughing, I led us up to a certain point and stopped. Looking down in the dirt, I noticed a small piece of stomped down paper, and leaned down to pick it up.

"What's this?" I asked, holding back a grin as I blew off the dirt, and handed it to her. She unfolded the paper, and instantly her eyes lit up.

"Oh, look, Peter it's a treasure map!"

I looked over her shoulder skeptically. "Are you sure? It could just be lines and squiggles -"

"No, no, I'm sure. Absolutely positive! See, there's a compass on the bottom right corner, and here's the water, over west, and these dashes are leading somewhere, through these… what do you suppose this could be?" She pointed to a repeated symbol surrounding one section, that looked like little spikes all around.

I froze, allowing my voice to drop to a low whisper. "I've seen that symbol before. It's supposed to mark the unknown territory. Some say it's dangerous, but it's so deep into these woods no one really knows." I gave a frown.

"Oh," she said, stumped. "Well, it seems you have to go through it to get to the treasure. Oh, why don't we just do it, Peter? Come on, it'll be fun!"

"I don't know, Wendy…"

"We can always turn back!"

"Oh, all right."

Sighing a little happy breath, she turned back to the map and immediately her joy faded. Once I inquired what was wrong, she looked to me in embarrassment. "I don't know which way is north."

I suppressed a laugh at her pure disappointment of this and guided her hand to point towards the sun. "The sun always rises in the east and sets in the west -"

"Well, I know that."

"Just listen. It seems to be starting to set in that direction, making that west -"

She spun around. "And that north! So we have to go this way!"

I nodded and we continued our trek through the woods, off the so-called "path" and into a deeper part of the forest. The grasses, moss, and vines grew thicker, and the trees clumped together more so it was harder to make it through, and at many points we were walking single file. But Ever was determined, and so we went on for about another half an hour until we reached our so-called destination.

"I-I don't understand. There's nothing here, except woods and brush and dirt." She looked around one last time, before deciding it final. "Oh well, you did warn against it, so I guess I should have listened. I did enjoy the hike here, it was awfully thrilling! But we might as well turn back now."

I stifled a laugh. "Oh, Ever, when are you ever going to learn that seeing is not believing?" I directed her confused self around and pushed her slightly forward.

She swung her head back over her shoulder, confused, but I edged her on. Then, taking one step forward, her foot gave out from under her, and the pretend flooring of vines and leaves and branches tumbled down through the slope in the ground along with her. She toppled downward, sliding against the dirt that had her falling into a covered recess in the ground until she at last hit the bottom with a loud "ufh!" I followed her, landing on the bottom as she got up, fists clenched, facing me.

"Oh Peter, you knew, you knew! What is this, some kind of trap?! Do you find this funny or is it just-"

I silenced her with a finger to her lips and turned her around to face the beauty of the underground cave we were in. About fifteen feet ahead lay a small pond, on the furthest side from us was a little opening from the coming stream up above, that had waters trickling down over the rocks which created a sort of glowing waterfall. The waters played in the light, and you could see little fish swimming along the pond floor. The moss-covered rock walls surrounding it gave the whole scene a comforting, welcoming feel.

Ever stood awestruck in front of me, taking it all in, then slowly turned back to me, no emotion displaying on her delicate face. "It - it was your treasure map. The whole thing was set up… you - you knew these woods and you lied to me."

I nodded solemnly. "I hope you're not mad. I thought you would like the -"

"Peter I love it!" She ran and threw her arms around me, kissing me all over. "It's the most beautiful thing I've ever seen! Thank you, oh thank you!"

I hugged her back with the most splendid feeling warming me. Knowing I had made her happy made me feel like a king. "Well, it's not over yet," I said with a beam, and led her over to the east wall, pointing to the words delicately carved out in the stone.

PETER & WENDY

Her lips broke into a smile and my heart soared.

"Peter," she whispered in the quiet, the only sounds were those of the of the dripping water and faint birds tweeting up above.

"Yeah?"

"I believe. You truly have taken me to Neverland."

Chapter Eight

Wendy

I sat in the little makeshift nook that Peter put together for me after I had decided to stay a little longer, and crushed a *lot* of berries as dusk started to sing a lullaby to us all. Never in a million years would I picture myself in this position. Yet, look at me now. Absolutely loving it.

Loving it when Albie curled up next to me every night. Feeling proud when I finally managed to get sweet Elli to talk to me about himself earlier today. Delighted with Will, who opened up to me enough to show me how to tell different animal tracks apart yesterday afternoon. Why, just a few minutes ago I was laughing with the twins, Thomas and Oliver, as they tried to teach me their card games, and I epically failed. I loved these boys with an incredible passion. They were so seemingly perfect. And then I realized they weren't, and I loved them even more.

It was heartbreaking that I had to leave these… angels. Children that had snuggled their way into my heart and refused to let go. Children I hoped to never forget.

I couldn't get the thoughts of how truly caring Elli really was, or how funny the twins were, or how cute Albie was, how incredible Peter was, or how kind Will was, under all that toughness.

I smiled so big as Peter came in, these sweet memories still clear in my mind.

"Wendy," Peter called softly. I looked up, startled at his anxious and troubled tone. "Can - can you, uh, help me with, er, something?"

I cocked an eyebrow, as he pointed outside of the little grove of trees surrounding our camp. What with all the secrecy?

"Uh, sure…" I let him pull me up, and away.

"What's wrong?" I asked, as soon as we were out of earshot.

"It's…" he didn't finish, but whatever it was, it was making him uneasy, and…

Was that fear? "What's wrong, Peter?" I repeated, putting a hand on him. With a deep breath, he continued.

"Tomorrow I'm taking you to the trails. Then - then you can go back to your mum. Take care of her…" I looked up at him, to notice his eyes were glistening with… tears. "Love her, be who she needs."

"And who do you think is that?" I asked bluntly, angry at the sudden turn of events. What was the cause of him saying these things?

He smiled gently. "You."

"But the week isn't up yet…"

He shrugged and shook his head sadly. "The longer we wait the harder it will be on the boys. I want you gone before they wake up tomorrow." He started to turn away, but I pulled him back.

"Why are you doing this, Peter? You *kidnapped* me, so I was forced to stay until I - until I fell in love with this little home! And now I have. Why can't I stay the rest of the week? It's only day four!"

He nodded, and I realized that I wasn't the only one counting the days until my departure.

"We're finally getting along, and you've just found your Wendy!" He turned his head away, and I gently redirected it back towards me. "Why, Peter? What is making you say this?"

"The boys, they'll-"

"The *real* reason."

He sighed, slowly raising his head. "Because it will be harder on *me* if you stay longer. I was gullible, I thought I could find someone to - to love me. But no one ever has, or ever will." He finished the last part with teary anger.

"You - you think I don't love you? You think I don't love my first real friend?"

"I think you don't love me enough to stay here."

"Peter, listen…" I started, at a loss for words. I wanted to stay, I did! But I couldn't, I couldn't leave my mum with a frightful worry of where I was.

"No, Wen-Ever."

I shook my head in confusement. That was the first time he had called me Ever since I had started to let him call me Wendy.

"You listen to me. Your mother has plenty of people, but I only have you. You say she doesn't love you like I do, like the boys do, yet you still choose *her*. Don't make excuses! You don't want to stay. You say you love me, that I'm your friend - but friends don't leave. At least, not true friends. I already said it, and I'll say it again: no one has ever loved me, and no one ever wi-"

And that's when I couldn't take it any longer. If words couldn't convince him, then maybe this would. And so, before I could stop myself, I pulled his face close to mine, got up on my tip toes…

And I kissed him. Okay, so I didn't really aim that good, and I got more cheek then lips. But still, I kissed him.

And it felt good.

Holding his face close to mine, we slowly broke apart. Peter had tried to push me away at first, in his surprise. But he quickly relaxed into the moment and kissed me back.

His breath fell on my cheek as we stood there for a second, and then, as if we both decided at the same time, we leaned in once again, but this time I had better aim.

I felt his hand skate around my waist, drawing me in closer. My heart seemed to flutter into my throat, leaving my gut to drop in a nervous, yet excited way. It was nothing I'd ever felt before. Like when Albie snuggled up against me or Elliot asked me to read, but different. Better.

Finally, I pulled away, my heels sinking back down to the earth. I leaned my head into his, holding tightly to his hand. We sat like this for a moment, our foreheads gently touching. Until finally, I broke the silence, saying, "you know, the painful thing is losing yourself in the process of loving someone too much, and forgetting the fact that you are special too. *You* are special, and I care about you, so, so much. Now, do you understand?"

...

Peter, from that point forward, had chosen to let me stay, making the best of the time we still had together. And in that precious time, we managed to share more moments, laughter, and... thimbles.

I tried to not think about the fact that I was leaving soon, to soon, and instead read to Albie, pretended that I was mad at the twins to "teach them discipline" from their atrocious pranks, spent quality time with Elli, and even got in some nice long chats with Will, who hadn't shown much liking towards me being here so far.

To be honest, I think he might've been a little jealous of how much time I'd spent with Peter. So I tried to back off, but boy, it was *hard*.

Yet, no matter how much I tried to not think about it, I sadly knew I would be leaving, leaving this camp, this forest, and not only the only people I love, the only ones that have loved me back. And too fast that week slipped into days, which flew into hours, which evaporated into minutes.

All too fast.

I had already said goodbye to Will, the twins, and Elli, who was trying so hard to suppress his sadness, yet tears still found themselves silently rolling down his cheeks. Thomas was even sniffling, and Oliver was unsuccessfully trying to conceal his sobs.

My departure had even managed to get Will with watery eyes.

But barely. Yet I knew I was still going to miss him a ton.

Albie might have been the hardest to say goodbye to. The more I thought about it, the more I noticed as much as I was his Wendy, he was my Michael. I had been trying to say goodbye to him for the past five minutes, but somehow, right now, he was gripping on to my legs so tight, even Peter couldn't get him off.

"Don't leave, Wendy! Don't leave us!"

Finally, with everyone's help, I kissed a sobbing, now screaming Albie behind.

I was crying in hysteria as I turned to Peter.

"Come on," he said, beckoning me to the edge of our - *their* camp. I could tell he was trying very hard not to cry too.

He would bring me near the trails, but not to close, for his and the rest of the boy's safety.

Once we were out of their earshot and sight, we both looked into each other's eyes. And then, as if we agreed on something, leaned forward and shared our last kiss.

Wow, he's a good kisser.

Finally, we tore apart, and both quickly became wet-eyed. We had only met each other less than a month ago, but it seemed like I had known him forever. You can't blame us for crying, we only had each other right then. And when I would leave, we would both have no one. No one that truly understood. Not even my mum.

"Ever, I'm - I'm really gonna miss-"

"No, Peter. No goodbyes. Never-never say goodbye, b-because goodbye means going a-away, and-and going away m-means... forgetting."

We sat in silence for a moment, until Peter finally spoke, with a sad smile. "I guess I'm not the only one to quote the book."

I smiled back, with a sad shrug.

"It grew on me."

...

We had been walking in silence for a while, me following him, both of us sniffling and trying to tell ourselves that at least I hadn't left yet. I kept being able to keep it in, and then Albie's cries would come back to me, and tears found themselves silently rolling down my cheeks again.

I hated that I knew that those cries would haunt my nightmares for many years to come. That the anxiety of wondering if Elli would ever be able to open up that much to anyone ever again would worry me every morning and every night. Each of the boy's personalities, that I had fallen deeply in love with, would hurt me for the rest of my life, every single day without them.

It was worse trying so hard, to *not* think of Peter, who I knew I would miss the most. Even more than Albie.

Just then, the things Peter had said in the past few days came rushing back to me, as if my life was flashing before my eyes. *They just have you and me. And I-I only have you… your mother has a whole world looking out for her… no one has ever loved me… never is an awfully long time.* His lips against mine, our hands intertwined, me on his lap as I read…

"Peter," I called out, startling myself on how I had reacted to these thoughts without even thinking about it.

Yet I knew I was right.

He sniffed and quickly wiped his red, raw eyes.

"I-I'm going to stay." I breathed in deeply, hoping this decision wasn't as selfish as I had once feared.

I saw a flicker of hope in his eyes, for a quick second, but it went away fast.

"What'd you say?" he asked quietly, without emotion.

"I *said*, I'm deciding to…" wow, he wasn't even listening. "Peter," I continued, lifting his chin to force him to look at me. "I'm going to stay."

He froze.

I grinned.

"Y-You were right, I only have you, and you only have me. It might have taken me awhile to realize, but we need each other more than my mother needs me. The boys need me more than her. And I need them."

He looked at me for a second, then smiled bigger than I had ever seen him smile before. Finally, now, after saying what needed to be said, I felt free. No longer in the grasp of my mother.

I wrapped my arms around Peter's neck and felt the happiness of being together.

Together. At last.

"Ever I… I," he fumbled, fishing for the words but failing desperately to voice them.

"Yes, Peter?"

"I… you look beautiful," he decided, releasing his grip around me with a meek smile. I thanked him and beamed, not because of the compliment, but in relief. He had tried to say those simple words, those special three, but he couldn't. And neither could I.

It felt good to know that he felt the same way. That he, too, wasn't ready to jump off the high cliff, with the chance of falling.

I had been thinking about them lately, those words, and I decided I didn't want to risk it. Risk the chance of falling. This was all so new, so overwhelming. I guess it was nice to know that he wasn't ready either.

Ready to jump.

Ready to fly.

Ready to say *I love you.*

Chapter Nine

Peter

"No, I just don't like it. I'm sorry Peter, but everything's changed. And just because you won't admit it, doesn't mean it hasn't." Will shook his head, his jaw twitching in its usual agitated manner. I frowned, twisting my water bottle to a close and storing it in the small hollowed out pantry. I then stood, heat rising inside of me as Will half rolled his eyes at my defense of Ever.

"Will, all the other boys absolutely adore her. Yeah, things may have changed, but it's for the better," I scoffed the retort, rubbing my temples with my palms. Wendy was bathing in the stream, washing off her clothes and taking a bit of time to herself, and the younger boys were playing slightly rough on the other side of camp, nevertheless laughing and throwing light hits. Albie kicked dirt that clouded Elli's face and then high fived the twins with a winning grin.

"No, I'm not saying I don't enjoy her," he sighed like I didn't get it. "It just seems to me that you're enjoying her a little too much."

My cheeks flushed red and I lowered my head, licking dry lips. "Will, it's not going to come to that. We're just friends."

"Friends?" He raised an eyebrow.

"Friends."

And yet, there was heavy doubt lingering in his eyes. "What would it hurt?" I pointed out, the back of my head pounding with the idea that I couldn't promise that *friends* would stay just that. I hadn't told any of them about the kiss, but the moment I was about to, my closest friend went off on me.

I knew from the minute his lips opened that he had this speech prepared. "Peter, you think it's all fun and games now - and it is. But what your underestimating is how much those boys look up to you -"

"No, I know -"

"Ah-ah, just listen," he cut me off. "Both of you. And what do you think happens when all of a sudden this sweet, united co-parenting 'friendship' gets taken a little too far. What do you think fills their heads? Peter, all these boys suffered the consequences of their parents being together. Albie and Elliot were left, probably because something happened between the adults, the twins watched both their parents die, mine - mine…" His voice trailed off and he recollected himself. "All these things happened to our *parents*."

I noticed he used the word *our.*

"So what do you think they're going to naturally assume when you guys connect in that same way. Because I'm betting all of the sudden they're going to feel less important, maybe the possibility of abandonment may cross their minds, or hunger, cold, loneliness -"

"Okay. Okay, I get it."

He pursed his lips and began carrying over the collected kindling for the fire. "Listen, I'm not meaning to -"

I turned and walked away.

...

"Did he take it well?" Ever asked, tying the bow on the back of her dress, and fingering it to ensure it had maintained it's neat structure she had when forming it.

I rubbed my forehead, agonizing over which words I would choose to form the sentence. She already knew.

"You didn't tell him." The disappointed frown dimmed the little flame inside of me. I opened my mouth, then closed it, stepping a little closer to her. I drew up her tender hand and placed it desperately up to match mine, only to watch it drop. I drew it again to my shoulder, and again, to watch it drop.

"Ever he went off on me, got all mad before I could even get the words out. It - it wasn't the right time."

"Well then find the right time." She pushed past me and disappeared behind the trees.

"Ever!" I called after her, running back to catch her. I spun her back around to face me, defeat in my eyes.

"Don't be mad. I can't have everyone against me right now. Just… don't be mad." I watched the sigh leave her lips and trail down to the grass. She fingered my palms and met my eyes with a sad sparkle in hers.

"I'm not mad at you Peter, God knows I could never be mad at you. I just don't want you to ruin this - you need to tell him."

"He *will* ruin it," I interjected, anger rising in my throat. "He got all mad at me today, just feeling like something might happen. Ever please, let's just keep this on the down low right now. Can't we just wait until there's actually something to tell?"

She stared at her shoes for a long while and looked up with a little smile. "What would there be to tell?"

"Oh, I don't know," I simpered, tapping my lower lip with a discreet smirk. She rolled her eyes, but couldn't help laughing, and pulled me along in the direction of camp.

...

The days following we kept our secret just that. It was thrilling, in a way, sneaking off at different times and being able to hide it from the boys who could only really see what was right in front of them. Will did give me the side eye a couple of times, and seemed to shoulder Wendy off, but I knew he would come around.

He had to. Because if I knew anything from my time spent with this most beautiful, amazing girl, it was that the only thing that could come between us was death and death itself.

And I didn't plan on dying anytime soon.

Chapter Ten

Peter

The crisp night air tickled my skin, getting to me even with the fire Will had built up. The sky was nearly black, and I sat next to the boys around the bonfire, enjoying the peacefulness of the night.

Ever smiled to me from across the clearing, and I gave her half of a smile back. She sighed, disappointed, and started to come over when sudden faint calls interrupted us. I turned around wildly, seeing with squinted eyes the bright gleam of flashlights in the distance.

A search team was here.

Tension aroused, the boys scrambled to their feet, but knew better than to make a sound. We had gone over this protocol hundreds of times. The fire was doused with water as the rest of us bolted to our trees.

"Our trees" meaning the ones each person was designated to and had practiced climbing before in case of a situation like this. Albie came up on my back, the twins shared the thickest trunk, and Wendy followed Will. I reached the highest supporting branch and clung to it and Albie, watching Will help a struggling Ever. Nevertheless, she managed, and we clung to the branches, the cold air stinging our cheeks and noses, looking out in the distance to the people scouring the area.

Thankfully, they didn't come close enough to discover the camp, but instead turned west of us and continued on their way. We waited for half an hour after being cleared, just for precautions, and then slowly slunk down the trees and found our beds, exchanging nervous glances.

...

I sat in the clearing a little ways away from camp, surrounded by the sounds and feelings of the wildlife around me. The leaves stretched towards the sun, green as freshest field of grass. The stream, only a bit off in the distance, trickled down towards me. I let the sound of the running water overtake me, closing my eyes with a smile. If only everyone could enjoy this. It was sad really, what we as a society had done to our beautiful, natural world. I sat on an old fallen log, a tree that used to stand tall like the others, point towards the heavens, and hold singing birds. That's what I loved about our forest, our section at least. No hands but ours had touched it. No damage had been done. It was it's own world; living, breathing, thriving.

And then, right beside me, was Ever. In her eyes, her own forest, her own world. And I loved it just as much.

"Hey."

"Hey."

"Peter, why is this still happening?"

I turned to her, trying to keep my face emotionless. "What's happening?"

She rolled her eyes and plopped herself down next to me. "You're still avoiding me. I told you, I'm here to stay. And nothing, *nothing* is going to change that."

I exhaled deeply, looking to her with desperate eyes. "But how do we know? We came so close to losing it all yesterday - what if your mother comes looking for you? What if the police -"

"Then we'll run. Like you've run. It's a huge forest, Peter, we have endless hiding spots." She stretched a hand around my neck, giving me a sweet smile that I couldn't help but return.

And just as quickly, it disappeared. "But what if you see her again and you want... and you want to..."

"Go back with her? Believe me, our home was nothing but... well, let's just say it was nothing like here." We sat there in a peaceful and happy silence, before she froze, then slowly let a playful smile creep at the edge of her lips. "Hhm, do you hear that?" She stood up.

"What?"

"The birds. It's almost as if they're singing a song just for us," she breathed and cocked her head. It was true, they whistled a pretty tune back and forth, and though I was pretty sure it wasn't just for us, I enjoyed the sound of it. "Get up." She took my hand, pulling me to my feet.

"Where are we going?"

"Not where, what." She started to sway, a mischievous look in her eyes. "Do you know what I miss the most about London?"

I shook my head, mystified. What was she getting at? Her whole aura, delightful and cheery, however pleasant, struck me as rather odd.

"The dancing. How everyone got lively when the music sped up, and would sway and twirl for hours. How at school if a boy likes you, he would come and ask if you could have a dance with him at the school ball. Or the girls who got tired of waiting would ask the boys themselves." She looked to the sky, a sparkle twinkling her eye. "You know, Peter…"

"Let me guess," I caught on quickly. "You're tired of waiting." She nodded, beaming. "But I don't know how to dance," I spluttered, watching as she lifted her hands to rest on my shoulders, and I tried to do the same.

"No, silly," she laughed. "Not there, *here*." She took my hands and placed them on her waist, and my heart fluttered with joy as pure as a child's laughter, a tingling in my hands where they collided with her. She started to oscillate, shifting her weight from one foot to the other, one foot to the other. I followed her lead, stumbling a little when she stepped back, but I stepped forward and moved to my right when she moved to her left and vice versa. I started to get the hang of it, and soon our hands were clinging to one another's, up by our shoulders. We danced around the clearing, to the beat of her soft hum. I had never had such a pleasant time in all my life.

"Twirl me," she laughed, pulling our gripped hands higher and helped me spin her around. She ended up further out, our arms outstretched, and suddenly she spun back into me, her dress twirling out with the momentum, and she landed in my arms, our faces so close that our noses were nearly touching.

"Hhm," she smiled, the both of us in a daze, and she reached up and kissed me.

A direct gasp from behind startled the two of us, and we pulled apart to see Albie, wide-eyed and serious. "Peter… Wendy? What are you…" He was so distressed he barely reached the end of his sentence, and turned and ran away as fast as his little feet could carry him. Ever and I met eyes, and we darted after him, all the while calling his name to gain no response.

"Albie! Albie, darling, come back," she called, the two of us stumbling into the camp to finding Albie already in Will's arms. He stared at both of us, the boys doing the same, and all was silent until our Wendy gave a quiet "oh."

I dropped Ever's hand. "Will, I can explain -"

"Can you?" he snapped. "We talked about this Peter! You said we were always going to be put first, that nothing was going to come between that."

"Yeah, and you are," I started, flustered.

"How are we supposed to know that?! How are we supposed to feel comfortable lying in our beds at night knowing you two may as well run off together and leave us?!"

"Will, we would never!" Ever gasped, hurt and attacked by the sudden accusation.

"Believe me, guys, it doesn't mean -"

"No. I liked her being here, I really did. But not like this. It's like we don't even exist anymore." He glared at the two of us, long and hard, before stalking off. Elliot looked at us with a gaze full of hurt, and turned around, following Will. Why, the thought had never occurred to me that they would take this in such offense! The twins followed Elliot, and lastly, standing there was Albie, in confusion and woe, before he, too, walked away.

"No, Albie! Come back sweetie," Ever called after him, a hand stretching out as if to grasp him. She turned to me with tears welling up in her eyes. "This is all my fault, Peter." She took a step away from me, her hands gluing to her sides. "No, we can't do this to the boys. They won't understand. For now, let's just... keep our distance."

And then she, too, turned and walked away.

I didn't even have the words to call after her. Speechless, I found myself wandering out of the clearing, tears springing up in my eyes. How fast had I just lost everyone I loved? I journeyed through the paths to places I hardly ventured through, digging through the overgrown forest. This wasn't happening, *couldn't* be happening. Just ten minutes ago I was dancing with her, and the next second, not only her but everyone else had decided it best to keep their distance. I kicked the tree next to me, crying out in rage when it only sent pain shooting through my foot. A pudgy hand tapped my side.

"Peter?"

I turned around to see Albie, looking up at me with round eyes, and sighed, slumping down with my back to the tree.

"I'm sorry," he piped up, sitting down cross-legged, or what he liked to call 'criss-cross-applesauce.' He said he heard it from a kid in the village.

"For what?" I asked, half in thought.

"For not accepting what you wanted and for judging you," He said plainly. They seemed like such big words for a six-year-old. "I know you love Wendy, and because I went running back into the camp and scared the boys now you can't love her."

He puffed out his bottom lip, all sad. I took him in my arms, sinking under his weight. He certainly wasn't a toddler anymore. "Listen bud, I *can* love her. And being kept from her doesn't mean I still can't with all my heart, it just means we aren't going to do the things we used to anymore. For you guys."

"Like laugh and play and dance?" he wondered with bright round eyes, looking up from the dirt he was spooning into his palm.

"Yeah."

"To tell the truth," Albie admitted solemnly. "I kinda liked it when you did that. At least when you were together. It was like the stories in the book. It's just when you kissed I-I… I don't know. I…"

"I know, bud," I smiled. "No more kisses."

Suddenly he crawled up close to me, alarmed. "But she can still kiss me goodnight on the head, right? I like it when she does that."

I nodded happily and wiped the dirt smudges from his hands and cheeks. "Let's go home."

...

Home became, well... just a term. It started to lose its meaning with Will still upset, Ever and I apart, and Elliot failing to keep the peace. Everyone seemed to be at each other's throats, the twin's couldn't get along, Will ignored Wendy and I, and Elliot seemed to not care so much anymore. I would look at Ever, and catch her looking back at me. When I tried for a smile she would return it, then dip her head back down as if to say, *no, we can't Peter.*

But we could! We could if we just tried. Maybe slower, maybe in a different attempt, but we certainly could. Except she wouldn't even entertain the idea.

Finally, enough was enough. Will rolled his eyes and shot up from the couch, irritation forming his aura. "Alright you two, we get it already! Just go - go patrol the walking paths or something. I've had it."

She jumped up, dusting off her new clothes. Will had given her an old t-shirt and baggy jeans to wear while we washed her dress. With the flats, they looked kind of funny, but at this point, she barely wore shoes like the other boys. My boots were already growing small and I barely wore them as well. "A-are you sure?"

"Yes."

"We'll be back by nightfall!" she cried, smiling at Albie who returned the grin.

I took her by the hand and we were off. Soon into our walk we were laughing and talking like it had been years. She told me of all the ways she had tried to entertain the boys and all the ways she had failed. I never dropped my grip on her hand and she never dropped her gaze.

"We can't let Will do this to us anymore," I decided at last. "I mean I get the 'taking things slowly' but that doesn't mean we can't be in each other's presence!"

"I know," she breathed. "I just thought it would be better for the boys. But it wasn't. We really do make quite the team."

I grinned. "What would I do without you?"

"Hhm," she laughed, pretending to think about it with a hand on her chin. "You wouldn't have any full cooked meals, that's for sure. And you wouldn't know how to keep Albie under control now that he's started his defiant screaming fits once in a while. And you most certainly wouldn't have received any *thimbles*," she snuck the word in slyly, biting her lip with a twinkle in her eye.

I laughed wryly and pecked her on the cheek, slinking my arm around her shoulder; the two of us walking in silence, enjoying one another's presence at last. We walked for miles, neither of us daring to say a word, to ruin the moment that had us wanting to live, right here in these woods, forever. Until she decided to prompt a question, simple and harmless, that killed something inside of me.

"I've heard everyone's backstories, I even got Will to open up to me about his past. The only thing that I just can't seem to get out of any of them is one story. Your's."

I was silent for a while, trying to find the right words and gaping breath. Eventually, I spoke. "That's because they don't know it," I stated plainly. I hadn't spoken of my past life in years; it was something I tried so hard to forget.

"What, Peter? What don't they know?" She squeezed my hand reassuringly and looked at me with widened blue eyes that wouldn't accept refusal. So I told her. My hands started to tremble, a tear even threatened to fall off my cheek, but I couldn't help it at this point. I told her everything.

"That once upon a time there was a young boy named Edmund. Edmund's family was poor, and he had no friends but the ones in his head. This didn't phase him because he was happy in his own world. He never knew his mother, but he liked to imagine that she was a beautiful fairy from a far-off land, always watching over him, always protecting him - even when he was alone. He liked it best to be alone, or just him and his nursemaid Mary. She taught him how to read, placed a book in his hands and told him never to give up hope. But then she, too, disappeared and never came back.

The boy stayed in his room a good deal during the day, and at night would sneak downstairs, quiet as a mouse, and fill his belly with the little food they had, for he was always hungry. Then to his room he would return, and stay there until night fell again."

"I-I don't understand," she interrupted. "What does this have to do with you?"

"Just listen," I told her. "Edmund's father was addicted to this - this drink. Little did he know it was what made his father go mad, do all the horrible things he did. Sometimes he would call him down, demand his presence and sometimes - sometimes he would do things with him. Take him fishing, or teach him how to be a "man." But most of the time he would find some, any reason to strike him, to beat him so badly he had to lay flat on his stomach all night for the bruises and sores hurt him when he moved." I paused, holding still to my quivering lip.

"And one day Edmund had enough. He saw all the other boys with their parents playing games, giving hugs, talking, *laughing*, and he realized he would never have that with his father. So, holding tight to his book, he ran as far as his feet could take him, not stopping until he was sure he was never going to be found by his father again. And then he met a boy, a boy named Will, outside his house. He was quite a few years younger than Edmund; he was found trembling outside on his front porch. Edmund asked him what was wrong, and together they watched the scene inside. Watched the boy's father hurt his mother like Edmund's father had done to him.

Edmund asked if the boy wanted to run with him, and knowing the boy was too scared to run, he said, 'I'll be back in two weeks. If this gets worse when I come, you can run away with me and never have to see this again.' The boy nodded and wiped his nose. And when Edmund went to leave, he called him back, asking one question.

He said, 'you never told me your name.'

And looking down at the book, Edmund decided he didn't want to be his father's son anymore, he didn't want to be scared or alone. He wanted to be like the hero in the book, help boys like him out of impossible situations. And so he told Will his name was Peter. And he's been Peter ever since."

Ever stopped, inhaling sharply. "Oh, Peter, that was you? I mean, I knew it was you because you said - Peter, I never knew your father was such an awful, awful man! I'm so sorry."

"It's okay," I spoke without emotion. "I'm over it now." I decided to change the subject, as I could bare no longer the thick tension that lingered in the air. "What I'm more interested in is your story. How did you get here? The *real* reason."

She ran her fingers through her hair nervously, figuring that if I had shared my story she might as well share hers. "My mother agreed to bring me anywhere I wanted, if I did things her way."

"Her way?"

"She wanted me to stop fighting, to stop ruining the dates she set me up on, and be a *darling* child, as she put it. Basically, she wanted me to live the life of a stuck-up brat and enjoy it. Or, at least, pretend to. So, she agreed to bring me here, and I don't know, I saw the woods and just... ran."

Confused, I pursed my lips and phrased a question. "But that night you came, you said you were lost. You were scared. If so, how come you ran away?"

She shrugged, tossing her blanket of hair off her shoulder. "I realized, after I was about a mile in, how stupid it was. Regardless if I hated my life, I had nowhere to go in these woods. I would surely die if I tried to live here alone, even to escape my fate back in London. And it was also the fact that I knew my mother loved me, even if she showed it in a twisted way. I didn't realize then, that *my* happiness mattered as well as hers. So, I tried to turn back and got lost."

"No," I corrected her. "You were found."

...

I hadn't even realized how far we'd gone until we could hear the sounds of voices and footsteps.

We were right on the brim of the trails. How could I have been so stupid?! It was dark, nearly pitch black, and yet there was still people out there.

Or at least someone.

"Help! Help!" We heard the cries and advanced a little further. A man, too shielded by the dark to make out, was dragging himself down the paths, clearly starved and lost. "Please, is anyone out there?!"

"We have to help him," Wendy decided, in her usual caring manner. She started forward, but I pulled her back.

"No! They can't see us. Everyone here must be looking for you, and if they spot either of us-"

"Peter, he's injured! I'm not going to leave an innocent man to die!" She stormed forward right as the moon passed over both of them. And in the dim light, I could see his face.

"Wendy, Wendy don't -" I called in urgency.

But she had already left. And I couldn't save her now.

Chapter Eleven

Wendy

As I ran towards the distressed voice, I noticed how this might be a bad idea. This was a random man calling for my aid, someone who was a stranger and could possibly be dangerous.

Yet still, he was calling for help.

Peter was right, lots of people are probably looking for me, who knows if this man's one of them?

Yet still, he *needed* help.

I shook these thoughts away. This person needed someone's assistance, and right now, that someone was me. I couldn't let my petty fears stop me.

When Peter had pulled back, I had lost sight of him, so I quickly followed the pained voice until it sounded like it was right in front of me.

Then *he* was right in front of me.

I have never been so relieved that I followed my instincts. This man *really* needed someone's helping hand, and now. In the time I had lost sight of him, his leg had gotten stuck under a tree log, his pants ripped and his face was smeared with dirt. He badly needed a shave, and a strong scent of liquor and wine was emitting from his entire body. It was like instead of a shower with water, he had bathed in alcohol.

Except, in the state he was in, you could tell he hadn't taken the effort to clean himself in a long time.

He looked up at me, and I have to say, he looked worse than drunk.

He looked crazy and mad.

"Hello, pretty girl," he croaked. "I knew you would come to help a... a poor, hurt man." The last part sent an evil grin up to the corners of his lips. He looked so bewilderingly triumphant, not so desperate for help any longer.

I choked back my fear.

"I... um, we can both pull at the log, that might get it off. If we can't with only us, there is someone I left behind so I could assist you. I can always run and get him."

"Oh, that won't be needed," the man assured me. "You'll do plenty fine."

"Um, okay..."

"The log is actually fairly light. So you should be able to do it," he smirked. "*Ever.*"

I froze. I had never told him my name. Slowly, I forced my shaking legs to walk backward, but I quickly bumped into a tree.

"I-I n-n-never told you my n-n-name, so… so…" I gulped. "H-how do you k-know who I a-am?" Slowly, my arms reached back and clutched the tree.

For what? The littlest protection?!

Yet still, it made me feel safer.

The deranged man sitting in front of me grinned madly, as if he had just won a great prize, and yet killed his opponent to do so. "How do you think I know?" he drawled.

I opened my mouth, only to close it. The small surging anger I had just felt towards him deflated quickly now that it was my turn to talk.

I shook my head and repeated the same words. "I n-n-never t-told you."

With a mad cackle, he sat there, not answering me.

My heart felt like it stopped at the suspense. Why hadn't I just listened to Peter? And what should I do now?

I would have to run, I noticed all too quickly. Maybe the fallen tree log would hold him for a little, but not forever.

Then suddenly, as if he knew exactly what I was thinking, he kicked the log off easily, and that's when I noticed it was dead and hollow inside, making it light as a feather. How could I have been so stupid? If it was real, he never could've gotten it on top of himself so quickly in the first place.

Before I could even work up enough adrenaline to run away, he jumped up with more ease then you would have imagined from an old drunk, and grabbed the neckline of the shirt Will had lent me.

I was frozen, yet still shaking with fear.

His breath smelled worse than his entire body, his teeth were yellow and crooked, and his eyes were dull, as if he hadn't been properly loved in a long time. I would've felt bad for him, if he wasn't holding me so high my feet only brushed the ground, trying to hurt me or kidnap me.

Why did he want me? How did he know my name?

"H-how?" was the only thing I managed to get out.

He smiled wickedly, as if he thoroughly enjoyed this, and then he finally told me.

"Your mother."

...

Why did I run here? Why did I fall, so... so stupidly into this trap of his?! Or hers! Of course it was my mother; who else would want to ruin my life when I had finally found my happy place?

At least my frustration towards myself was better than my petrified fear.

"J-j-just f-for..." I glared at him, telling myself sternly, *don't be afraid.* "J-just for you to know, I was with people when I w-went to help you! So, many people are behind me. And when I say many, I mean *many* many. Like, they would outnumber you by a lot. And they should be here..." I looked at my wrist, then remembered I didn't have a watch. "Any time, now," I finished lamely.

A flicker of... fear (was it?) passed through his eyes, but in a snap was gone, making me wonder if it was really there at all. He opened his mouth to say something, but just then a loud noise interrupted him.

The noise of a person.

"Ever!"

Peter looked like he had been trying to find me for a long time. Leaves and twigs were stuck in his hair, and sweat glistened on his forehead.

"Ever, I... put her down! Let go of her!" I guess he realized that I wasn't alone a bit later than he found me.

"I said," he repeated angrily, making me so grateful for his bravery, "put her d-" and then both the madman and fearless Peter looked at each other. The crazy stranger's evil grin grew bigger as if he had been waiting to find not only me, but Peter as well.

Peter, meanwhile, grew deathly pale, and all the strength and courage that he had had before disappeared quickly.

"Hello," the man sneered. "*Edmund.*"

The boy cringed.

This man was scary, but scary enough to frighten even Peter? That didn't seem possible. And how had he known Peter's real name?

My mum wouldn't have sent for Peter too, she didn't know who he was!

Did she?

Luckily, Peter being afraid made me lose my own dread, for I felt like at least one of us should be strong.

"What do you want?" I demanded.

He laughed. "Found your voice, have you now? Well, I will answer you, but I think you know already." He leaned in a little closer, leering down at me. "You."

My hands started shaking again.

I hated it.

Chapter Twelve

Peter

I tumbled into the clearing, my breath coming in short rasps, and sunk to my knees, my hands on the grassy dirt floor.

"Peter?" Elliot asked, trying to get a good view of me in the dark. I could see that he had been put up for watch that night; the boys didn't like to have everyone asleep and vulnerable when I wasn't around. I stood, still catching my breath from my run through the forest, and looked to Elli with wide, fearful eyes.

"Wake the boys."

Confused, he nodded and shuffled over to the swaying hammocks, alerting each boy with an urgent shake on the shoulder. "Get up!" he called over and over again until four sleepy-eyed drones were slinking out of their beds. Their eyes grew larger when they saw me: dirty, tired out, and clearly distressed.

Will was the first to speak. "Peter! What's wrong?! Where's - oh God, she didn't leave because of us, did she?" He looked at me, compassion swelling in his eyes as tears swelled in mine. "Peter, I'm so sorry. This is all because of me, I didn't realize -"

"N-no," I said shakily. "It's not that. It's - it's much worse."

The twin's eyes grew wider, and they spoke with the same thought.

"Well then -" was started by Thomas.

And "- what is it?" was finished by his other half.

"He took her - a - man... he - he took her." It was all I could get out.

A collective gasp was followed by an uneasy silence. Will was the first to gulp down his fear. "Was he a man - looked almost homeless, very tall, smelt of alcohol... and did he have this look in his eyes, like - like he wanted to -"

"Kill you? Yes."

"Oh my God, Peter, it's that man!" Concern grew in his voice like a rapid-fire, thickening the tension in the air. I nodded.

"This is all my fault," I muttered, my breathing shaky. I started to pace, back and forth, back and forth, my hands going to my head, then my sides, then wringing themselves out - not sure of what to do. "This is *all* my fault."

"No it's not," Elliot tried. "I bet you tried to stop the man in the first place. Why would it be your fault that he was there?"

"Because he was there for me!" I bellowed, watching Elliot shrink back in fear. Realizing my fear was turning to anger, I calmed myself, and forced all my fright into my clenched fists, repeating more quietly with closed eyes, "because he was there for me."

"Why would he be there for you?" a voice rang out dubiously.

I stopped pacing, placed a hand on my quivering lip and took a deep breath. "There's something you don't know." I instantly looked to Will, seeing agitation spread over him like an illness at the thought of another secret. "That man - he's - he's my father."

I had to sit down after that, tell the boys my story. It was hard - having to relive it all once again - but I left out a single minor detail. That my name was Edmund. Part of me still wanted them to believe in me, believe in magic, in the story of Peter Pan. And if they found out that my name wasn't actually Peter, I don't know, I thought they may lose some of that belief. And I couldn't have that. So as far as they knew, I was still Peter. Peter Pan.

And then Will asked me how my father got to our dear Wendy, and that story was even more painful to share, as I had to tell them how I failed her.

...

"Wendy - Wendy don't!" I called after her, watching in agony as she tore through the bushes and onto the trails. The moonlight passed over her, sparkling on her hair and moving to the injured man. Or at least, the man who *claimed* to be injured. And right as I saw his face in the dim light, my stomach dropped to a sickening feeling and I began to feel faint. He wasn't injured - that was for sure - and his intentions were most definitely otherwise. And now there was nothing I could do about it.

I peeked through the branches of the trees, trying so desperately to get sight of them, but as the moon's light faded, I could only hear the dialogue.

"Hello, pretty girl," I shuddered as I heard him say. " I knew you would come to help a… a poor, hurt man."

The liar! My fear slowly started to evaporate into anger. No, not anger - rage.

"I… um, we can both pull at the log, that might get it off. If we can't with only us, there is someone I left behind so I could assist you. I can always run and get him," Wendy started. *Yes, yes!* I cried out in my mind, my delusions of hoping she was secretly a mind reader enveloping me. *Come back and we'll run, far far away!*

"Oh, that won't be needed, you'll do plenty fine."

My teeth gritted.

"Um, okay…"

"The log is actually fairly light. So you should be able to do it. *Ever.*"

Stomach bile rose in my throat. I had figured he was here for me - he had to be! But he knew her name, meaning he wanted her. And I couldn't let him hurt her.

The rest of their conversation seemed to fade away, the fear churning in my stomach overtaking me. This man had ruined so much of my life and hurt me in unspeakable ways. I couldn't let him lay even a finger on her.

I zoned back in when Ever's tone became sharp with fear. She stuttered, practically pleading for help. Conflicted, I followed the sound of her voice, my feet dragging slowly because I was so scared. But I loved her too much to let him get to her. Yes, I loved her. I told myself that over and over, growing stronger with the feeling.

"H-how?" she squeaked in fright, stuttering as he got closer to her.

"Your mother."

My fear evaporating into the roaring winds, anger turning my cheeks pink.

I crouched low beneath the protection of the bushes, trying to swish spit behind my teeth to give me something to focus on, but finding my mouth bone dry. "J-j-just f-for… J-just for you to know, I was with people when I w-went to help you! So, many people are behind me. And when I say many, I mean *many* many. Like, they would outnumber you by a lot. And they should be here… any time, now." Ever looked nervously around, and I knew that was my cue. Mustering up enough bravery for both of us, I stepped out from my cover and called out to her.

"Ever!" My courageous and strong-willed words I had been thinking up failed me once I laid eyes on the man, and I stuttered out, "Ever, I…put her down! Let go of her!" The cruel man only smirked at my loss for words, a look which he had given me countless times before. As if saying *you never had it in you, Edmund.* "I said, put her d-" His grin spread wider, like a father's proud smile when he found himself admiring his son's accomplishments, except in the most fear-surging, twisted way. I heard his voice in my head, tearing me down. *You've finally found your voice, Edmund. Well, it's about time. I tried to teach you, again, and again, and now look at you. The man I always dreamed you up to be.* I could see the words in his eyes, and they clouded my head, making me cringe as I recalled his way of teaching.

"Hello… *Edmund*." I slunk back in fright. Suddenly I wasn't the strong, protective Peter Pan anymore. No, I was only the little boy who never had the strength to fight back. *No! That's how he wants me to feel!* And yet, I couldn't help but feel just that. The way he emitted his power and control over me was just too much. The memories were too much.

"What do you want?" Ever demanded, and it comforted me that she could now be brave for me. My father only laughed wryly. "Found your voice, have you now? Well, I will answer you, but I think you know already." He leaned in closer to her, and some fury replaced my fright. "You."

Ever started to shake, uncontrollably now, and without thinking I ran at the man with all the might I could rally, only managing to push him off of her, to make him stumble back into the tree. "Run!" I screamed as he stood back on his feet, furiated as ever now. But Ever didn't move - couldn't move - and only stayed there, trembling like a mouse.

"Oh Edmund, you just don't know what's good for you," he sneered, wiping dirt from his face. "But I'm going to teach you a lesson. Just like we used to. You remember our *lessons*, don't you?" His sneer turned into a low growl, resembling a fierce lion, and I started to tremble more than ever. I was still, except for the shaking, unable to move, unable to think - completely helpless. Yes, I remembered our *lessons*. They were, and are, what haunt my sleep at night, fill me with nightmares I can't soon forget, and make me relive the past so vividly it jolts me awake with tear-stained cheeks. I remember it so clearly because *every* night I relive it, as a little boy who just wants love - just that! He asks for nothing more, cries over nothing, not even food to fill his belly. No, all he wants is care and love, one person to give him those two simple things. And when his father gets angry, beats him to teach him something no child needs to learn, he lays awake at night and wonders why he can't have a father who cares?

And now I was that little boy again, wondering the same thing. Only this time it wasn't a dream.

I shivered as my father got closer, his lower lip curling in disgust. "Well, aren't you gonna do somethin' boy? Aren't you a *man*, now? Or are you just gonna let me hit you like I did when you were a boy?! You know, Edmund, if you just fought back *one measly time* I wouldn't have kept on. I was trying to make you stronger! But you were too weak." He breathed the last sentence down my neck, chilling me to the bone. I shook my head. And then, with his hands already placed on my shoulders, he shoved me hard into the tree behind me. I hit it with a thud, pain ringing throughout my spine as I heard a cry of distress from Ever, who let go of the tree and started to run over, but stopped with a screeching heel when my father whipped around to her.

"Oh, aren't you a doll? Well miss, your *Peter*, that's what you call him, right? He's going to have to go through a lot more than this, unless of course…"

"Unless what?" She snapped defiantly, clenching her fists like a child.

He fingered his lip pathetically. "Unless you were to come with me."

"You think I'm going to blindly go with you? You're a - a mad, twisted man, and I certainly won't go anywhere with the likes of *you*!" Her words weren't very intimidating, but she ended it with a wry laugh at his angered frown.

"You sure?" he pouted.

"Yeah, I'm pretty sure I've made myself clear." Her confidence faltered, though, when my father wheeled back around to me, his raised outward palm striking down against my cheek. I winced, bringing a hand to the wound and tasting the metallic savor of blood in my mouth. Right as I did so, I dodged another blow, only to have yet another fist strike me in the stomach. I doubled back, pain erupting inside me and making me sick.

"How does that feel, son?" He snapped his knuckle, and a sickening feeling clouded over me. "Want another?" Baring his yellowed, crooked teeth, he sent his heel straight into my knee, making me collapse on the dirt ground, and Wendy scream in protest. I could hardly see the fist he raised in the air over me, for now, black spots danced around in the sky, growing larger with every passing second. I could only hear now, really, as Ever ran over to me, throwing out her hands in an attempts to guard me against his next strike.

"Stop! Stop!" She swallowed. "Just... stop."

He grinned evilly. "You're either really stupid, girl, you like the taste of blood, or you'll -"

She didn't let him finish, completing his sentence. "I'll go with you."

I tried to call out in protest as I struggled to get up, but realistically it came out as more of a pained moan. Ever pushed me back down on the ground, my head hitting the hard, cracked dirt, and kissed my lips.

And then she was gone.

Chapter Thirteen

*P*eter

I started to feel faint close to the end of my story, and though there was nothing left in my stomach to throw up, I could feel stomach bile rising in my throat yet again. My jaw hurt from where my father had struck me, my stomach, sore and upset from the blow to it, churned with fear and anticipation. He had her, he had my Wendy! And it was all because of what? Her kind heart, her willingness to go with him to save me? No… it was because I wasn't strong enough to save her myself.

I wasn't strong enough to fight my father.

But I wasn't going to make that mistake again. I stood, staggered, and brushed the dirt off my knees. "We have to help her. There's still time! There is no way they've made it to the village by now, and the moon's nearly full so we'll still have light to-"

A wave of nausea rushed over me, and I stumbled back down. Will caught me with expecting arms, and sat me down, my back against the rough bark of a tree. "It's all my fault," I mumbled softly, my vexation turning to a pathetic inconsolable grief. "I have to help her."

Will felt my head for a fever, his expression rather concerned. Behind him, all the boys watched with wide-eyed dismay, leaning in to listen closer as Will spoke softly. "Yes, and we will help her, but right now you need rest -"

"No, nothing-of-the-sort," I moaned in protest, my words jumbled. But he was right, I could barely keep my eyes open. And still, she was out there somewhere, alone, probably scared and hurt, and I couldn't rest knowing that.

"Just *listen*. I'll take Oliver tonight into the village - that's probably where he's taking her - and we'll look to see when the next train leaves for London."

"London, why-"

"Because you said her mother wanted her. And her mother lives in London." As he spoke, he signaled something to Elliot, who then scrambled over to fetch the water bottle from the pantry. I nodded sleepily, alarmed that even in this state I wasn't able to connect those points together. "We'll be back before the sun rises. Then in the morning," he continued, "We'll all go down and save her before the train leaves off. Alright?"

Again, I only nodded. Will took the water bottle and gently lifted it to my lips. I obliged, and downed most of the water, realizing how thirsty I was after sprinting miles on an empty, beaten stomach. After finishing off the water, I stood shakily and was helped to the couch where a blanket was laid over me and sleep welcomed me with open arms.

...

I awoke in a field of swaying grass, each blade as tall as I was, sharp green and reaching for the sun. The sky held no clouds and shimmered with the most beautiful unrealistic blue, as bright and playful as the sea. Looking around I saw the same scene in every direction, and no matter where I turned or where I went everything was the same.

Until I saw her. Farther off in the distance was a girl, her hair light brown and curled in neat pretty waves. Half was tied back with a light blue ribbon that matched the sky and it seemed to lay so perfectly on its bed of hair. Her dress was the same blue, the top made up of a sheer light material, coated with light blue flowers that created an elegant sweetheart neckline, and trickled down to cuff her wrists. Beneath that was a simple ribbon that synched her waist into a perfect bow in the back, and under the bow was a skirt that sank down past her feet, it's material made up of layers of the sheer blue over a solid skirt, each one flowing and dancing in the winds. Even though I couldn't see her face, she was absolutely breathtaking. And then I heard her laugh, a sweet sing-song sound that seemed to echo throughout the field. She beckoned for me to follow and I didn't hesitate a second to run after her, chasing her through the field and soon finding myself in a forest. I hadn't even noticed the change of scenery until I couldn't find her any longer. I had been so focused on the girl that I didn't seem to notice where I was going. Nevertheless, I hiked past trees and bushes of leaves in any attempt to find her.

"Peter," I heard her voice ring out once I met a gathering of wild blueberry bushes. "Come find me. You *know* where, Peter." As I listened to the echoing words, I tried to pinpoint where they were coming from. But I just couldn't. They seemed to be coming from every direction, and then at the same point nowhere at all.

Then it struck me. I knew these woods. Every square inch of them. And I knew exactly where to find her. Turning and tearing through the trees, I picked up my pace until I reached the vine curtains that draped down, twisted and turned, and I pushed my hands, then myself, through them.

Sure enough, I found her, splashing and playing in the waters, her dress still flowing in the winds and the waves, but not seeming to get wet. She smiled at me, her eyes twinkling with a mischievous, delighted look. I could see her face now, clear as day, and she was exactly who I expected her to be. Who I *wanted* her to be.

"Wendy!"

"Peter, you found me!"

I nodded happily and followed her into the water, overjoyed that she was there, that I was with her. I dove into the lake after her, determined to reach her, but every time I waded closer she seemed to slip further away. Again and again, I tried to get closer, all to no avail, as she seemed to go deeper in whenever I moved. "I don't understand," I faltered. "Why won't you -"

And then she was right there, right in front of me, grabbing onto the collar of my shirt. "Get close to you?" She snipped. I jumped, slightly, surprised at her abrupt change of position.

"How did you…" My words trailed off as she leaned in and kissed my lips, a soft gesture that should have filled my heart to the brim, my stomach with butterflies and made excitement trickle to my fingertips. But instead, I felt… nothing.

"I can't stay here, Peter," she said after she pulled away. "Not here with you."

"Why not?" I asked plainly, trying to kiss her again, but she dodged away. I wanted a second kiss. I wanted - no, I *needed*, to feel something this time.

"Because you might let go… again." Along with her words, she let go of her grip on my collar and started to fall back into the water, nothing to balance her weight. I grabbed on to her hand, my grip slipping as the waves started to crash directly under her. Her tender hand slipped out of mine and she fell, disappearing into the waves.

I didn't even have the time to scream. Shook, and terribly upset, I dove under after her, but this time she was nowhere to be seen. I searched around underwater, desperately trying to find her before I ran out of air until I heard a muffled cry from up above.

"Peter! Help me! Peter! Help!" The cry got louder and louder, more ear piercing the closer I got to the top. And when I reached the crisp air above, I was further away from the shore than I had ever been before, and there was no bottom in reach of my feet to stand on. But even with the distance, I could see a clear picture of what was happening on shore. Her dress was now stained with blood, which poured from a wound on her side and other smaller injuries on her legs and arms. Her eye was cut and swollen, her face and neck bruised in various places. Her hands were chained down with black chains that came from the sands and wrapped around her wrists, climbing up her arms gradually. The longer I looked, the higher the chains enveloped around her, the more blood poured from her wounds and the louder her screams and pleas for help were. I tried to swim to her, but no matter how far I went, I was the same distance from the shore as before. I tried to yell to her, but she couldn't seem to hear me.

And then the strangest, most horrifying thing started to happen. Her image began to flash. One second she was her normal self, beckoning me over with a smile, perfect in her flowing blue dress, and the next she was back in the black growing chains, bloody and crying out in pain. I couldn't bear to watch, because the longer I did, the more the horrid image overtook the good one, and the cries overtook me. The waters at my feet started to churn and swirl, sucking me down with them. I battled them furiously, trying to stay afloat, trying to get to her. But I was already weak from treading the water for so long, and the more I thought of her, the more I seemed to sink. Further and further down until the waves splashed over my head and sunk, taking me down with them.

...

My eyes flew up and I sat up suddenly, drenched in sweat. My blanket was on the ground, it had apparently been kicked off in my sleep, and the cold night reminded me dreadfully of the cool surging waters in my dream. The sky was still dark, not a star to gaze upon, so I let my head fall back on the arm of the couch.

I sighed. How I wished it was Ever's arms I could fall into at this point; or that she could fall into mine. It didn't matter, whether I was comforting her, or she me, because in a way we both found comfort in one another and that was enough.

Unable to bring myself back to sleep in fear of another nightmare, I stood and strode over to the pathway out of the clearing, my feet paving my direction without thought. I walked and walked, passing the hidden bushes of wild berries, past trees and brambles and moss-covered logs, down the path all the way to the curtain of vines that twisted and turned. I pushed my hands through, making enough space to inch past without disturbing the nature of things.

The view past the vine wall was just as beautiful at night. The waters were still and blanketed the sands with foam. I sat down on the dry part of the shore, hugging my knees to my chest, and looked up at the sky. The billowing clouds shifted out of the way to reveal two simple stars, one slightly northeast of the other.

"Second star to the right and straight on till morning," I spoke in a whisper, the ghost of a smile tugging at my lips because I knew, wherever she was, Ever was looking out at the same set of stars. I let that smile take me over, closing my eyes in the moment.

It wasn't long before I heard a voice. "Hello? Hello? Are you there?" The sound of it was light, warm and feminine. My eyes flew open, and I looked around eagerly. Wendy?

But this voice definitely did not belong to my sweet Wendy. No, it was older, a bit cracked with age, and I thought it to be the voice of someone who had trailed off the path and lost their way. But then something odd occurred to me. The voice had said 'are *you* there', not 'is *anyone*', or 'is *someone* there'. It was as if they were looking for someone already, that they suspected someone they were acquainted with was already there. Wherever 'there' was.

I stood up, trying to locate where the sound was coming from, and it was all too much like my dream. "Who's there?" I called out sharply, thinking it to be just my imagination. But it wasn't. Because right after I spoke a woman ducked out from behind the curtain of vines. I stood there, staring dumbly at her as she smiled at me. She was beautiful and captivating in her own way. Her blonde hair, loose in the winds, had been blown into a complete mess, but it was a wonderful mess. And her smile, it was so pretty and welcoming, like you just wanted to give her a great big hug right when you saw her. She wore a simple white dress, but that was just enough to make her look stunning, because it let you focus on her alone.

"A-are you lost? It-it's the middle of the night."

She walked over to me and sat down, looking out at the horizon and the waves, and at last saying. "I know, but it's a beautiful night."

I stared at her, feeling like I was completely underwhelming her. This stranger had just come through to my secret special place in the middle of the night and sat down on my beach, and I - I didn't know how to react.

"Yeah it is, I guess." I had admired the beauty of the place countless times, but on a night like this, I just couldn't appreciate it. A question still nagged at my throat. "Y-you said 'are you there' like you were looking for someone… were you?" I failed to find any other words.

She turned her head to face me with a twinkle in her eye. "Why yes, I was." And she gave me no other explanation until I inquired who it was she was searching for.

"You."

I stood there stunned, stuttering with speech. "I-I-I... do - do we know each other?"

She shook her head, her focus back on the still waters. "Sadly, no. You don't know me, but I know you, Peter."

This time I couldn't even stutter. I was completely speechless. She motioned for me to sit down, and I did, like a lame, trained dog I sat. "H-how do you k-know my name?"

She smiled and seemed to give warmth to the cold winds blowing at us. "Don't you know, Peter? Don't you know?" she said again, and I did know. I knew full well, it was just... impossible.

"No, no," I gulped, staring at my feet. "You died in labor. I never even got to see you. It was always father. I - I -"

"And yet I'm here now. I'm sorry Peter, for what I put you through. Maybe if I had been stronger you wouldn't have to have gone through that. I could've protected you."

"No," I said, yet again, in total disbelief. She wasn't here, not *really* here. But then again, she was. And part of me knew that even if this was a dream, I didn't want to wake up.

"But you've been so strong," she continued. "I'm so proud of you." She ruffled my hair, an endearing look on her face. "I've been watching over you."

"Then - then you saw what happened. How father got to Ever. I - I couldn't save her." I dropped my head, my hands hitting my forehead and sliding back to my neck.

"You did all you could. You'll find her and save her - I believe in you. Your father is a... a broken man. But he loves you."

I scoffed crossly. "Would you hurt someone you loved like that? Would you take everything from them until they had nothing? No one? I had nobody who cared for me, mother, no one! And now the one person I found that loves me like that he takes."

"Look around you. The boys, me, we all love you."

I gave her a sad look. "But you're not really here, are you? You can't be here."

She returned my look with a sad smile. "No, I'm not. You're dreaming, Peter. But whether or not you choose to believe I'm real is up to you. I just came to tell you that I love you." She kissed my forehead, and I hugged her tight, tears now streaming down my face. I had just met her and yet, yet I felt like I'd known her all my life.

She let go of my hug, and I found that she, too, was crying. And soon she started to fade away. Slowly her image got dimmer and dimmer. "I'm waking up," I sniffled, clinging to her hand like a little boy.

She nodded and then said in a soft, loving tone, "You know that place between sleep and awake, that place where you still remember dreaming? That's where I'll always love you. That's where I'll be waiting."

I smiled through my tears at the quote. "It was your book, wasn't it? *Peter & Wendy*. The one that Mary gave me when I was a little boy. It was yours."

She nodded, her image now fading from view. "I love you, Peter."

I opened my eyes and lifted my head, looking around in an instant. My mother was nowhere in sight and the sun was rising. I must have dozed off sitting down, which would explain why my head had fallen into my knees. I stood, dusting the sand off of me, and wiping my eyes groggily. The dream had been so vivid, she had been there, and then, just like that, she was gone.

As I trotted back down to the path, I pondered on whether or not she had really been *real*. Had I just made up my mother to comfort me? Can one do that? Can one simply make up a person in their head, just like that? I supposed so, but I also wanted to believe otherwise. It wasn't like I had been thinking about her before I fell asleep, she had just *come*. And if I believed in fate, in the story of Peter Pan and the lost boys around me, then why couldn't I believe in her? I did, after all, have a mother at one point, and it made sense that if she died and she had the power to look after me she would do so.

I left the decision at that with no more thought to it and picked up my pace on my journey through the woods. The boys would certainly be alarmed if they were to find me gone when they woke up, so I sped briskly through the forest in an attempt to get back before they arose.

I seemed to have arrived just in the nick of time, because when I got there, Albie was about to wake Elliot, looking back at the empty couch and the tossed blanket.

"Albie!" I hissed as I darted over to him. "Albie, don't wake him up!"

"Oh, Peter!" he cried, loud at first, then quieted his tone. He ran over to me, excitement in his eyes. Besides a fit of coughing, Elliot remained in his sleepy state and rolled over on his side.

"Where'd you go, Peter? Did you get Wendy back?"

I shook my head sadly. "No, buddy. But we're going to do that. I promise. We will get her back. Alright?"

He nodded solemnly, and I picked him up and brought him over to the couch. We both laid there silently for a while, snuggling with the blanket over us, watching the sunrise in the distance. Finally, he couldn't stand the silence any longer and squirmed over into a sitting position to face me. "If you weren't saving Wendy, where did you go?"

"Can you keep a secret?" I asked with a smile, laying him back down. He nodded his head vigorously. "I went to my special place and I looked up at the sky and saw two stars, one to the right of the other. And you know what they say -"

He didn't let me finish. "Neverland! Did you go there Peter, oh did you?!"

"No, no," I laughed. "But I fell asleep under the stars and in a dream, my mother came to me."

His eyes grew wide as saucers. "Your mother?! Isn't she dead?"

Again, I nodded. "She may be, but I think she's up in Neverland. And sometimes, when I sleep under the stars, she likes to come down and visit."

Albie smiled, peering up at the stars with the most amazing curiosity. "Maybe one night in my dreams my mother will come to me, too."

"Maybe," I repeated uneasily, then told him to go get the book so we could read. He got up gleefully and went over to grab it, coming back with the cutest grin as he flipped through the pages.

"I'm on this page, right… here!" He placed his little finger on the paragraph where I started to read. *"Not the pain of this but its unfairness was what dazed Peter. It made him quite helpless. He could only stare, horrified. Every child is affected thus the first time he is treated unfairly. All he thinks he has a right to when he comes to you to be yours is fairness. After you have been unfair to him he will love you again, but will never afterwards be quite the same boy. No one ever gets over the first unfairness; no one except Peter."*

"What does that mean?" Albie interrupted.

I took a pause, thinking up the right way to phrase it. "It means that if someone wrongs you, like really hurts you, you can forgive them a hundred times, but once they wrong you part of you will always remember how hurt you felt."

"So you can't love them anymore?" he asked innocently.

"No, no, you can love them. Like Wendy, she loves us even though we had her tied to a tree at the start. It doesn't make her love us any less, it just doesn't go away."

He pointed to the words on the page. "But it says 'no one except Peter'! Does that mean *you* can forget it? Like what your father did to you? Can you forgive him and forget?"

I sat, staring at the little boy in my arms, trying to say something. "I-I don't know buddy. My father hurt me, again and again. Maybe one day I could forgive him, but I don't think I could ever forget. And I certainly won't forget that he took Wendy."

"Yeah," Albie agreed defiantly. "No one takes our Wendy."

It was at that time that Will and Oliver came running into the clearing, panting and clearly out of breath. "The train…" Will said between breaths. "Leaves… at noon."

I stood up, gently closing the book and handing it to Albie as all the boys looked to me. "Then what are we waiting for? Let's get our Wendy back!"

Chapter Fourteen

Wendy

I cried and cried until it was impossible to have any more tears. Yet still, I let my hurt, depressed, angry shoulders shake, and my dry eyes continue to look for any wetness.

Luckily, Peter's dad was driving his rusty, well worn-down truck, and I got thrown into the back seat, so he didn't have to watch me in my bitter distress. Though sometimes he heard me let out a soft whimper, and even then he would yell at me to shut my mouth so he could focus.

He was a little happier, though, now that he had what he wanted.

Peter out of the way, me in his wretched grasp.

I glared at him in the front, hating him with every bone in my body. He had ruined my life.

The pathetic life that had been so dull, so empty. It had been the same thing every day.

And then had I run away. And I got thrown into a swirl of emotions. First fear towards the "lost boys," who kidnapped me with no reason, then a mixture of confused love. For I had started to fall in love with these boys, when *they* had hurt me. *They* had stolen me away. *They* had forced me into their little Neverland.

Yet I loved them.

Then, after I kissed Peter, yes, *I* kissed *him*, I felt guilty about wanting to leave these crazy lovable, innocent, sweet boys. Even when I knew my mum needed me.

Finally, I realized that I needed them more then she would ever need me. And so I felt... well, good. Right at home.

Then she ruined it, like everything else. She sucked all the happiness out of my life, and when finally I found a little light, hidden where she could never find me, she somehow still found a way to ruin that, too, even from afar.

And so I cried all night until I finally fell asleep.

The next morning I woke with a start, a gruff hand shaking me awake.

Where was I? Who was this man? Was this a dream?

As he raised his hand to slap my groggy face, I suddenly remembered. I ducked, but still felt the sting of his harsh hand, for I had been too late. Gasping in pain and eyes wide that he would dare to do such a thing, I lifted my head up and glared, fighting the urge to bring my hand up to my bright red cheek.

But as soon as I looked up to his unsympathetic, twisted face, my courage faltered. He pulled me out of the back seat and threw me on the ground.

"Don't even think about running away, or else I swear I'll go back and kill your beloved *Peter Pan.*" There was something absolutely awful about his voice that convinced me he would make well on his threats.

I shuddered and gulped down my fear.

"Also, hide your face. Wouldn't want anyone recognizing you now, would we?"

I stumbled towards the cheap motel as he pushed me in front of him. I looked at the ground and tried to pull my tangled, dirty hair over my face to hide it from view.

I was so worried that people might notice I was a girl, yet a girl that wore dirty pants and an eternally dirt stained, very large shirt.

A sad smile was brought to my lips as I remembered valiantly trying to clean this shirt - as I insisted all the boys learn how to do with their clothes - and not being able to get a single filthy stain out.

I thought about the laughter that that night had brought. The smiles.

The love.

Would anyone ever love me like that again?

"Get a move on," Peter's father sneered, pushing me so hard it took all my might to not fall over. As soon as we got inside, I realized that my worries were for nothing. Everyone wore dirty clothes, and though a few in long skirts, not one girl was in a dress.

Of course, I should have known this. Why would he bother to get one of those nice hotels, like the one my mother and I had once stayed at? My mum probably offered him some nice deal, so why would he be spending some prize money just so I could have some... some fancy dinner, some comfy bed, or some luxurious bath to scrub off all the dirt I had accumulated in the past weeks?

...

In fact, I did take a bath. The next day I did, in a tiny, cracked, ancient looking bathtub. Then, I put a scratchy, yet clean red dress on. Once I was good to go, I gave myself one more look in the mirror, before leaving the bathroom -

But I stopped. I looked back into the mirror, looked back at the girl in front of me. She was actually quite pretty, now that she was all clean. You could see her dazzling blue eyes through a thick, long layer of dark eyelashes. Her once tangled dirty blonde hair was now brushed and pulled back out of her face by a pretty white bow, which matched her pearly white shoes. She wore a simple ruby red dress, with a pale pink ribbon at the waist.

Yet, besides her breathtaking appearance, you could tell that she wasn't happy. In fact, she was deeply depressed.

This same girl, this same beautiful young lady, had cried all night. This girl had finally found happiness, only for the little light she had once discovered to be snuffed out. This girl had taken a chance, for it to be taken away from her just as fast.

This girl staring back at me, this broken young lady, I knew much too well.

Chapter Fifteen

Peter

The rain dampened the grounds we marched over, endlessly as we made our way to the village. The trees seemed to bend over around us, not so tall and green they stood, hunched over like they bore the weight of all our sorrow since Wendy had left. Even little Albie, who hadn't made it two miles before without complaining was as silent and sober as a crippled lamb.

The dreams from the night before had me crippled as well. I had wanted to believe that the vision of my mother had been real, or at least a sign or had some sort of reasoning behind it, but that also led me to believe similar things about the first one. What *if* my father had hurt Wendy? What then? What if he had…

"Stop thinking that way," Will said coolly, wringing out the folds of his shirt, which were soaked from the downpour that had showered us ten minutes ago. Now it was only sprinkling, but barely only that.

I peered at him with confused eyes. It was as if he had read my mind. "How…" I wondered, rather aggressively.

"Oh please," he added with a roll of his eyes. "Don't act like in all the years I've known you that I wouldn't know the look on your face when you start to fear the worst. When your eyes gloss over like they're going to start watering, but never do. And your nose scrunches up, your teeth clench, and your face just looks overall soured. Let me guess, you're wondering how hurt she'll be, or if she'll even still be alive when you get there." He stated the fact so bluntly, it almost made my already watering eyes spill over. "But don't worry," his tone softened. "She'll be there, and in one piece too."

"How would you know?" I grumbled, slightly taken aback by his sudden change of tone.

"Because I know you. And you wouldn't let that happen to her -"

"But -"

"*And*," he cut me clean off. "I know what kind of scummy half-brained pirate we're dealing with. He hasn't taken Wendy to try and hurt her, but rather to get something in return. Clearly, her mother wants her back, and she's willing to pay the highest bidder."

"What makes you so sure?"

"Because he has no reason at all to hurt Ever, except of course if he were he trying to hurt you. But if that were the case, and *I* were that twisted of a man, I would have done his worst to her in front of you, so that her suffering would ebb into you like a thorn, agonizing to get pierced from, but far more painful to pull away from."

I laughed wryly. "You really have this all thought out, don't you? What are you, a silent killer?" I cocked an eyebrow.

"Something like that," he joked back, and I realized how grateful I was to have a friend like Will. He could make me laugh even in the grimmest of circumstances. His heart was always in the right place, his head in the right game, and he seemed to always know what was best for me and the others. I had thought poorly of him in the past, since he had gotten so angry with Ever and I for, well, sharing thimbles too often. But looking back, I couldn't blame him. I loved him, and all the boys, like brothers, and I found that that love had been temporarily subsided for a girl. And although that girl meant the world to me, I couldn't forget about my true family.

We continued on our trudge through the forest, staying clear of the trails until the very end, where we made our entrance into the village. People buzzed about, couples holding hands, doors opened and closed, cars drove through the streets as we made our way around them. The train station was on the other side of town, so we walked the distance and tried not to meet eyes with anyone in the village.

It was a quaint town, nothing like London in the stories, and was a size small enough for everyone to know everyone but enough for visitors to stay, walk through the beauties of the forest and make their way back home. I could recognize some of the faces I saw around, although I was comforted to know that they didn't know me, as I was good at keeping down low.

"Excuse me, sir," Will addressed the man to my left with a polite tone. "Do you by any chance know what hour it is?"

He looked down at his wrist, pulling over the cuff of his sleeve and check the time. "It's ten till twelve, boy."

Will looked to me with widened eyes. "And would you by any chance know the fastest way to the train station?" I asked. "We're really in a hurry."

"Down the road, and make two rights. Now would you boys quit bothering; I've got places to be."

The lot of us fumbled out an "of course", a "yes", or a small "sorry", all of which ending in sir, and we were off. Down the long road which seemed to go on endlessly, making one right, and then another, until finally, we were there.

Only 'there' was a sea of people. People trying to get off, people trying to get on, others saying goodbye, and next to them a joyous hello. And in the mix somewhere was Wendy. Somewhere.

Will and I tore through the crowd, our eyes peeled for a girl in baggy jeans and an old white t-shirt.

And then I saw him. Walking straight for the entrance to the train, but keeping his eyes out and aware, he stood with tall posture, one hand on his side, and the other slunk around a girl's torso, and held her tight by the waist.

If I hadn't seen her face when she turned I wouldn't have recognized her. She wore a brilliant red dress with a fitted top and a flared skirt, with a thin light pink ribbon that laced around her waist and tied in a small, neat bow in the front. Her feet were in white heeled flats, and around her neck, bright pearls were strung. Her hair was done up in a big white bow, and simple makeup decorated her eyes and lips.

But she did turn around. And I did see her. She looked at me with the most alarmed eyes, a face that pleaded *"help!"* until an aggressive hand grabbed her by the chin and pulled her face back forward. Anger flooded my cheeks, made my blood boil and bones rattle. I tapped Will on the shoulder, pointing to the two of them and then I was off, him close behind me.

Thankfully I was faster than the drunk old man, and I caught up to them swiftly. I took Wendy by the hand, holding it tight and watching with a smile as she turned back to me. I pulled her in as my surprised father stood stunned, and hugged her reassuringly, then put her behind me for protection. My skin bristled as my father's face hardened, his fists clenching by his side.

"So, you've finally gotten the courage to stand up to me."

"Do your worst, *father*," I snapped back, gritting my teeth. He smiled, a wicked, greedy glare, then did the most unexpected thing. Grabbing me by the collar of my shirt, he pulled me up so high that my feet barely hit the ground and my face was only centimeters from his. Ever clung tight to my hand, and my fear drained from me into her.

He leaned close to my ear, and I could feel his hot breath sink into me. "*Don't* test me, boy." And then he threw me to the ground, or should I say, he threw me into Wendy who fell to the ground. I groaned, turning over and finding myself on top of her, our hands still connected.

"Help! Help!" My father started to call out, as I wiped my eyes groggily. "HELP! He's threatening my daughter! Help!"

At his last words, I was completely alert. The crowds began to gather as my father kept hollering, and I looked up right as a man kissed his wife on the head and pushed through the crowd to get to me. He was probably 6'2" and was the largest man I'd ever seen. His expression was stone cold, his eyes in a fury, and his large arms tense. Too shocked and frightened to move, I stared at him, watched him approach until he was standing a foot away from me.

"Alright kid, get off the lady."

"No, no, no you don't understand… he's here to hurt her -" I pointed to my father who looked innocently at the stranger.

"Just help my daughter," he pretended to cry, emotionless tears glistening on the corners of his eyes. The stranger turned back to me, his gaze dropping. Ever tried to talk to me, the crowds mumbled and I could hear the police already in the distance, but already everything around me started to get fuzzy. But I didn't move. I held my ground, clung to Wendy, convincing myself that there was no way I was going to allow my father to take hold of her again. The man grabbed me by the arm and pulled me up, holding me back as I subconsciously fought, kicking and screaming as my father stooped down and helped Wendy up, grabbing her dainty hand and practically forcing her to her feet, then slipping his hand around her waist once again. I fought harder. He whispered something in her ear as I fought the man, who soon had me down on my knees, my arms behind me.

My father finished talking to Ever, pushed her forward and I saw tears staining her face as she looked at the man holding me down and choked out three words.

"Thank you, sir."

And then he took her through the crowd and onto the train.

Will, who had been trying to help me with no success, ran after her, only to be stopped by an angry crowd and upcoming policemen. I was taken by one of them, and in the short second that I was being passed from the stranger to the cop, I broke my arm free and attempted to land a punch in my oppressors face, which was dodged, and followed by a hard kick to the back of my knee joint, causing me to fall to the ground. Handcuffs were snapped onto my wrists, yet still, I fought, even without meaning, and they tightened around me, pinching my skin and drawing blood as they clicked tighter. The officer brought me up by the arms and I saw that Will, too, was in the same situation as I, for he had been fighting on my behalf. And just the same, both of us were being walked from the train station and through the wild crowd.

I turned to look back, catching the eye of a girl, watching me through the window of a train. She wiped tears from her eyes, gave a sad smile, mouthed *goodbye*, and the train started up and rolled away.

...

I looked around the bleak room, seeing nothing of interest. The walls were gray, the floor an even darker shade of cement, and there were only two small windows too high for me to look out of. It was only the brown wood table and chairs that drew any attention to the scene. And the woman who sat across from Will and me.

I tugged at the handcuffs around my wrists, hating the feeling they gave me. Not that they had pinched my skin, drew blood, or pressed a profuse amount of pain on the sore wound, but that they were one more thing holding me down. One more thing in between Wendy and I.

"That man was your father?" the woman asked dubiously, restating the fact I had just shot at her. She turned from me to Will, desperate for information that made sense. Will looked to me, telling me clearly to shut up, and continued on with his story.

"No, ma'am," he corrected, his expression softening. "I can explain. About a month ago there was a fire. We were able to make it out, along with our mother, but our father and sister weren't so fortunate." He took a depressing pause. "Our mum brought us here hoping we would "find peace in the forest walks", but really it was just to get away from home for a bit. The - the girl, she looked so much like Lucia, I-I guess we just lost ourselves. It's been a hard month for all of us." I followed Will's gaze and let my eyes water up, not really thinking about his fake sob-story, but really of Ever's face as the train rolled away, my father's grip on her, how I may never see her again. Will, too, looked so heartbroken, and I wondered if he was thinking the same thing.

"Oh…" The woman looked baffled. "I, um, I can let you off with a warning. What's your mother's name?"

"Oh, no, no please!" Will cried out abruptly. "Please, my mother, she's taken everything so horribly these past few weeks, worse than us, surely! If you tell her we got in trouble like this, it will certainly push her off the edge. Please, ma'am, don't tell her."

She cocked an eyebrow, studying Will who kept the same desperate face on all the while. "Alright," she finally sighed, "but if this happens again -"

"It won't." Will shook his head vigorously.

She pulled out a key from her pocket, clicking open both of the cuffs that held our wrists and gave a short smile. I pulled my hand away in an instant, and under the table so that she wouldn't see my bruised and bloody wrist and try to keep me here any longer. "You two boys have a good day."

"Yes'm, you too."

Then she got up and opened the door, calling over a man in the other hallway to escort us outside.

The second I got a breath of fresh air, I took Will by the arm and ran. Confused, he broke free of my grip and ran after me, all the way back to the train station. The departing schedule was printed on a large bulletin board, and I scanned down the lines until I found the trains to London, then I read the times:

Train No.	A624	A626	A628	A630	A632	A634
LONDON:	12:00	1:00	4:15	7:00	8:00	10:30

"One!" I exclaimed, out of breath, and turned back to Will. He was more focused on examining my wrist; had the scab that had already started forming not broken open when I scraped it on something during my run he would have left it alone.

"Peter you need to get this checked out," he decided, lifting up my forearm to see the bottom of the wound. I yanked it back from him.

"No! We don't have time. You need to get the boys and take them back to camp. I'm getting on that train."

He looked up incredulously. "*How?*"

"I don't know," I shook my head. "I'll try to pickpocket some money or something. You just need to worry about getting to the boys and getting them back to camp. I'll find you there with Wendy."

For a brief second I thought I saw a hint of disappointment on Will's face, and not letting it fade too soon, I inquired the reason for it.

"Nothing," he said quickly. "You're right, you need to get to her."

And then all too soon, the usual distressed look washed over Will, and he licked his lips nervously, glancing around. "What?" I demanded impatiently, following his gaze to where he was looking.

"The boys… they were… right…"

"Oh God," I muttered, my hand cupped over my mouth. Had we… lost them? "Let's start looking. We can split up and search the -"

"No," he cut me off, turning to face the little clock tower by the ticket booth. "No, we only have like twenty-five minutes before you have to get on that train. I'll find the boys and bring them back to camp, don't worry. You - you need to get our Wendy back."

I nodded gratefully, silently noting that he had said 'our' Wendy and not 'your' Wendy, grabbed his arm reassuringly, and then I was off.

...

"That's mine!" she shrieked, yanking back her wallet. I had managed to slip it from her purse, but not undetected. The young lady must have been just in her twenties, and based on the large diamond on her finger, she certainly had someone waiting for her back at home that was very rich.

"I need to get on the next train," I pleaded, my foot tapping again and again on the floor. "Please."

"Then steal someone else's money!" she cried, stomping down on my foot with her heel and storming off. Pain seared through my foot, but I didn't let it deter me, for I only had ten minutes left. I went around to everyone like a beggar, asking for money, and managed only to scrape up a couple of pennies and nickels, which certainly wouldn't do it.

I looked nervously to the train, which was being boarded hastily. And then I watched, crestfallen, as the doors closed and the train prepared to leave. No! I needed to be on that train - no matter the costs. I looked back at everyone, hoping I would get one last look for Will to see if he had found the others, but saw nothing.

Then I turned and ran. As fast as my feet could carry me, I pounded down the left of the tracks, getting as far ahead as I could possibly get before the train started moving. Soon I was out of sight of the villagers, and far ahead of the coming train. It chugged slowly along, picking up speed but not too fast. I waited as it passed me by, all the way until I was right alongside the bay window caboose, running, running, running and then I jumped.

For a second, I was simply airborne. And then I slammed into the side wall, pain searing through my shoulder and left knee. Dizzy from fear and hurt, I grabbed onto the metal railing that sided the step, hanging on with my life as my foot slipped out from under me. Frightened to death, I pulled myself onto the step and climbed into the little porch on the back on the caboose, sitting down out of sight. I wasn't leaving this train until I got to London.

Until I got to Wendy.

Chapter Sixteen

Wendy

I sat across from Peter's dad, trying not to think about all the horrible things that had just happened to me. But it was hard, for I had lost Peter and the boys, my only friends. I was currently with some drunk oaf, and soon I would be reunited with my treacherous mother.

That was the part that scared me the most. I would be back to her, who would force me to do whatever she likes, would make me feel bad about my appearance, and wouldn't let me be friends with anyone unless she approves of them.

So basically, no one.

Also, soon, I knew she was going to start making me meet some boys "I should have interest in." Her high, squeaky voice came flooding back to me, our last "talk" - the thing that had made me run away...

"Ever," she had started. "I think it might be time, where you start taking a bit *more* interest in… boys."

"Mum, you do realize I'm only fifteen, don't you? I thought you said sixteen is when I should take that specific... interest."

She had thought for a moment. Finally, she said, "Yes, but you're so mature for your age. So... ready." She smiled her crooked smile, that she seemed to think was a winning one. She did, in fact, have a pretty beautiful one, but she saved that for when she was flirting with one of *her* boyfriends. It wasn't worth showing off to me.

Whenever she could tell I wanted to argue with her, she would give me a compliment, like saying I was mature. This way, it made me sound like the unfair one.

"Thank you, Mum," I replied, forcing a smile out. "But, there just hasn't been many boys I have taken interest in yet."

"Well, naturally. I wouldn't think so, so I started looking for you." She threw another smile my way, but this one said *your welcome.*

"Oh, really? Thanks for being so... thoughtful." Every word pained me to say.

"Yes, yes," she said, acknowledging my forced words with a wave of her hand. "Anyway, you might already know him. His name is Dean, and he lives down the street. He seemed *very* interested in you."

And that's when I threw a hand over my mouth, horrified. I did indeed know Dean. Though he sent most girls swooning over him with his extremely good looks, he was quite an idiot. Also, was extremely nasty to all the girls he'd ever dated. I had heard bad things about him from all the girls at my private school.

"Um, there was a few boys I was already thinking of, Mum. Please, I-I think they would suit me better."

"I already told him you would be wanting to come over this Friday," she continued as if I had said nothing.

She also did this a lot, to "avoid an argument."

"Please, Mum. Anyone, I swear, anyone but him!"

She gaped, then gasped dramatically. "Are you saying that *I'm* not good enough to see what boy would fit you best?"

"No, I just-"

"Who is older, *Ever*?"

"But-"

"WHO IS OLDER?!"

"You," I finally mumbled.

"And who is wiser?"

"You," I whispered.

"Who?!"

"You," I repeated, louder and clearer.

"Good. Now, I know you Ever, you surely aren't one to think *fighting* with your mother would solve your problems, the mother that only wants the best for you, but I do know where it comes from."

I looked up, confused.

"That brat, Addison, is it? She's surely rubbing off on you the wrong way. I don't want to you see her again."

I gasped in a pained sort of way.

"I've heard many things about that girl, and none good either. She's very peculiar, and there have been rumors about how she *doesn't* want to marry. Wouldn't want that getting to your head, now would we?"

Addison was my best friend, and the only one that ever truly understood me. My mum didn't approve of her, though, for though her parents were extremely nice, they weren't very wealthy at all. Plus, she was right. Addison didn't want to marry and was quite the tomboy. My mother had been trying to find an excuse to get rid of her for a long time, and now she finally had hers.

"Please, Mum, I'll meet up with him, I'll do anything you want, but please…"

"Oh, yes, you will meet up with him, without a doubt." And she briskly walked away, throwing an "end of discussion," over her shoulder as she left the room.

Addison had been the only good thing in my old life, and so once I realized that I might never see her again, I couldn't take it.

And the rest is history.

Hate filled my heart as these heartbreaking memories filled my head. I truly detested this wretched woman, who had lied to me, who had broken my heart, who...

Who I was soon going to be forced to go back to once again.

...

I tried to keep my mind off Peter, my mind off the fact that all I wanted to do was run into his open embrace, and cry into his shoulders for hours.

I would give anything right now, just to be able to see his face once more, to be able to meet lips one more time.

This made me start thinking what would've happened if I hadn't run away.

Thoughts of me snogging Dean came flooding into my mind's eye, and I suddenly felt like I might throw up.

It was hard not to think of Peter right now, though. His dad kept impatiently tapping his fingers in the same pattern and way Peter would tap his foot in, when he himself was impatient.

Finally, the irritable tapping came to an abrupt stop.

"I'll be in the bathroom," he grunted.

And he walked away.

I took a large breath. Finally, he was gone. Finally, I could breathe freely. Finally, I was alone.

Alone.

And all of a sudden I wanted someone. I needed someone. I was alone, and scared, on this big train. When I had company, I hated it. When I was utterly alone, I wanted someone.

But he was gone, and I was too afraid to run away. Too afraid for him to do something to Peter out of his anger of me escaping. So now all there was left to do was wait for this train to bring me to my destiny. The destiny I had tried so hard to get rid of.

The destiny that was getting closer by the moment.

And as the tears fell, I didn't try to stop them this time.

Chapter Seventeen

P_{eter}

The train ride took longer than I thought, even though the car seemed to be flying fast. Never before had I just sat and did nothing for *so* many hours. There were always things to do, places to explore, games and fun to play. I tried to sleep to no avail, not even able to shut my eyes with the excitement coursing through me and a nervous twitch that kept me up.

Things changed, my boredom evaporated, when I wasn't alone any longer. Abruptly, and out of the blue, a girl came running out of the back car, and not even realizing I was there, clung to the back railing, heaving and wringing her hands into the metal.

She was rich, no doubt, and wore a fit and flare, knee-length dress patterned with grey-blue and white chevron stripes, synched at the waist with a tight, breathtaking red ribbon, matching her red flats, and a short sleeve white bolero that complimented her little white gloves. Her hair was down in loose, side-swept curls, which sat nicely on her right shoulder, as well as the glittering diamond necklace around her neck.

I watched her without taking a breath, fearful she might turn around and find me there, but she didn't look back. Instead, she clung to the rim of the roof, stepping up with one, then two feet on the top of the railing and inhaled sharply. She shook tremendously, trying to prepare herself.

I couldn't sit by and idly watch her like this. "Don't do it," I said in a calm and eerie manner.

The girl turned, so startled that she leapt down from her position on the rails, and took a pace away from me. "I-I didn't know anyone was-was here. I-I wasn't going to-"

"It's okay," I said quietly, standing up and walking over to the rail, pretending not to notice how she kept her distance. When I said nothing more, she wiped a tear from her eye and strode over, pulling my attention.

"Please don't tell anyone," she cried in a heavy British accent, sitting down on the deck and hugging her knees to her chest.

And she began to ball. And even though she looked to be a couple years older than me, maybe eighteen, when she curled up like that she merely looked as helpless as a child.

"I won't if you won't tell anyone I'm here," I noted with a small mischievous smile. She looked up as I sat down across from her, my arms folded. "Now, tell me…"

"Isabella."

"Isabella, tell me, what made you try to do that," I gestured to the railing, and farther past it.

"I wasn't *just* going to try - I would have succeeded if you didn't give me such a scare."

"Okay then," I nodded solemnly, "go ahead. I'm not stopping you now."

She gaped silently, remained still, and shook her head subconsciously.

"I thought so," I continued. "So, let me rephrase. What made you *want* to do that?"

She sniffled, wiped her nose, and attempted to glare at me. "Why should I tell you? You're just a filthy boy I know nothing of."

"Exactly," I piped up, cocking my head. "You know nothing of me and I nothing of you, so what's the harm? Who would believe me if I were to go in there and say you tried to jump when you yourself denied it?"

She took my point gingerly, sighing and staring at the door to the inside of the car. "My parents want me to get married." And she said nothing more.

I tried for a comforting smile. "Well that's not so bad, is it? Love is a beautiful thing when you let it take course."

"But that's just the thing!" She cried in protest. "Love hasn't got anything to do with it! They're practically forcing me into a life I don't want. I hate him! With all my heart and soul I hate him. I just... I didn't think I could do it - I mean, I still don't.'"

I studied the girl, for a long while, watching her take slower, gasping breaths in an attempt to calm herself. I dropped my gaze to her gloves, now on the ground, and to her long fingernails which were digging into the skin on her wrists until they left little red welts.

"Well, have you tried talking to your parents about the other boy?"

She looked up, surprised. "How do you..."

"You have that look in your eyes. I saw it in a girl once a while back. The look of longing for something when you know you're supposed to be or have something else. In your case, it's another love. Your hatred for you betrothed is not really towards him, but towards the fact that he's stopping you from being with someone else."

Isabella sat quietly for a couple seconds, then shrugged her shoulders. "I guess."

I turned and looked off at the forest we were passing by, and my heart ached for home.

"That girl... what did she long for?"

I looked back to my new friend and spoke with a silent beam. "For a new life."

"Huh," she said with the ghost of a smile tugging at her lips. "You speak in riddles. Tell me more. About this girl you talk of, what was she like?"

I closed my eyes and pulled back memories from the past month, the words pouring off my tongue sweet like pure honey. "She was like a cerulean bird, who learned to fly regardless of her clipped wings. And when she took flight, she was beautiful. She had the ferocity of a thousand lions, but the heart of a dove, and her voice sounded like the music of the mockingbirds. Wildflowers grew where she stepped, life was brought back up and joy arose from her kindness. She felt pain, but she didn't show it, she knew reality, but she lived a dream, she had nothing, but she gave love. And she was mine. Not because I wanted her, but because she let me. She was my cure, my darling cure, not of my past but of my future."

Isabella sat and listened contently to the sound of my voice, joined me in my memories. And at the end, she opened her eyes and smiled, but then thought over my words a second time and confusion washed over her face. "I-I don't understand. A cure? How so?"

I grinned an unpleasant grin and looked to my wringing hands. "Let's just say I didn't have the most fortunate childhood."

"Oh, your father was poor," she concluded sadly.

"No," I corrected her. "No, he had a good job. He could have been rich if he chose. But he was too busy getting drunk and beating me for it to worry about money."

I froze. I hadn't even meant to tell her my true story until the words slipped off my tongue. But, as I had said before, I didn't know her and she didn't know me. So what was the harm? We would soon part as unlikely friends. So I continued. I told her of everything, how I found Will, the other boys, gave them hope. I left out Wendy and my belief in the story of Peter Pan; I had already given her a pretty clear description, and felt I couldn't bear to press any further.

"Oh my God," she muttered softly, cupping a hand to her lip. "I feel so foolish, not wanting to live through the life I was given when I have parents that love me." She began to play with her hair. "I mean in a very controlling, intrusive way, but yes they love me. You…" She gulped.

"Everyone has their own battles to fight," I told her kindly, "They aren't to be measured or judged."

She smiled a simple smile, and reached her hands back behind her neck and began to unclip her necklace. "What are you doing?" I asked, not understanding how the two things connected.

"This," she said, pulling the strung jewels down in front of her. "Is my kiss to you. It's the least I could give you for saving my life," she pressed the necklace in my fingers and watched as I stared down, wide-eyed. I had never held anything worth so much in the palm of my hand.

"I-I don't understand. How - how is this a kiss?"

"Oh," she laughed shortly, folding the pleats of her dress. "You must have never read *Peter & Wendy*. My mistake. Well you should, it's very exciting. I don't have a thimble, but I thought that to be the next best thing."

I stared up at her speechless.

"You'll understand when you read the book."

And still, I said nothing.

"Anyways," She smiled, closing my fingers around the diamonds, "sell it, make some money. Use it to save your girl."

I didn't think my eyes could grow wider. "How -"

"You have that look in your eyes."

Chapter Eighteen

Wendy

I walked off the train carefully, noticing that Peter's father had not turned back to help me as a real gentleman would have.

But then again, when had he ever done something like a gentleman would?

I stumbled a little but caught myself before falling. I then took a nice deep breath of fresh air and felt the relief of finally being off that prison of a train.

That same train that would have my sorrowful tears etched into it forevermore.

I looked up into the fresh blue sky and wondered whether Peter was looking into this same sky. And in that moment, all I wanted to do was fly.

Away.

I wondered if I had just been brave enough to say the words, if I had just had a little courage, just enough to be able to say *"I love you,"* would it have been different? Would we have ever been able to fly away together if we hadn't been so worried about falling?

"Come on!"

The words jolted my eyes away from the clear sky.

"Staring at the heavens won't help you get your beloved back," Peter's father sneered. "Do something helpful now, and hurry up, wouldn't you?!"

I hastened to fasten up, but gave the back of his head the biggest glare I could muster.

...

The sky started to darken as we waited for a taxi. Finally, one came, and we both climbed in.

It was the most tension-filled ride I have ever been in.

I looked out the window, and watched London roll by. I was potentially home. But then why was this so hard?

Just then, a little girl who I had ever only dreamed about filled my vision. Standing over her was a kind featured man, with a wrinkled face and a few white whiskers.

"Grandfather," the young girl said, sounding quite sophisticated for her age, *"Tom, from school, told me that one day he was going to run away. And I*

said, I said to him, 'but won't you miss home?' And he replied back, saying, 'I ain't got no home here, for home is where the heart is, and my heart is quite a ways away.'" The girl then stopped, looking up at the gentle man. *"What does he mean by that, grandpa?"* she implored. *" 'Home is where the heart is.' Do you believe that? Where is my heart anyway?"* And the man smiled at her, in a fatherly sort of fashion, and replied, *"My darling Ever, that is, I believe, a mystery people far older and wiser than you have yet to discover. Where does one's heart lie?"*

The memory slowly faded back from where it had come from, leaving me bewildered, and even more lonely.

My grandfather had been the last person to ever love me. He had been the father I had never known nor had, the kind friend who you could trust with all your secrets. He had died when I was really young, but once in a while random memories of him and I would pop up in my head.

I could never even begin to express how dearly I missed him.

Home is where the heart is, I mouthed, as we pulled into the front of the hotel. Now, when I finally knew what that meant, when I finally knew where my heart was, when I finally found my true home, I was pulled away from it.

...

As we walked into the run down house, the first thing I was told was, "I'll be back soon. And don't even think about running away."

Which was fine by me, for I had gotten quite sick of him lately. And he didn't even have to say the last part, I wouldn't have dreamed about running away.

Well, I would have definitely dreamed about it, but wouldn't have ever actually ever done it.

Anyway, now away from his forceful watch, the thing I was doing was sitting in the bathroom, on the ancient looking sink, and looking at the girl staring back to me. The puffy, red-eyed, dirty, broken girl staring back into my devastated eyes. I wanted no more of this... pain. I was done with the train ride of hills and valleys, ups and downs. Especially when most of it was downs and not ups. I wanted it to be over. I was so sick of it.

What was the point of living anymore anyways?

I have to say, that might have been the scariest thought I have ever thought before. The fact that my life was so bad, so terrible, it seemed almost better just to end it. Of course, it had gone as soon as it came. I didn't want to end my life, not when there was still the tiniest hope of redeeming it, of finding Peter again.

Finding myself again.

And so I pushed those horrible thoughts out of my head. Because even if I had to survive not only looking at this heartbroken girl in the mirror, but actually *being* her…

Well… it would totally be worth it if one day, I would be reunited with my beloved Peter Pan once again.

…

I knew something was wrong the moment he came in. He looked scary.

And drunk.

"Um, sir…" I began, but he didn't reply. I didn't know what I should do. I desperately didn't want him to do something bad if I didn't help him. But with the same amount of desperation, I didn't want him to see or notice me at all.

But a second later, I thought *too late for that.*

For he had spotted me.

"Sir…?" I started with deep uncertainty.

"Where is she?" he demanded with a grunt.

"Um, I'm right here, sir, let me just-"

"WHERE IS SHE?!" He demanded.

"I - please, I don't know what you mean…" My voice sounded far away. I wanted to disappear. I think I liked him better when he was angry and churlish, even to the extreme. Right now, he was more than evil and twisted.

He was eerie and chilling.

And that was what I was thinking before he hit me.

Screaming as his cruel hand met my cheek, I fell to the floor, clutching my raw, stinging face. Tears blurred the dark room, as he got ready to strike another time.

"Where did she go? TELL ME!" he bellowed and threw another punch.

But this time I managed to roll away faster than he swung.

"Please!" I gasped, openly crying now. "Please, I don't know what you're talking about!"

But he didn't seem to care.

This time he was faster than me. I ducked his third blow, once again in the face, but he then his hand met my gut, full force.

The breath was knocked out of me, for seemingly forever. As I gasped for air that finally was starting to come again, I heard a loud "thump".

Tears stinging my stinging cheeks, I looked up to find Peter's father, unconscious next to me. The blow must have taken the last bit of energy out of him.

And now fear and time and pain all caught up to me, pulling me towards sleep. Tiredly obliging, I let myself slip under.

Wishing to never wake up ever again.

Chapter Nineteen

Peter

I hopped off the train as it was tiring out, coming to a slow stop. I was then able to disappear into the sea of people at the station, and it was odd not having to fear anyone's recognition of me. I did see Isabella with two older people, I supposed to be her parents, neither of them looking very cheery. But she caught my eye with the hugest delighted grin and the brightest eyes, and I knew she was happy.

Not only happy. Free.

I felt success in her joy, but I quickly pushed it aside, as I wasn't going to let it deter me from my real goal. Ever. I pushed past grumbling people, muttering sorry to every third person or so, and scrambled over to the ticket booth. A man, rather short, with a mustache he was clearly growing out to curl, looked up at me, and seemed as if he was rolling his eyes all the while.

"Can I help you?" he asked in the most monotone, plain voice I had ever heard. It was like, if his voice was a color, it would be puke green - no, not even puke green. It wasn't even that exciting. Brown.

The dullest brown you could think of. I held back laughter, thinking about how Albie would react if he were here.

"Uhm, yes. The last train that pulled in from Kielder, departed about an hour before us… do you know when that came in?"

He puffed out his lips and attempted at folding his stocky, pudgy arms. "Do the math, son. If it left an hour before your train, when do you think it came in?"

I scoffed. I didn't have time for this. "No," I snapped back shortly, "I was wondering if it had any delay."

"No, delay, son."

What was with this guy?! "Okay," I tried for my most polite tone. "But did you see a girl get off. Red dress, light brown hair with a white bow, a pretty face you wouldn't soon forget -"

"I am not permitted to tell you the whereabouts of our travelers," he cut off sharply, "If you have anything else you need help with, feel free to ask. If not, get out of my sight."

I pursed my lips, attempted at saying something, then stocked off.

I searched the area to no success. No doubt my father had taken her somewhere far, and fast. Burned out, I strode over to a bench. How was I to find her? Heck, I couldn't even find my way around this place, no less all of London! I slumped down on a bench in distress and felt something crinkle in my pocket. Feeling around, I pulled out a little tag from food from the market, all bent and folded from sitting in my back pocket. I turned it over to the back and smiled when I saw the writing on it. Half in Albie's messy handwriting, and the other in Will's neat slanted letters, it read: "*The moment you doubt whether you can fly, you cease forever to be able to do it.*"

Oh, how the boys knew exactly how to cheer me up. Every quote had a deeper meaning, something from them that I knew I could hold onto. I took a second to analyze this one. It wasn't just telling me not to give up hope, it was telling me not to give up on them, or Wendy. That I shouldn't doubt myself because they were with me, and if I did, even for a second, that doubt could overtake me. What I could get from one little quote!

I started to wonder, as I got up and continued on through the streets, how the paper even ended up in my pocket in the first place. I hadn't recalled them ever slipping it on me and felt like I would have felt it on the five-hour train ride. But maybe it was just meant to show up at the perfect time in the perfect place.

Suddenly I thought of the boys back home, and my heart ached a bit. I hadn't been this far away, well, ever. This made me even more determined to get to Wendy, because I needed to get home. To Will, to Albie, to Elliot and the twins.

I picked up a slight jog. Where was I even heading? I tried to think like my father. Where would he take her? He wouldn't take her right to her mother, because there was no doubt he would've wanted payment first. And he wouldn't spend money on some motel, because he had nothing to spend yet. So… where?

Puzzled, I slowed my pace, coming to realize that the further I ran blindly, the further I could be running in the wrong direction. My hands went to my head in frustration, and I let out a quiet but angered cry.

"Are you alright?" I turned to see a woman, who seemed to have come out of nowhere on the small abandoned road I was on, smiling at me gayly. My first impression was that she was sweet, but not somebody you would want to get on the bad side of. She had light brown hair like Ever's, almond eyes and flushed cheeks. She held herself similar to Ever, and, in fact, the more I looked at her the more scarily she resembled the girl; although at the same point, it was like she could not have been more different.

"Yeah," I mumbled, rubbing my cheek, which had become sore from my clenched jaw. "Yeah, I'm fine."

She looked concerned, like, overly concerned, and wiped a smudge of dirt from my face. "Oh, sweetheart, but you're so dirty..." she examined me thoroughly. "And thin!"

Something about the way she said it sounded so familiar, but I just couldn't pinpoint it. All I knew was that my gut was telling me to get away from her, and fast.

"I'm - I'm fine," I pushed her off of me, trying for a smile. "Just going for a run, that's all."

"No, no," she decided, slinking an arm around my shoulder. "No, I must get you home and clean you up. Your father certainly won't be proud of his son returning home like this. Please, my house is just around the corner."

"My... my father?" I stuttered, every word she spoke making my skin crawl.

She stopped short, a feared expression passing over her, and then ever so quickly it was gone, making me wonder if it had truly been there at all. With a plastered smile, she pulled me along, saying, "Well, you do have parents, don't you, boy?"

I nodded slowly, and followed her, completely unsure of how to get out of the situation. It wasn't like she had threatened me, but at the same point, that's *exactly* how I felt. Like if I tried to leave, I would regret it.

So I let her pull me along, talking about everything and nothing in a pleasantly happy manner. I ignored her words, dragging my feet, and quickly realizing I should have been documenting my surroundings. I took a brief survey of the area, sweeping it over with my eyes and finding how quickly the poor neighborhood I had been running through had turned to a rich one, with streets full of big bright houses, green lawns, and cars driving every which way.

"I - I really should be getting home soon, my - my father wants me back before -"

"Oh, nonsense!" she exclaimed, not even letting me finish. "I'm sure dear-old-dad won't mind if we spend a bit of time cleaning you up. I don't think he'd be too happy to hear that you were running down *those* streets, now would he?" She said it with such hatred and disgust, it made me shrink back in fright. If she only knew where I actually lived.

We marched up her driveway, past her gleaming light blue car, and into the house. I slipped off my muddy boots right as we stepped into the hallway leading into the living room, and saw her nose wrinkle at the thought of them touching her floors.

She hurried me through and upstairs, so fast I hardly had time to see around the house, and with all that had occurred that morning, the home seemed rather much like a blur of crisp colors. I was whisked upstairs to the bathroom, a towel and a fresh pair of clothes forced into my hands and the water turned on. The women merely said "ta-ta!" and flounced away.

Completely flustered, I turned to the gushing water and watched the white tub fill up with sudsy liquid. Wanting to be defiant, and then seeing nothing coming from it, I began to take off my clothes and gave in to the warmth of the water.

When I was done, clean, soaking cold and wet, I hugged tightly to my towel and looked down at my old clothes, versus the new ones. Hesitantly, I decided on the fresh new tunic and pants, and kept my old little green vest, then left the room in a hurry.

The aromas that traveled up the stairs from the kitchen were nothing like that of the humidity of the bath, and I felt instantly drawn to follow them. I would have followed the warm scents, had the slightly cracked open door to my left not drawn my interest. Instead, still gripping my old clothes, I wandered over to the room and pushed open the door.

I immediately felt at home. The room had this smell that welcomed me, like roses in a lake, and though the walls were a bland pink, the window was big and showed a great view to the trees beside the house. A little bird's nest sat on the window sill, breathing in the fresh air of the creaked open window. Around the room were little trinkets, old and new, that filled it with a homey, exciting feeling. I strode over to the desk, running my fingers over little metal figurines and smiling when I hit a thimble. Without thought, I grabbed it, pressed it to my lips, then put it in my pocket, and continued my search.

And then I found something that made my head spin. An unopened envelope, from a Dean Miller, sat there on the desk. It wasn't who it was from, but rather who it was addressed to that shook me.

A Miss Ever Kingsley.

I clutched the letter, every point, every feeling that had stirred up inside of me suddenly making sense. Why, I had been so wrapped up in the whimsical magic of it all that I hadn't even stopped to think. This was Ever's room! Ever's house, and - and that woman down there, she was… Ever's mother.

I trembled, dropping the letter and my old clothes and ran over to the window. How had this all happened? How had she been right there when I was lost, how was her house even that close to the train station? It couldn't have been more than two miles based in how long I was running for. My life had felt like one coincidence after another since Wendy came along, so much so that they all seemed to jumble up and confuse me.

It was too high of a jump, and the only other way down to earth's level was the stairs in the house, that led right into the living room, which was directly beside the kitchen where her mother was.

I decided my best plan was to act oblivious and try to get home to my so-called father. Cooling my nerves, I stumbled my way down the stairs and tried for a smile when I approached Miss Kingsley. She was cooking, a white apron over her deep pink dress, and she to a pause to wipe her hands on her apron right as I met floor level.

"Th-thank you for the bath, but I really must be going now."

Stopping what she was doing, the endeared woman came over to me and combed her fingers through my hair. I let her do so but cringed at her touch. "Oh, nonsense, I'll talk to your father about why you were gone so late. You do want me to drive you home, don't you?" she asked, not caring much for an answer and continued on with, "Come right along. I'm making salmon sandwiches. Oh, do enjoy a meal with me, I do hate to always eat alone." She sighed, checking the salmon she was cooking.

"You have no family?" I inquired with a tilt of the head, meanwhile observing the room. Everything was too clean and well kept, it was underwhelming. The counters were shining and spotless, nothing left on the table tops, the floors gleaming, the drying towels folded precisely, and even the sink had nothing but a damp rag to fill it. I could understand why this home could be a prison for someone so wonderfully unique as Ever.

"Oh," she began blatantly, her back turned to me as she prepared the meal. "I did once. But that was years ago. My husband, he… he left."

She refused to press on and soon the silence became too much to bear. "I don't mean to pry, ma'am," I began politely, and she waved her hand to reassure me that nothing I could say would be wrong. "But there was another room across the hall that looked like a young girl's room."

She fingered the bread on the plates. "Oh, that door was supposed to be closed. It's only a guest bedroom, that's all."

"But if it were a guest bedroom -"

"If you don't mean to *pry*, Edmund, then I suggest you shut your mouth!" she snapped impatiently, and all too soon realized what she had said. I snatched the opportunity.

"H-how do you k-know my - my name?" I pretended to stutter. "I-I nev-never told you."

She whirled around, tucking the kitchen towel she had been using into her apron. I didn't think much of the act except that she was accepting plan B with open arms. "Did you not tell me? Well then, that certainly is a curious thing." She advanced towards me, and I backed up slowly. "Seems to me like we have a little *issue*," she babied last word, puffing out her bottom lip pathetically.

She continued to advance, and I continued to back up until I found myself tucked in a corner, and no way out. "Your Ever's mother, aren't you? The one she ran away from."

"Well she only has one mother, doesn't she?" She bit back aggressively, pushing me against the wall.

I shook my head in defiance, trying to think up a way to get out the situation, and something to say to keep her stalled. "You aren't going to take her from us! She's found her real family now!"

I sounded like a pathetic crying child.

Ever's mother rolled her eyes. "The only real family she has, boy, is me." At her words, I attempted to kick her shin, but all too soon she grabbed me by the neck, and reached under my jaw with her bony fingers. Squeezing hard, she pressed upward in an unbearable manner and I began to feel woozy and faint almost instantly, not being able to think right. I struggled against her grip, kicking and fighting with all the energy I had left, but ended up going weak in her arms, the only thing on my mind being Ever's safety, but even that seemed to be slipping from view.

Miss Kingsley lowered me to the ground with a knowing grin as I trembled, childish fear returning to me for the first time since I saw my father in the forest.

My stomach churned as black swirls spiraled around me, getting closer and larger by the second. The last I saw was part of her grinning face before I finally gave way to the sleepy feeling that was pulling me under.

Chapter Twenty

Will

"And I -" Albie shook with unsteady breaths, wiping his nose sloppily on the cuff of his sleeve as he tried to calm himself. He took in breaths in little hiccups, continuing to rub his wetting eyes as he trembled with the excitement and fright. "Couldn't - find you... and then - there were so many - many people - I -I -"

I pushed his overgrown hair out of his face and tried for a comforting smile. When that didn't help, I pulled him in for a tight hug, tears springing up in my eyes. In less than two hours I had managed to find Wendy, lose her again, get arrested (in a way), talk myself out of it, lose the other boys, see Peter off to London, and find Albie. My head was a jumble, my feelings a craze, and I was at that state where you are so completely out of sorts that you sort of forget what it feels like to feel normal.

I don't know, maybe that's crazy. And then again, maybe that's just where I'm at at this point from living in the woods for years over years.

Albie squeezed me tight and his trembling seemed to go down. He had gotten split up from the others, lost in the crowd, and went into little kid panic mode when he could find anyone he knew. I had found him first, thank God, but was yet to find all the other boys. I knew Thomas wouldn't split from Oliver, and that Elliot was too shy to venture off on his own, so I could bet that they were all together, but who knew in this sea of people pushing and pulling to get this way and that.

At last, pulling away from Albie's hug, I managed to smile and looking him in the eye, offered a piggyback ride. He obliged gleefully, jumped onto my back, and clinging to me like a frightened pup. "Let's get the other boys!" he said in pure childish hope, and the words struck me like a stone to the head.

I had honestly no idea how I was going to find the rest of the boys. They could be anywhere. Anywhere. Looking around in the overwhelming crowd, I began to panic. And I don't mean just down to earth semi-freaking out, I mean *panicking*. It was as if all of the sudden, my mind began to spin in a million intertwining circles, my head pounded and beaded sweat and my entire body began to clam up. I knew it was serious when my dominant hand began to shake. Tense and uncontrolled, it trembled and shook vigorously, and I grabbed it with my other hand, but the movement seemed to spread up my arm and to my jaw. My breathing came in short, undecided rasps, and the more I tried to calm myself, the further I found myself away from that aspect of serenity. I let go of Albie's legs, and he slid to the ground, tapping me on the back and trying to ask what was wrong. But I didn't turn around; I couldn't.

I was frozen.

Frozen, trembling, and lightheaded with fear. It overtook me like a crashing wave, pulling me down and back in, only to wash me up on shore and do the same thing over and over again. I wasn't the person that let stress get to him, I wasn't the friend that poured out all his problems, or sought comfort. No, *I* was the comforter, the stress-reliever, the low-issue sidekick that lived to help. I took comfort in the trees, the waters and nature around me. I found the small things and focused on them. But now, now there was nothing to focus on. Only that the boys were *my* responsibility. Not Peter's, not Wendy's - *mine.* I clammed up, my palms sweating, and sunk to the ground, not caring what the people surrounding me thought. Hugging my knees to my chest and tucking my head in, I rocked back and forth, my mind a blank slate. Albie's tapping on my shoulder became more violent, as well as the rasps of my breathing.

I couldn't do it. Couldn't. Couldn't. Couldn't. And the more I shook, the more I told myself that. Because for the first time in what had been years, I was breaking down. I couldn't help the shaking that was taking me over, nor the tears that were streaming down my cheeks. I couldn't slow my breathing, or stop my head from pounding. It was just all happening, all so sudden, and I couldn't change it. And if I couldn't change it, then how could I find the boys. How could I get them home and care for them until Peter came back? And what if he didn't come back? What if his father got to him?

What if?

What then?

What now?

And I know it's not in the slightest bit cool to have a mental break down in the middle of a train station. But there are just some things no one can control. Like my childhood, that sucked. And the way I had let myself be a push-over my entire life, or chosen not to take initiative when Wendy came also sucked.

Because she didn't come alone. She brought me fear along with her.

...

I usually don't write things down, but it's the middle of the night and I have no one to talk to. Not that that would change had it been daytime anyways, as Peter and the other boys are so engrossed in our new "Wendy", but I'd prefer to use the time of day as an excuse.

Things just haven't been the same since she came. It's almost like my whole purpose is just disappearing. I used to be so close with Peter. I was the only one old enough to really understand him and I could make him laugh and cry and smile, whatever. The point is I was always there for him. And now am I not only not there for him, I can't be there for him. And it's the same with the other boys. This girl that has come in has completely taken me over. She does everything! She is always able to help him out, comfort and keep his spirits light, and love all the other boys, all individually. I don't let her get too close to me, and I can't help the distance, it just doesn't feel right to sugar coat my emotions around her. But she cleans (what she can), and cooks, and cares for, and just does just about everything! Everything that covers the half of what I did. It feels like, if I were to leave and never come back, no one would even notice! The boys rarely pay attention to me anymore and I feel like

I'm just biding my time until I'm pushed so far away that I'm just... out.

And I hate it. But I can't change it. I can't change that they want her over me, or that I feel invisible, and I can't make the boys love me over her. She loves them, and they her, and the thing is, I care for them too much to push her away because they do love her. But I can wait. I can wait and watch, and love them as much as they'll let me, and let her love them. And if she goes away, I can search for her until I get her back to them. And I'll wait some more. And maybe they'll see. Maybe they'll tell.

But for now, I'll just wait.

...

"Will! WILL!" Elliot shook me back and forth, pulling my hands from my ears as most of the crowd watched. "Will get up!" He pulled me to my feet and slapped me to my senses, telling me with a fierceness in his eyes that we needed to leave, fast. I nodded, shaking myself out of a daze and let him lead me along. And as I ran alongside Elliot, I noted that the twins and Albie were with us, leaving the crowd in complete confusion. We ran and ran and my lips broke into a free smile. Don't get me wrong, I was still hurting, I was still in shock, my hands still slightly shaking, but it was different. The craziness, the overwhelming fear became less overwhelming and the hope that something could be a bit better, maybe even a little bit better, came through. Elliot, the twins, Albie - they were all fine.

And that meant, so was I.

We kept running until we got to the brink of the woods, and realizing no one was on our case, slowed down the pace and turned it to a brisk walk. Elliot caught up to me and began walking in synch, side-by-side with my footsteps.

"Peter - er, I mean Will… what happened back there?"

I sighed and ran my fingers through my tousled hair. "Exactly that," I admitted solemnly, letting him catch on. "I can't *be* Peter, or Wendy for that matter! I thought for so long that Ever had taken my place, and I really just realized that she hadn't - she had only stepped in when I couldn't fulfill the place I was put in. There are so many things - "

"Slow down!" Elli cut me off in my ramble, his hands raising slightly. "What are you even talking about, Will? No one's expecting you to put on a show. We don't *need* a leader, we're a team. But what happened back there - it can't happen again."

"I know, I know," I moaned, having been focusing on the wrong speech. "I guess I just got overwhelmed -"

"Overwhelmed? You call that *overwhelmed*? I think that's a bit of an understatement." We met eyes. "Okay, okay I'll let you finish."

"Like I was saying, I just *broke down* because I finally let the stress get to me. I guess I hadn't realized how much I had let build up until I let a little through."

He wrinkled his nose with pursed lips. "What do you mean? It hasn't been that stressful, has it?"

"It's going to sound really stupid."

"Spill."

I rubbed my tired eyes. "I thought Ever was replacing me. I thought that I didn't matter anymore now that she could do *everything*. I didn't know who to help or how to do it because she seemed to give you guys all that you needed. I guess one girl really is worth more than twenty boys."

I could've sworn Elli was about to laugh. I didn't even have the emotional capacity to take offense. He cupped a hand to his mouth for half a second and placed it on my shoulder. "Will," he said, "when are you going to let yourself be one of us? You're so focused on trying to help people you can scarcely help yourself! Even *Peter* has moments that he needs to be cared for, or he feels sorry for himself. Stop trying to live in tomorrow and realize that you have a whole day ahead of yourself!" He finished the conversation with a sequel of wheezing coughs, all of which I disregarded as I was focused on his words.

His advice was so blunt and sharp, that being fully honest, I was dumbstruck and completely taken aback. I stopped, thought it over a minute, and started to laugh.

Yes, I laughed. And I don't regret it, either. Because being at that state, having just had a mental breakdown, prequelled and followed by all the events that had occurred and barely sleeping three hours that night, all I could honestly do was laugh.

Elliot, confused, his facial expressions slightly altered from my unexpected response, joined me in my laughter, and soon we were all laughing, out of the mere bliss that we had made it back to our home territory.

It was only Thomas who remained silent and stone cold. Even his shy, lesser in size and personality, self had cracked a smile, whose shaking had turned from fright to joy.

"What's wrong?" his brother asked him, landing a playful punch on his shoulder. He shook his head, a stressed aura coming from him and surrounding us all.

"Where's Peter? And Wendy?"

I stopped. I realized I hadn't told them where our famous couple had gone. They must've figured that we weren't able to save Wendy, but we were so focused in the moment of trying to get away from the alarmed crowd, that none of them had paid much attention to who was where. I hadn't mentioned it to Albie when I found him, and for some odd reason it just never got brought up in my conversation with Elliot. Maybe it was that I hadn't brought it to attention.

"I - um… he's… he's going to London."

Albie's feet skidded to a stop. "London?! Like where Wendy lives?"

I nodded slowly and the younger boy's eyes widened.

"But it's so…"

"Far away."

"Are we ever going to see him again, Will?"

I looked to Albie, my eyes watering suddenly. I wouldn't tell him no, I would never tell him no. Not even thirty years from now. But at the same point, could I say yes? Could I place false hope in the minds of the young kids that looked up to me? False hope in Peter?

In me?

Honestly, I had no idea whether or not we would see Peter again. Don't get me wrong, I had faith in him, I just didn't know whether or not he could beat his own father. I mean, even in his own territory the drunken man nearly had him killed. Now he was in London, a totally unrecognizable different arena, and his father had the upper hand. His father had Wendy. And as long as that was the case, Peter would never win. Because as long as his father had control of what Ever was put through, how much she suffered, Peter couldn't beat him.

So, would I ever see my best friend again? He would tell me to have hope in him, but the more I thought of his predicament, the more I realized that it was all just... talk. How could he win?

And how could I replace him if he failed?

I ruffled Albie's messy brown hair. "He'll come back," I promised, picking up the pace to the front of the group and muttering to myself.

"He has to."

Chapter Twenty One

Peter

Darkness filled the void in which I stood, spinning my head and wrapping around me like a cold, chilling blanket. Although it's color did not differ from the rest, I could sense some type of wisp floating around me, tickling my ears and sliding up to my lips.

"Don't go with him, Peter. Don't go!" It hissed, tensing the very bones in my body. It got so close, so overwhelmingly loud, that I sunk to the ground and covered my ears, squeezing my eyes shut.

And just that fast, they were open. I awoke to the smell of something warm and familiar and turned to press my nose into the comforter blanketing me. The sweet reminisce of Ever should have brought me cheer, but it only jolted me awake further, flooding my brain with the recollection of how I had fallen asleep in the first place.

I sat up to find myself in Ever's bedroom, looking exactly as it had when I had checked it out the day before.

Was it the day before? I couldn't tell.

But that wasn't what was exactly on my mind. Jumping off the bed and feeling instant lightheadedness, I ran to the door and twisted the knob with all the strength I could muster, unable to open it. The words from my dream had me scared, and I began to kick and thrash the barrier blocking my way out of this house.

I could faintly hear Ever's mother in the kitchen downstairs, and knew that she could hear me yelling and kicking as I tried to beat down her door.

This sudden wave of anger that had overtaken me lasted, by no surprise, only a couple of minutes, and I soon gave up on my attempts to break the wood and knob keeping me in the room. My back to the wall, I slid down into a desperate sitting position, my hands pressing on the sharp pains pounding in my temples. And in the quiet, I heard the sound of Ever's mother even louder now, coming from the right side of the bed. Curiosity took the best of me and had me ambling over to the location of the sound.

Sure enough, there was a vent there. A vent that somehow led to the kitchen. And if I could hear her humming, she could definitely hear me. I pressed my face up against the dusty vent, inhaling sharply.

"I KNOW YOU CAN HEAR ME!" I bellowed through the echoing tunnel. "AND I KNOW THE ONLY REASON YOU

HAVE ME HERE IS TO GET EVER BACK! BUT LET ME MAKE SOMETHING CLEAR: YOU WILL NOT HURT HER! SHE HAS FOUND HER FAMILY, AND YOU AREN'T NOT RIP HER FROM THEM! SO DO WHAT YOU WANT WITH ME, BUT LEAVE HER OUT OF THIS! AND IF YOU WANT TO COME UP HERE AND UNLOCK THIS DOOR TO TALK LIKE CIVILIZED PEOPLE THAT WOULD BE MUCH APPRECIATED BECAUSE YOUR VENTS ARE PROBABLY THE ONLY THING IN THIS HOUSE THAT ARE NOT CLEAN AND I DO NOT LIKE TO PRESS MY FACE UP AGAINST THEM!"

I finished my ramble and sat up, feeling significantly better about myself, that is until the clicking sound of heels echoed from the kitchen up the stairs. I froze. I hadn't expected her to answer my call that fast.

But she had, and given what I had just screamed, I needed to be prepared for every and all outcomes. I braced myself in front of the door, preparing to dart just as it opened. The sounds of the heels grew louder, and closer, until the clicking of the lock on the door made the hairs on my neck stand tall. The door swung open, and without waiting a second, without looking, I charged, my body slamming into Miss Kingsley, and something sticky and hot. The two of us toppled to the floor, and I rolled over, a sharp, piercing pain shooting into my chest.

The black spots before me dissipated, and I struggled to sit up, seeing the horrific scene around me. Miss Kingsley was on the floor as well, covered in the sticky, steaming substance of what appeared to be hot tomato soup. Beside her, large broken pieces of a glass bowl lay, and as I stared at them, it dawned on me. Looking down at my own chest, also sticky and hot with the soup, I felt a crimson liquid bleed into my shirt, where little pieces of glass were shattered into me. It must have happened when I dove into her, my chest taking the heat of the thin glass bowl. There was only a few, which were too small to be very deep but still hurt awfully, and I winced as I pulled myself into a sitting position, trying to catch the mixture of soup and blood from dripping onto the carpet. It was a lost cause, though, at this point, as the entire landing was stained red with soup.

"You foolish, stupid boy!" Ever's mother shrieked, slowly getting up and looking over her sticky red hands. She rose to her feet, gaping at her ruined carpet and then at me. "Get up!"

I didn't stir.

"I said *get up!*"

I scrambled to my feet, wincing as the little glass pieces ebbed into my skin. She met my eyes, and the focused in on my wound. I gritted my teeth, trying not to show any weakness, even with the glass in my skin making my insides scream.

"You're hurt," she sighed pathetically. I nodded. "Oh, no that won't do. You're fa- *I* can't have you dripping blood all over my house, now can I?" Though her words weren't so, her tone seemed very sympathetic. She advanced closer to me and I didn't stir, half of me hoping she had some human in her that would take pity.

The woman grabbed me sharply by the shoulder and I jumped, my fingertips trembling. "*Clean it up,*" she snapped, looking me over. "All of it." And then her eyes drifted to the carpet, the tomato-stained rug and glass pieces.

I dipped my head, finding no triumph in defiance, and spoke through gritted teeth. "Yes."

This wasn't enough for her. "Yes, *what?*"

Holding back the urge to roll my eyes and give it up all completely, I muttered quietly, "Yes ma'am."

A smirk formed her lips, a victorious, twisted grin, and she let go of my arm, dusting off her hands. "Good. Now go into the bathroom and get yourself cleaned up. In the drawer directly beneath the countertop, you will find a pair of tweezers to get the glass out. You might as well put on your old shirt, I'm not going to waste any more good clothes on you. But," she raised a pointy, bone-like finger. "This won't do. Your jacket is stained and torn. Let's be off with it."

I looked at her with pleading eyes. I loved this jacket. I had had it since I could remember. It was what made me Peter Pan, and I didn't care if it was red or blue, stained or torn. I needed it. But Miss Kingsley wouldn't have it. She shooed me with her hands to hurry up, and I slipped it off with a quivering lip. "I expect all *this*," she gestured to the landing, "to be gone within the hour."

I nodded solemnly and sped into the bathroom. I looked to the mirror and took a shaky breath at what I saw. A boy, my age, same hair and clothing, stared back at me. But that was about all that was the same. His face, although clean, had lost the smudges of dirt and soot that represented the life he was so proud of. His cheekbones were sunken in, eyelids dark and ringed with sleepless marks, and the eyes that stared back into mine were not at all the same. Dim and cold, they displayed a whole different scene behind them than I had seen before.

Hopelessness.

And covered in blood, soup, and glass shards, that's all I could feel. But then I imagined Ever next to me, safe in my arms, and oh how much brighter did those eyes seem to shine. I could get through this, I could, I could!

I looked down to my stained tunic. It was ripped where the glass had cut through, and I knew that I needed to take out the bigger pieces before removing the shirt completely. So, with a controlled breath, I opened the depicted drawer and pulled out the tweezers, clamping them on the biggest piece of glass, and began to tug. With tears springing up so fast, I realized that it couldn't be like ripping off a band-aid. I needed to take it slow. If I didn't they surely would have gone through ripped the skin and embedded little pieces inside, making my teeth grit up against one another. I threw down the bloody glass onto the counter, gulping down fear. There was only one more piece that hadn't gone fully through the shirt. And then another under that. *Three,* I told myself, undermining the wound. *Three pieces of glass won't kill me.*

And it didn't. Surprisingly. I let my determination to see Ever cloud over everything else, as it was just another step to finding her. Yes, that was it. Whether it would get me closer, I had no idea. But, by the end, I was a tear-stained, bloody mess. I tore off the rest of my clothes, and turned on the tub water, hoping it would refresh the cuts. But right as the cool liquid hit the bloody surface, I let out a pained, uncontrolled cry, that I was sure all of London could hear. Not having much experience with wounds like these, I wasn't expecting it to sting so, but it did.

It did. Nevertheless, I still had a whole carpeted area to clean up, and supposedly within the hour. So, I winced through the pain and rinsed myself off, then changed back into the pants and my old tunic. The clothes gave me somewhat of a comforting feeling, for though before I would have regretted not taking the new ones when they were available, it felt good to have something from home.

After getting cleaned up and changed, I walked out to the landing to find a bucket of sudsy water and two rags, one to remain dry and the other to soak in the water. I picked up one of the rags, and covering my hand with it (careful not to cut myself again), picked up the glass and set it in a pile to my left, then dipped the other rag into the water solution, and began scrubbing the carpet. I honestly had no idea how I was supposed to get this red stain out, but I could put as much effort into it as possible.

And I did. Thirty minutes, actually. Thirty minutes of bent over back, scrubbing the carpet and trying to get the red, now pink stain out. The color was as stubborn as Albie during bedtime, I decided, and the thought made me smile. I managed to get it out enough that there was the faint recognition of tomato soup and the worn down scrubbed carpet looked worse than before. But that may have been what I was trying to do.

Maybe.

I looked up from my work, wondering how easy it would be for me to sneak out of the house. I mean, if I just managed to get downstairs without making a sound and -

"I see you're done here," the snapping voice of Ever's mother shook me from my thoughts. "Well, then get on, back in the room."

Again, I didn't move. Rolling her eyes, and pushing up her sleeves like she couldn't bother to get them dirty, she snatched me by the arm and pulled me back into the room. I put up as much of a fight as I could muster. Clawing at her bare skin, and digging my heels into the floor, I fought back to her surprisingly strong grip, even though I knew it was a lost cause. It was a lost cause to think I could beat her. It was a lost cause to think I could get to Wendy in time before my father did something awful.

But it wasn't a lost cause to have hope.

So I fought, and thrashed, and spit, and *may* have bitten her, and all the while ended up on the floor of the room behind a locked door. Wiping my nose with an angered grimace, I ran to the door and pressed my ear up against it, only to hear her heels clicking down the stairs. On that note, I went over to the other side of the room and once again pressed my cheeks up against the vent. I could hear the clicking wheel of a dialing phone, and ever so faintly I imagined I could hear it ring.

But, alas, that ringing didn't last forever. Even though I wished it had. A woman's harsh tone followed her throat-clearing grunt, saying,

"I wanted to let you know I've considered your deal, *Rufus*, and I've decided to make a trade... No, I'm not going to give you money for her!" Her volume sank in a chilling way as she sauntered into what came next. "But I do have something I *think* you will find quite worth the switch... what? Your son, darling. Yes. No. I've already arranged for Dean to pick her up there tomorrow at three from my place, so she needs to be here before then. Alright."

Suddenly she paused, and I could feel her uneasiness rise. I held my breath. "What else? You said there was another boy. *To keep him company?* Rufus, don't pretend like you actually care! No, no, that won't do. I can hardly only handle one. For God's sake, Rufus, when will your own son be enough?! How is he? Oh, he's the nastiest, disagreeable, shoddy child I've ever met! I mean he..."

I let her voice drift away as I sat up. There was nothing more I could gain from listening in on her conversation. I laid my head against the back of the bed and tried to process what I had just heard. Wendy's mother was going to trade me for her.

What, as if we were property?! But that's exactly how I felt at the moment. At least Will wasn't being dragged into all this. I had Miss Kingsley to thank for that. But I couldn't help the fear crawling up my throat that my father actually cared enough to go back for him. I guess I just had to make my presence enough.

And then I thought of Wendy. And for that little while, I couldn't help but actually feel happy about this whole arrangement. Because even though her mother had somewhat abused her in different ways, she still loved her, and I knew with her she wouldn't be hurt. Not like she would be with my father. I had told myself I would take a thousand blows for her, and this way, I felt I could actually do that.

Looking around the room, I saw something I hadn't noticed before. On the corner of the desk sat a small, quaint typewriter. It was littler than a normal one, or so I thought at least, but it fit the slim view of paper sitting in it. The piece had been freshly put in, only allowed about two inches of white to sneak out.

Getting up, I strode over to it, and pulled the entire thing to the front of the desk, sliding into the chair. I straightened out the top of the paper, and four little words were printed in black at the top.

I want to fly.

A smile crept to my lips, and I wondered if the adventure I had given her actually allowed her to do so. And then that smile faltered. Would she ever fly again?

And truthfully I doubted whether I would ever see her again.

Trying to make the best of it, I straightened my posture and placed my hands on the keys. I wasn't a fast typer, but I managed. I wanted her to have a letter to remember me by, so even if she never got to hear my voice again, she could hear it in my words and never forget what we had.

Dearest Ever,
My Wendy Darling,

If you are reading this letter it is probably because you have made it to your mother's and we did not manage to escape back to our home, yet. Yet. But until then I hope that there is a part of this, a part of me, that you can take and find comfort in.

That morning, before we met, I was broken. I wouldn't let myself forgive my father, and did everything abiding by how he treated me. I loved those boys with all I had, but it was never enough because part of my heart was always filled with hate from a past life. And one might say you couldn't blame me, but I still blamed myself. The thing is, all of it changed when you came. You were the sunshine that tore through the clouds and lit up my surroundings. You showed me that a heart without hate, a heart full of love and promise, can turn any story, change any person.

And you, my darling, changed my story.

Your smile was the one that I looked forward to seeing every day, and what I went to bed at night dreaming about. I love your thoughtfulness, your tender heart, and sweetness. I love the way your voice sounds whispering in my ear and how you have the ability to find beauty in everyone and everything. I love how much you cared for the boys who hurt you, kidnapped you, tied you up. I love your willingness to see the good in people and to change the bad. I love the second chances and kindness you give even to those who don't deserve it. I love the feeling you give me when your around, the way you make my stomach drop and heart crawl into my throat. I love the sweet sound of your laugh and giggle, the way you dance and play for hours. I love so many things about you, my dear, I can't even begin to count.

Because, Ever, I love you.

And I'm sorry I never said it before. I'm sorry I waited until it was too late. Because the truth is, I was scared. And I wasn't ready to fly. But just like you said up above these words, I wanted to fly. And I realized the first step is the jump.

Maybe I will fall, and maybe I will crash and burn and never leave my father's grasp, but I will never regret that I jumped. I will never regret choosing to keep you, and trying to win you over. It may have been the cause of all this, and it may cause us both pain, but I would rather live the rest of my days out in that pain with the memories I shared with you alongside me.

I also want to say that I am sorry. Because you may not have wanted all this, and that being I was selfish. You would have never had to meet my father had I not forced your hand in staying with us. But I do hope that you enjoyed our time as much as you seemed to. I do hope that we gave you the adventure you gave us. And more so, that that adventure is not over.

And though this all may seem scary, I promise it will get better. Because as twisted as your mother is, she loves you. And maybe, maybe my father loves me too.

We'll get through this, whatever the end result may be. Regardless, I want you to live the rest of your life happily and find new adventures to replace the old. Because if you keep trying to fight this endless war, you will never get the chance to fly. But I swear to you, that the moment my feet touch free ground, I will never stop searching for you. And will it be thirty years from now, who knows?

But it won't stop me.

Until then, find joy in the laughs we shared, comfort in the good moments, and protection in knowing that we are all still looking out for you. Never give up on that, and don't ever say goodbye, because goodbye means going away and going away means forgetting.

And I never want you to forget about me. As I will never forget about you.

So when it's hard, when you fail to see the light at the end of the tunnel, read this letter and look up at the stars. Find the second star to the right and make a wish, because somewhere, in some place, so will Albie, and Will, and Oliver, and Thomas, and Elliot. And so will I.

And then, someday, we'll see you there.

In Neverland.

Peter Pan

I folded up the note and placed it on the dresser along with the diamond necklace I had kept this long. I knew with her it would be safest.

Chapter Twenty Two

P_{eter}

The coldness of her voice sent a chilling shiver down my spine. "Up! Now!"

I didn't hesitate to respond. Throwing off the covers on Ever's bed with a mixture of regret and longing, I stood before the angered woman. Not only had it been the second, and most welcoming bed I had ever slept in, I felt that she was there with me when I did.

I wanted more.

But today, that wasn't in the cards. Today, the cards I was dealt were rough. Ever's mother didn't bother to have me changed, feed me or let me freshen up. I was simply handed a glass of lukewarm water and told to stay hydrated.

Hydrated. As if my biggest, most pressing problem was hydration.

And then she took me to the car. That was when it hit me. I was really going to have to face my father. I couldn't let this happen. Wild emotions stirred through me as I was pushed into the back seat of the car, and all I could think was *I can't give up yet. Not now. Not without one last fight.* Because realistically, if I did give up now, if I didn't fight, I would be on the losing end of the battle for the rest of my life.

So when she got into the front seat, rumbled the engine and began to pull out of her driveway, I tried the door. It was sealed shut. So, next, I began to crank down the window. Slowly, and in a steady pace, I put it down a little bit at a time, so that she wouldn't notice. And she didn't.

I didn't have much time to focus on her, but if I had I would've noticed how stressed she looked, how her eyes fought the tears threatening to come and how tightly she gripped the wheel, wringing her hands out on it. One who saw something like that might have felt bad for her, might have even cared.

But I *didn't* care. So, slowly cranking down the window, enough so the barely existent wind wouldn't affect her, I waited for the car to slow to a stop at a yellow, turning red light, watched the grass on the side of the road slow from zipping by, and didn't wait a second.

I pulled down the rest of the window, readied myself, swung my legs over and dove out. Instantly I regretted my decision. Having gone feet first, I felt the sharp pain soar up my ankles when they landed just by the grass on the pavement, give out from under me and have me tumbling down to the ground.

I think I may have blacked out for a couple seconds, because I honestly don't remember anything until I stood up. Sore and pained from the cuts, scrapes, and bruises I had given myself, I watched in frozen hesitation as Wendy's mother exclaimed and pulled her car to a screeching stop (the light had just turned green), and got out angrily, huffing as she made eye contact.

I met those eyes, the fierce blueness of them so similar to Ever's, it killed me inside. But there was something different, and I had to hold onto that. Her eyes were full of hate, longing and despair. Like she would rather kill than love again. Ever's were different. The blue storm inside swirled around a mixture of compassion, love, and the willingness to take risks.

I didn't have long to ponder that comforting thought, for the moment I met her fierce gaze, I turned and fled. There was about ten feet of grass from the side of the road, and then behind that a lining of trees that you could hardly call a forest, much less a wood. Nevertheless, I sought comfort in the trees and dove inside, trying to find one to climb. I passed by branchless trunks until I finally seized the perfect structure and clung to it. Swinging myself up with the force of a wild animal, I climbed higher and higher, at last finding myself a sitting spot far up, and looking down to see Ever's mother, and her heeled feet, glaring up at me.

"Get down here boy!" she screamed up at me, then cautiously looked around to make sure no one was watching. I shook my head in disagreement.

She continued to yell at me in all hopelessness, and at one point tried to climb, but when I ascended further, she gave up on that as well. Finally she stopped in her storming rage, placed her hand on a tree and smiled a wicked smile. And that was when I knew, instantly I knew, that in some twisted way she had bested me.

And it wasn't fair. Because as long as the game lasted, she would play dirty. And I had to keep my hands clean.

Looking up with that same plastered smile, she decided to make sure I knew that, "whether you return home to your daddy or not, Ever will be back where she belongs. And Peter, I can either make that an easy, comforting process, or an oh so very painful one. So, if you claim to have any feelings for my daughter at all, I suggest you climb down from that tree this instant and get *back* in the car."

Like I said, I knew she had bested me. And I also knew she would keep her word, no matter the costs. Sulking and infuriated, I slipped down the tree, and to her winning smile, strode back to my place in the back seat of the car.

The ride to my father's was the most painful and tense ride I had been through. And given, I had been through a lot. The air was so thick and strained with apprehension you could cut it.

I couldn't breath.

Pulling into the driveway of the old, seemingly abandoned hut gave me the worst stomach ache I had felt in years. It looked like something you'd find in a horror film. Wood beams were falling off the walls of the crest of the bay window, paint was chipped and cracked in various places, and the creaking sounds from the winds I couldn't locate sent chills down my spine.

Miss Kingsley exited the car, and when I stayed put, came around and opened my door, pinching my arm and dragging me out.

I was actually here. It wasn't just a dream, a night terror or vision - no, I was here.

And then he was there. Dressed in moth-eaten clothes, an old stained button down top and ripped, faded jeans, my father stepped unsteadily onto the front porch. His blood flecked eyes bore into me, and the crooked yellow teeth behind his lips watered cruelty, as I couldn't help but notice how he hadn't changed a bit. The whiskers on his face he refused to shave had greyed, and he seemed to have lost weight, but other than that he was the same.

He was the same man, cruel and twisted, that chased even demons away.

I watched as he continued on past the porch and down the driveway, ascending towards me. All the bones and muscles in my body tensed up, freezing me still, and I watched him come closer and closer.

And then he stopped. Not in front of me, I knew as relief flooded through me, but in front of Wendy's mother. "Is she in there," I heard a mutter come from Ever's mother as I tried to listen in. My father looked at me, shook his head no, then whispered something in her ear.

And then he smiled, and that awful, crooked smile bared its teeth at me, as his hand slipped around the woman's waist, and he drew her in for a kiss. Minutes were years as they embraced one another, all the while I felt like I was going to throw up.

Not only did I find this twist in the story to be the most vile, disgusting turn out as could be, the first thought that flashed through my head was that they were actually a couple.

And couples date.

They spend time with one another.

They get to know each other.

And they get to know their significant other's children.

Meaning my dear Wendy was not done with my father. No, that battle wouldn't be over for a long long time. Not until the day he died. And if he's held on this long, than how much longer will it be?

I decided against that thought, trying to convince myself that in the poor health he was in, it wouldn't be forever. But be it as it may, it would feel like forever.

My father broke from his girl, leading her over by a loosely connected hand, to me. I shrunk back, but managed a to glare daggers through his skull as his boney hand seized my chin.

"I thought we discussed him being in… a good condition." He suggested the matter as if I were merely a piece of merchandise.

"Nothing of the sort," she mewed hastily. "And I didn't do this to him. The boy managed that quite well all himself."

My father smirked, still not taking his eyes off of me. "I'd rather you had."

And she, too, smirked.

They took a pause, both staring at me in abhorrence, until my father at last opened his mouth. "Well, dearest, you must excuse us now. Edmund - or should I say *Peter* - has a lot to see before the night closes in."

She nodded and flashed him a triumphant smile, placing a hand on his chest briefly before pulling away and dipping below the ceiling of her car.

I had never been so panicked at her going away.

Without waiting a second, my father snatched up my hand, raw from wringing, and pulled me along inside.

The inside of the house was almost exactly as I had remembered it. It freaked me out a little, seeing the same picture of the terror I had put behind me, now in front of me in the same condition. The living room, if you could call it that, was to the first left you made when going down the rickety hallway, filled with an old battered couch (in worse condition than the one back at camp), a matching armchair, and red stained rug.

And the bottles. Yes, the empty bottles lined the place, and were sand to a beach sprinkled around the room. They made it the place I had known so well, and they remained in the picture up until then.

To the right of the back hallway was the bathroom, frightening to enter, and caused a frantic hasten to leave. The kitchen was across from the living room, and there wasn't much to say about it, as it was one of the rooms he actually kept decently neat.

"You remember where your room is, son?" The voice behind me made me jump. I nodded as he handed a little brass key. "Good. Go up there, I be there shortly."

I obeyed his command and walked briskly up the stairs, down the hall and into the second door. I unlocked it with a creaking click, and pushed open the wooden door.

Instantly when I saw it my eyes welled up with stinging tears. The place looked *exactly* the same as it had before. And I'm not just talking like it gave me the same feeling or some of the furniture was the same, it literally looked as if the door had been locked and not reopened until now.

The bed, tucked into the corner, was made neatly with old blankets and a single pillow. Directly across the room from it was the cracked full-length mirror. I remembered staring into it as a young boy, thinking that it was possible that there was another boy on the other side sharing my same pain, and that I wasn't alone to drown in it.

To the left of the mirror was my chipped brown dresser, it's second drawer down half open. I, for some reason, distinctly remember leaving it that way, and I couldn't fathom as to why.

On the dresser was a picture, blurred out and bent, of my mother and father together. Their faces were too disoriented to make out, but you could see their joy in their body language alone as they embraced each other.

I remember staring at not only the mirror, but that picture, and wondering how a man like my father could have the ability to love someone that much. To put an arm around someone with such compassion, and then to another throw them down with such hate.

I threw myself on the bed, reminding myself over and over that I didn't want to be here, like for some reason that would help my predicament. I had done it - I had run away and lived in the woods. It seemed like some type of an impossible dream that I had somehow been living in, and now that I was back, it was merely a far off imaginary land.

"Edmund," my father rapped his knuckles on the door, and came in instantly, ripping me from my thoughts.

"It's Peter now," I said without thought, my teeth gritting against one another.

He rolled his eyes and muttered something inaudibly under his breath, then met my eyes and scratched his head. "I just wanted to say... er, I wanted to say that -"

"What?!" I snapped, not letting him get out the words. "What could you possibly *want* to say to me now after you taken everything?" I rose to my feet, the blood boiling under my skin. "You ripped me away from my life, the people I loved and who loved me back, you took me away from all of them! WHAT COULD YOU POSSIBLY SAY?!"

"What," he sneered in mock return, "Will Wendy and the boys be a little *lost* when they can't find their beloved Peter Pan? Will they *stop believing?*"

"That belief kept me alive! It kept all of them alive. I wouldn't be here right now without it, father, I wouldn't! It saved me!" I felt spit fly from my mouth as I yelled back at him in rage, all the anger I had kept under for him rising to the surface.

"From what?" he bellowed back. "From what did you need to be saved?!"

"FROM YOU!"

"I made you strong!"

"NO!" I screamed as loud as my voice would go, hearing it crack with fury. "ALL YOU DID WAS MAKE A LITTLE BOY WONDER WHY HIS PARENTS DIDN'T LOVE HIM, WHY NOBODY CARED WHETHER OR NOT HE WAS IN PAIN, OR WHETHER HE WAS WORTH ANYTHING AT ALL! YOU MADE THAT LITTLE KID CRY HIMSELF TO SLEEP EACH NIGHT AND FEAR THE WORST IN THE MORNING, AND TRY TO

UNDERSTAND HOW HIS TEACHER COULD BE SO KIND TO HIM BECAUSE HE DIDN'T THINK THATS HOW ADULTS WORKED! ALL YOU DID, FATHER, WAS MAKE A LITTLE BOY NEVER WANT TO GROW UP. YOU MADE ME *WEAK* AND YOU CALLED IT STRENGTH!"

I heaved recollecting breaths and lowered my finger, which was jabbing in his face. He opened his mouth to speak, not able to find the words, and then for a brief second began to raise his palm, for that was the only way he knew how to fight back.

"What are you going to do," I spat, "are you going to strike me, father? Well, I can tell you now, it won't work. Because I'm not that same little kid anymore. If you strike me I *will* strike you back."

The hesitant hand lowered.

"All I was going to say," he said soberly, "was welcome home."

And he left, closing the door behind him.

Chapter Twenty Three

Wendy

I sat, slumped against the bedroom wall, thinking of any way to get out of this impossible situation. I had to take it back, think about it from a bird's eye view. From after the fight.

...

The next morning, he seemed to have forgotten the wretched events of last night. He had seemed to come back to normal. The worst thing Peter's father had done so far was yell at me for not waking him up sooner.

And, of course, turn a blind eye to my bruises and cuts.

He did, though, seem to be a bit more quiet than usual. Was it possible that he felt a little, the very smallest, bit of remorse?

The ridiculous thought brought a cold, crude laugh to my lips that didn't seem to be truly mine.

But, in the same way, that didn't seem like a true statement. In all honesty, when have I ever done something that was truly me? Really my choice, for me, for my happiness?

I knew. I knew in an instant. Deciding to stay with Peter and the lost boys. I knew that was my decision from the very moment I made it, because of the way it made me feel. Free.

I sat there for a minute, pity and anguish for myself washing over me when I heard his voice outside my room.

Curiosity seeped through me, and I crept a little closer to my door.

Peter's father's voice was carried towards me.

"Finally!" he cried, his voice rigid with a mixture of anticipation and excitement. "So you did end up coming to your senses... how much did you decide on? I - what?" His voice turned to curious suspicion. "Wha- Edmund? But how... you'll have to give me time to consider. Fine, but he's not enough. There was another boy, taller, stronger. Well, yes - to keep him company." He shrugged the words sheepishly. "Well then... yes, fine, I'll give her to you. But don't expect her to be in the right way for a little date with that boy you said she's meeting at three-"

What? Peter was here?! And with my mother! How fate mocked us so. And could she really still be so keen on me meeting Dean - after all that had happened?

"-seemed to fall in love with my son, there, and... well, you said Edmund's nasty right now. But he's only that way because we *deprived* him of his love." I could clearly hear the sneer in his voice as he purposely tried to annoy my mother. "She's the same way, forcing her to meet this so-called 'Dean' might not be the best decisi-"

This time I heard my mother's voice through the phone and its effect was immediate. Goose pimples were starting to cover my body.

"DO NOT TELL ME HOW TO RAISE MY DAUGHTER, THANK YOU VERY MUCH, RUFUS!"

Rufus, I thought. So that was his name...

I skulked to the other side of the room, slowly. I didn't really want to hear the rest of their conversation. The only thing it had brought so far was unneeded knowledge.

Knowledge that only brought pain.

Furthermore, I continued to sit in my room for a while, thinking.

No, not about Peter. About my old life, actually. About what a little princess I used to be. But, not like a fairytale, where the princess is the savior or is saved because she ends up so kind and wonderful and deserving. More like… a princess at the beginning of the story.

Like Snow White.

She probably had gowns and treasures, maids and butlers and servants, ready to do anything for her, once she gave the command.

Yes, that was definitely somewhat of my old life.

But Snow White also had an evil stepmother. Who was cruel to her…

She even tried to kill her.

You see, like me, Snow White probably would have given up all the jewels, and the gowns, and the castles - even the grandest - for a chance at having a real, living mother that truly loved her.

I was a broken princess who didn't know her true identity yet, didn't know who she really was...

Lived her whole life listening to her mother and allowing herself to be pushed around, waiting for something - that now, I knew, was her prince charming.

Except, that princess didn't get her happy ending. She was given a poison apple, yes. And her prince, her beautiful prince, was snatched away from her.

And she was left to sleep in darkness for the rest of her life.

That's how I felt. Hopeless bitterness surged through me. I didn't know what to do, having all these treasures my mother gave me, riches and beauty and gold...

Yet not being happy.

And so yes, I was thinking about myself. How much I had changed. Going on as one person, ladylike and beautiful. Optimistic and willing to hope, having a little flame inside of me that refused to be snuffed out, no matter how many tearful nights it cost it.

Then, becoming a broken young girl, who had been put through so much, and become so hopeless, that she didn't find a point to life anymore, and was even willing to think, even for the briefest of seconds, of the option to... to end it all. For she found very little reason to live anymore anyways. Not when she had had that taste of joy, pure joy. Not when she loved it so much, and then - then it was taken from her, with not even the smallest chance of regaining it. Just like that.

I had changed. So much. Become so different, it was weird knowing who I once was.

But that hopeful young girl, who thought she saw good in the world, was wrong.

And now she was gone.

I laid my hot face against the cool window, tired. I wanted to fall into a dreamy sleep, where I could see Peter and my faraway father. Maybe I could meet Peter's mother, too…

And we would all be happy, on a flying ship, full course to Neverland, with no more parents to tell you no, or angry Captain Hooks.

"Listen, I don't want to see you out of your room for a little while now, alright?" Peter's father's snarly voice said to me, awakening me to full attention.

Not looking at him, I kept my eyes plastered to the window, and murmured "Alright-"

When suddenly, something caught my attention. Peter's father's reflection was on the window, but something was wrong. Though his rough, stubbly appearance was close to the same, something was not right.

And then I noticed. His left hand had disappeared! In place of it, a shining hook, with a pointy tip, and a…

I turned around, quickly, looking at him.

Then my eyes met his left hand...

And exactly that. His left hand. No hook.

I turned back to the window, to his reflection. But it was just him, looking confused.

"What?" he shouted, sounding annoyed.

"I... nothing, never - never mind..."

...

There had to be way to get out of this.

But no matter how hard I tried, I couldn't find one. Not even the smartest person in the universe could find a way to fix this, I didn't think so, at least.

She had me. She beat me. I had fought valiantly, but in the end, she won.

My heart silently wept as he led me away. Led me to my unknown, unwanted destiny. His hand reached towards the knocker, and I desperately wanted it to stop, for it to just go away.

But no matter how much I hoped, it didn't go away.

The next few moments were so terrible, made me feel even more depressed than I already was, I don't want to even explain them.

The doorknob turned with a creak, and the despondent clouds were the only thing I could see in a miles view that wasn't *perfect*. The house, the car, the lawn, everything about the scene was so sneeringly perfect it killed me. But the clouds, looming grey on this fitting day, were something I could relate to.

At least I had something.

But it didn't matter the moment my mother stepped out the front door, her heels clicking down the steps of the porch to the area below in which I stood. She smothered an endearing look on her face as she approached me, her arms going to my shoulders, but there was no hug. There was never any hug.

"Ever, darling, you look..." on second thought's hesitation, she frowned, and looked me over. "I like your dress."

It was as warm as a welcome from her could get, but in her cold dark eyes, I could see what she was really saying. *We'll talk about all this later, young miss.*

In short, she was her awful self, seemed barely even relieved that I was safe home, cheery nice to Peter's dad, and was cruel and absolutely dreadful to me.

And then their lips met, and the world shattered beneath me...

That's all I can say. It pretty much sums it up, anyway.

Henceforth, approximately thirty minutes later, I found myself sobbing on my bedroom floor; the remnants of a shattered mirror beside me, once again locked inside this prison. I remembered, with a heart full of hate, the fight that had left the mirror broken.

It surprised me that I had any more tears left in me, that I had any strength left to make any noise at all.

Suddenly, the thought that there was no more reason to live anymore, the thought that even death seemed a better option than this, once again came, threatening to overwhelm me.

And, my whole body trembling, I picked up a broken piece of glass. I was clutching it so hard, the sharp edges cutting into my hand.

Bleeding, and not caring, I raised my hand.

I felt an urge to stop, but it was like my hands were moving on their one accord.

Agonized tears streamed down my cheeks, blurring my eyes to what I was really doing. I stretched my cut hand towards my neck, vibrating and shaking and trembling so hard, I was like a plane getting ready to take flight.

My hand was so close to my throat, that every time it shook, it came nearer to cutting it.

I was so close. So close to it being over, to it disappearing.

The pain.

The hurt.

The heartache.

Yet I couldn't do it. I had gotten my violently trembling hand, with the shard of glass enclosed in it, so close. I just had to move it less than an inch closer, and then, maybe, I could fly.

Fly...

Not have to be myself, trapped in this awful person I knew I was. And then I thought of Peter. About what he would tell me if he were here. *Don't do it Ever,* he would say. *You're stronger than this. Believe in yourself. You're beautiful.* I let out a heart-wrenching shriek, my whole body shaking vigorously.

"I AM ENOUGH!" I screamed, collapsing onto the floor in sobs.

And the glass fell from my hand.

Chapter Twenty Four

Wendy

A girl walked to the window. Her hair was put up in a braided knot along the back of her head; shiny, golden brown. Flowers; yellow, gold and white were placed on top. She wore a white lace dress, with a golden ribbon wrapped just above the waist. Simple, but lovely. The stockings matched well with her skin tone, and on her feet, she wore golden-yellow flats. Glittering blue eyes shone through dark, curly lashes. Her cheeks were rosy pink, and her lips a light shade of red. And the necklace, yes, the dazzling diamond necklace that gleamed against her skin, held all the worth that met her gaze, but not because of the cost, nor even its beauty, but because it was the thoughtfulness, Peter's caring heart, that meant the world to her. Because it was from him. In some way, it had to be.

I looked back at the girl in the window. She really was incredibly stunning to the eye, like a flower dancing in the wind.

And this girl, this very same girl, was me.

Me.

But I didn't feel too beautiful. I didn't feel like a glowing flower. No. Not at all.

Inside, I felt broken, dirty. Like a flower that had once hoped to reach towards the sun, only to get squashed underfoot.

Yes, that seemed right. That seemed me.

A squashed flower.

I sat on my window seat, my "used to be" favorite spot of the house. Well, I guess it still was. It had a perfect view of our large cherry blossom tree, and if you looked from the right angle, it looked like the sun seemed to shine even brighter when it hit our roses.

When it rained (and it often did here, in London), the water would glisten on our neatly trimmed lawn, looking like a sleek sheet of green.

It really was quite beautiful. But never enough, not like the forest, not like love.

It would never be enough.

As I thought about this, I wondered if I was going to cry. But even though I felt sad, my eyes were not wet at all. I guess I didn't have many tears left in me, anyways…

"Ever," My mother's sing-song voice called from below. "It's almost three. We wouldn't want to be late now, would we?"

Once again, I took a glimpse at my reflection. "Ever!" she called once again. For someone who sounded so sweet and innocent, it was hard to imagine her being so cruel.

Nevermind, not as hard as you might think.

"Coming," I called back, heading towards the door.

Just then, I stepped on something sharp. "Owwww," I sighed, clamping a hand on my foot. I quietly cursed under my breath, something I hadn't done until I met Peter and the lost boys.

There was so much I did out of habit then, because of them.

I looked to the floor, directly beside my nightstand to see what I had stepped on, when I noticed something. It was a note, folded up thick and laid on the ground sideways, which would explain why it caused me pain. It was crinkled and held no dust, so it couldn't have been here for a while. Nevertheless, it had fallen and was waiting here.

Waiting for me.

I recognized it to be from the ink of my typewriter which was in front of me on the desk, and for a moment, joy seeped through me like the brightest of lights.

Dearest Ever,

He had written me a note! I had found a note from him!

But then my mother, once again, interrupted my one happy moment.

"Ever, where are you? We cannot have you being late!" She now sounded angry, and fearful of her coming up and seeing the letter, I quickly looked for a place to put it, where it could be safe, and close to my heart.

Close to my heart…

I slipped in the little bird's nest on my window sill. I had fought with my mother to keep it there. Sometimes, when it was warmer, little birds would come and peck at it, or see if it was worth making their home.

It felt like the only place in the room worthy of keeping Peter's words. And so, there it sat, in the little birds' nest.

"Coming, Mother!"

…

"I want to see manners, kindness, and best of all, ladylike behaviors, as that it is exactly what you are: a young lady." She dug her sharp nails into my skin, and I winced in pain. "Do you understand?" Under her harsh gare, I nodded my head quickly.

"Good, now look here." She held my chin tight in her hands, looking me up and down, checking to make sure I was good enough for this *ever* so important date.

Or, more accurately, good enough for her.

When she was satisfied, she straightened and ran a hand through her perfectly neat hair, ruffling it a bit, just a bit.

This must have been very important to her, if she was so worried that she would risk ruining her hair for it. I decided that this must, *must* go well if I ever hope to get on her good side again.

Must.

I sighed, letting my tiredness go, before standing up straight, broadening my shoulders just a bit, so my posture would match hers, and tried to smile.

Tried to. But I didn't think I could ever smile again.

Not now. Not when all hope was lost, once more. You see, the only way I could cope with the situation was telling myself the truth, no matter how hard it might be. The truth. That I would never see my beloved Pet- Edmund again. I shall never see Edmund again. The truth.

Sometimes, the best way to remember things is to repeat them so many times again and again until it is etched into your skull.

The truth.

The truth.

The truth.

Taking in a low, sharp inhale, I let my eyes go upwards to meet my mother's. She studied me again, but this time looked directly into my eyes. To see if I was going to make this her day, or destroy it into mine.

I tried to smile again, for my earlier attempt had lost its glamor awhile ago.

Your day, I tried to say. *Yours.*

Finally, she nodded briskly.

"Ever, I just wanted to let you know something."

I would look everywhere but her, everywhere but her.

"Ever..." her voice spoke in a manner I hadn't heard since I was very young. Almost... gentle. And, without thinking, I let my eyes trail up to hers.

And I saw something unheard of.

I saw tears.

"Ever." I could hear a faint plead in her voice now. "Ever, I just want to make sure you know... I-I'm doing this for you. All for you."

I had to look away.

"And, my darling, I love you. This, this is all for you. Okay?"

I couldn't say anything. How dare she... how *dare* she... she apologize...

"Ever, please..."

Why were tears so wet?

"Sweetie..."

If I just looked at her, maybe I could see love. Like, a true mother's love. Maybe, maybe then, it would be easier to forgive her. Maybe, if I saw that love, we could start over. But I... I just couldn't. After all that she put me through?

After everything?

We are all imperfect; she simply made a mistake and was now asking for my forgiveness. And I *should* forgive. Like... like a good daughter would.

"Ever, please look at me," she entreated.

And I could. I should. After all, she was my mother.

But this, this was the first decision she let me make on my own, *my* decision. I took a deep breath, and...

And I looked away.

...

I watched trees blur together, as my chauffeur drove me to Dean's house.

Her name was Sofia, and she came from America. She had come here looking for a job and took the first one she was offered. My helper.

I guess the "American dream" didn't always stand true. But then again, was London any better?

She was my best friend; that I was actually allowed to see, at least. Sometimes, when she could see I was really down, she would tell me about the other country she once knew.

She also had my favorite accent in the entire world! She tended to over-pronounce her R's, flatten her A's, turn her T's into D's. And when she talked, it sounded carefree and happy, instead of orderly and smooth, like most accents around here.

But ever since I had come back, she had seemed a little angry, a little far away.

I wonder what I did.

My hands were shaking as we pulled into Dean's wide driveway, but I didn't know why. My fear from earlier seemed to have evaporated into a weird stillness. Calmness.

I glimpsed at his large, neatly mowed lawn, and his widespread flower garden, dampened from last night's rain. There was a large maple tree in front, with a sturdy oak beside it. My expression hardened as I thought of this.

Will had taught me how to tell trees apart.

Whenever sudden thoughts like this came up, I no longer felt sad. Instead, I felt defiant, as if thinking, *I won't let this knock me down. Not now, not ever.* And then all I had left to do was to hope it was true.

I guess that just seemed easier.

I clutched the car door tightly with my hand, opening it before Sofia could. It helped my quivering hands, to be doing something, instead of waiting.

"Do you want me to-"

"No thank you," I said quietly, cutting her off. "I am fine myself, thank you very much."

And I was going to be. I was.

Taking a deep breath, and ignoring my friend's concern written all over her face, I started up toward the house.

Because I have no sense of precognition, and I was much too worried about what was about to happen to me, I didn't foretell that this was the last time I was going to see Sofia ever again.

I suppose if I had known, I would have at least waved. But I didn't. So I left without even saying goodbye.

...

I have to say, it surprised me when he opened the door. I guess I just thought that because he was rich, he was probably lazy and selfish, and would have thought too highly of himself to open the door. But there he was, right in front of me.

The second thing I noticed was why girls adore him so much. He was one of the most good-looking men I had ever seen, with innocent dazzlingly hazel eyes, light brown hair that was messy, but in a slick, handsome sort of way, perfect white teeth that would surely shine even brighter if he smiled, and muscles that were bulging from beneath his shirt.

And the last thing I noticed, was that he, like me, didn't seem to be too keen on this date idea. But if he wasn't (and he obviously was not), then why did he say yes to my mother? Or did she lie; was it not him who said yes?

He took a second longer to look me up and down, then I him, but when he was done, our eyes met, just for a second.

And then a minute.

And then a year.

Finally, I noticed what I was doing, and looked away. I was not his to stare at, and he was not mine. I felt that if I stared any longer, I would be betraying Peter somehow.

Yet, he was still staring at me.

"Er," I started, wanting to break his trance, not knowing what caused it in the first place anyway. I wasn't that exceptionally beautiful, he ought to have met much prettier girls.

"Shall we get going then, um, Dean?"

He stared at me a second longer, giving me a calculating look, then said, in a deep and strangely handsome voice, "I suppose so."

And then he started walking.

Just like that.

I stood on the spot, confused, then stumbled after him.

"Wait!" I called. "Where are we going?!" I eyed the picnic basket in his hand, shaking my head in confusion.

"There's a pond a little ways down the road, a spot most girls like. I thought you might, too." He said all this without stopping.

I raised an eyebrow. "And what makes you think I'm like most girls?"

To be honest, I don't really know why I asked this. I mean, all girls in London act the same way, don't they? They're girls, for goodness' sake! But, for some reason, I felt like I had to prove myself to him or something.

He paused for the first time and looked at me again. "And what should make me think that you're different?"

He let me ponder this for a second and then continued walking.

We got there pretty quickly, and he was right, I did like this place. There was a big willow, concealed in water, lily pads, and flower petals which all decorated the top of the pond. Birds tweeted in the distance, and the sweetest baby red squirrel watched us with big, innocent and careful eyes.

"Wow," I whispered, turning in circles to suck all of it in. "Wow…"

"Ready?" I heard Dean call behind me. I turned around, to find that he had already set everything up.

"Wow," I repeated, though this time for a new reason. "This looks delicious."

"Just a snack," he said modestly. "Cherries?" He handed me a cup of the ripe, juicy fruit, and I took it gratefully.

We sat there in silence for a few minutes, enjoying our food, me trying to find the courage to ask him a burning question.

And the longer I watched him in quiet, the more burning the question seemed pressing until it was impatience, not courage, that managed to ask him what I had been hoping to since he answered the door.

"Um, Dean?" He looked up.

"Ever?" I suddenly felt good. I liked how he pronounced my name. I didn't even realize he knew it. But I guess he ought to have, for why would he go on a date with someone who he didn't even know the name of? My mother must have told him, obviously.

"I was just a bit - er - surprised, I guess, when I saw... um, met... er, well, it's just... I've heard rumors about you, and it's not that they're bad, it's just... well, I guess, you're - you're just a bit different than I expected."

He looked at me inquiringly. I decided to continue.

"Dean, what I want to know is... well, I guess... who are you, really?"

He looked at me for a second, opened his mouth, closed it, and then shook his head.

"You know, that's a really good question."

We looked at each other again - once again a bit more than I think Peter would have appreciated - and then he looked away, and continued eating.

Chapter Twenty Five

Will

A starless sky. A shielded moon.

The heavens had closed.

The shortened day had only told me one thing: that soon it was going to get colder, and we needed to prepare. I wasn't about to let Peter's absence stop us from our season routine, nor was I going to leave the boys in their misery without him. "Come on!" I called, hastening them up as the twins carried in dry logs for fires, and Elliot gathered the dry leaves to stuff the blankets with. During the upcoming fall and winter season, we would layer two blankets and stuff the insides with leaves, then tie the edges for insulation. Then we would buddy up in the hammocks to keep warm. I usually went with Elli, the twins together, and Peter with Albie. But now with Wendy here I didn't know how it was going to work.

Well, she wasn't *exactly* here.

I pushed the thought aside and focused more on what I was doing, which was cooking the game I had caught. It seemed an impossible task to most, and some days it did take hours, but hunting isn't actually too bad in these parts. I mean, it's pretty much all nature except us, and I rotate areas each day or so, so that the animals don't leave their habitats behind.

Today I had gone fishing. I had caught three fish, one small and the other two fairly large in size. I had gone nearly every day this week and planned on catching at least three in hopes of storing them for later. Today, as noted, I had met that goal.

"Will, I'm tired," Elliot moaned, looking up from his job of sifting through his pile of leaves and picking out the dry ones.

"I know, bud," I said back in a soft tone, rotating the fish over the fire. Elliot coughed, but said nothing more and return to his work. All was well for about five more minutes until Elli looked up once again.

"Will, I want to go to bed now," he sighed, slumping down and giving up on his job. I looked to the sky and the faint hint of the once setting sun.

"Why, it can't be past eight o'clock! Just a few minutes more."

He puffed out his lip, and sat back up, once again returning to his job. There seemed to be something off about him, so I watched closely to his movements and reactions, trying to see if anything was truly wrong. It seemed not so, but in only a matter of seconds, I watched in horror as his eyes rolled back into his head and all of the sudden he slumped to the ground, lifeless and stone cold.

I screamed his name and darted over, my gut dropping. Taking him in my arms, I checked for a pulse and felt my breath return when I felt one, however faint. Just to double check, I held a finger to his nose and again felt a small bit of normalcy regain when I could feel his hot breath on my skin.

"Elli? Elli?" I tapped his cheek, trying to wake him as the boys crowded around in nervous excitement. I felt his head, then cheeks, and neck with the palm of my hand, all of which burning up his pale, sallow complexion. My rasps of breath began to come faster, I noticed, and I told myself not today. *Not now.* I squeezed his hand and watched as his eyes started to flutter, so faint and so brief that I started to doubt whether they actually did, but a stirring of his hands told me they had.

They were almost fully open now, and his were teeth chattering. Barely even meeting my eyes, he began to cough. I helped him sit up as he sputtered out his hoarse throat, trying to cover his mouth with a trembling wrist. It was then, in the dim sunset glow, that I noticed the blood being coughed up on his arm. Some of the crimson saliva mix was rolling down his chin, and more came up as he continued to wheeze.

"Get him some water!" I screamed to the other boys, my voice shaken with fear. They obliged, all running over to our supply of old plastic water bottles and brought one over. I helped him drink it, with a ginger touch, and tried to wash down the blood as well as stop my hands from trembling. To my relief, after the water, his fit stopped, and I immediately thought it a good idea to bring him to the couch. He was a rather small boy and seemed even lighter than before, and I have always been taller and stronger than even Peter. So it was with ease that I picked him up, and like a sleeping infant I brought him to the couch, hearing soft moans as I laid him down.

"What is it?" I asked gently. "What's wrong?"

His lower lip began to quiver as he managed to keep his tearing eyes open. "My chest hurts. It hurts, it hurts." He mumbled the words over and over, and with every deep breath let out a half cry when he exhaled. It was pitiful and sad, but I didn't know how to help him. I laid a blanket on top of him, and watched the boy cling to it greatly, seeming younger and smaller than ever. He closed his eyes, and despite the coughing and shivering, seemed like he was falling into sleep. So, leaving him be for a little while, I got up and addressed the other boys, who looked as pale and frightened as I felt.

"Is he okay?" Albie squeaked, as I took him in my arms to bring him to bed. I nodded solemnly, not knowing what to say next, and all I could manage was, "Yeah, he's fine."

"Yeah he's fine," was all I said to Thomas, and then Oliver as well, as I tucked them in without a smile, and kissed their foreheads goodnight.

And "yeah he's fine" was all I told myself as I knelt beside the battered couch and his sleeping person. Even in an unconscious state, with each breath, I felt his wince of pain and the occasional blood that tainted his lips when he would cough.

I can't even tell you how long I sat there. It seemed to be forever, with no moon or stars to watch, nothing to determine the time of night or how long it would be until he started coughing again. And again and again my eyes began to doze, and I would pinch myself awake, take a brief walk, and return to his bedside.

Peter if you're listening right now, I need your strength. I need your courage. I need your faith. I looked up into the speckless sky and wished upon a hidden star, hoping it was the right one. And then, without control, I felt my head lay down against the corner of the couch and my eyes droop closed.

...

I awoke to the sound of quiet sniffling. Jolting awake and instantly turning to Elli, I could feel the blood surging through my veins move a little faster. But he was fast asleep, and I calmed down. I looked to my left and right with less urgency than before, trying to locate the sound.

And then I saw him. His back to a tree that fenced the camp, little Albie was curled up into a tight ball, trying to contain his sobs. My heart lurched at the sight, and I rose groggily to join him. He didn't really notice my presence until moments before I squatted down next to him, my hands on my knees.

"Hey bud," I said softly.

He didn't respond, but looked up, and I saw the tears streaming down his cheeks. I wiped them gently, trying for a smile. "Aw, what's wrong?"

"Is - is h-he going to d-d-die?" he blubbered, his palms rubbing his red cheeks.

"No, no," I sighed, enveloping him in a big hug. "No, Albie he's not."

I looked to Albie, then to Elliot. The slumbering boy did indeed look weak, and never before had I seen a sickness like this. I had seen fevers, chills, and fatigue. But I had never seen something like this. I hadn't seen the blood from coughing, the trembling and chest pains. He seemed so weak all of the sudden, so different from his usual self, I didn't know how to handle it.

"It-it's just that every-everything," he heaved a great big breath and calmed himself before continuing. "Everything's changed. Peter's gone, Wendy's gone, and now Elliot… why does everything have to change Will?"

His almond eyes were round as moons, so innocent and sweet, something I couldn't bear to ruin. But the truth was I needed some time to myself to process this. Everything *had* happened so fast, and I - I didn't know if I could handle it even as well as Albie was handling it.

But I was in charge now. There was no 'take-a-break' or leave someone else in control. Heck, Elli couldn't even watch them for ten minutes so I could go take a walk.

The stakes were high now, I couldn't mess up, I couldn't stress or freak out or assume the worst because these boys looked up to me. I was their new leader, and my emotions, my feelings, and my thoughts were what trickled down to the rest of them.

And that was what scared me the most.

...

The next few days I spent by cooling down Elli's fever, using dampened rags and by dipping him in the stream. These effects only helped for the hour or so, as his fever and symptoms continued to get worse. The coughing up blood happened at least once a day, and the pains in his chest only grew, as well as the sudden temperature changes. He slept a lot, and sometimes his words wouldn't make sense.

And then he stopped responding. It was only for a quick while, but I swear it stopped my heart. I had just finished with the lunch meal, had cut some fruit into smaller pieces so it was easier for him to swallow, but when I brought it over to him there was nothing.

"Elli?" I shook him. Eyes open, still and staring at the clouds, he remained motionless. I set down the platter of food, concern swelling in my chest. "Elli? Elliot?!" I shook his arm, my cries growing louder until all of a sudden he shook himself back into reality and looked at me, instant tears welling in his eyes.

"Sorry, I... uh... sorry," was what he decided on, and with a hesitant glance, I picked up the meal once more. Spoon feeding Elli made me realize that I had never once done that. It had always been

Peter. Even in the stress of the storm, he was able to fit everything in, attend to every need. He was someone that you overlooked when he was there, but when he was gone you realized how much you really needed him. Like even though the world was always crumbling, somehow, he was able to fit the pieces back together. Without him, they would just... fall. Maybe into place, maybe out of place, however the pieces chose, but the point was that he was able to direct those pieces into harmony. So that they could thrive.

I couldn't compare.

Chapter Twenty Six

Wendy

We continued to eat in silence, enjoying the sweet fruit, salty caramels, crunchy granola, and everything else he had brought.

It was actually really quite delectable, and he told me he chose it all himself.

But, you see, that was the only thing he told me. We didn't talk, besides exchanging that bit of information. I suppose it was a bit awkward, but every time I opened my mouth, I felt like I was going to make it even worse, so I just copied his quiet eating.

After a little while, though, he was finished. I hadn't eaten anything in forever - my mum didn't want me spoiling this meal with him - so I was still very hungry. But I didn't want to seem like a pig or anything, and knowing my mother, the same person who would nearly starve me to death if she saw I was getting the slightest bit chubby, would highly disapprove. So I ate the same as him.

When he was done, he chose to stare at me some more. This made it even more awkward, so I decided to talk, wiping my red and juicy hands on a napkin in front of me.

"When you said 'who are you really?' earlier, if you don't mind my asking, what did you mean by that?"

He looked at me a second longer, and then slowly eased himself into a leaning position on the tree beside him.

He had set up our picnic blanket right under a big tree, whose branches intertwined with the willow tree in the water.

With a sigh, he started. "The truth is, those rumors, they were probably right. I'm not a very good person. At least, I wasn't." I didn't let him stop there. "The thing is, I've lived my whole life with my father. And everything I did, I learned from him. I saw, my entire life, him treat women like objects. They were just simply toys that he had for his purposes. He could use them to his advantage, and then dispose of them when he was done."

My eyes widened and he sighed again. "And… well, I followed suit. I just thought as he had taught me to think, 'well, they are women, they are not as good as me. What does it matter?' I know. A terrible way to live. But you have to see that this was the only thing I had known. This is what I was taught! You can't blame me for it!" The pleading in his voice surprised me.

"So... yes, that's exactly what I did. Most girls thought of me as pretty handsome, like my father, and by the age of fifteen, I had gone on what seemed like hundreds and hundreds of dates. You see, I had nothing else to hold onto.

And then she came. My mother. Eight months, and twenty-seven days ago. She was all of a sudden here. I hadn't even grown up with a mother; I had never met her! And then, all too fast, I had one.

And she changed me. The thing is, she left because my father had abused her in that way. He had only eyes for her physical beauty, instead of the true beauty she really had, and had threatened her into dating him. I guess he had kind of forced her into prostitution; she was poor and didn't think she had any other options. She also just really wanted to find the good in him, even the slightest bit. She thought, if nothing else, she could change him. And that's the exact kind of person she was. Never for herself, always for someone else. You see, she was sick. Really sick. And she came back here once more, just so she could see me. Once more, before she died. So I would know that she was there, someone who truly loved me. *She* showed me true love. *She* showed me what it was like to really live.

She showed me that people like you, girls, like the ones I had abused and selfishly used, as worth so much. Equality - that's what we need in this world, more than ever."

He looked far off, as if he had forgotten I was still there.

"And then," he finished in a small, sad whisper. "She died. Her last act was to save her son from wickedness, and the whole time, she was fighting a battle herself. Cholera. When she had fled from my dad, she had no money. She couldn't afford medicine, or clean water for that matter. If she had just told me, I could've helped her. I would have gotten her some, but no... I never saved her..." I saw how sad he was, though somehow, it made him look stronger, instead of crushed, like me.

"It wasn't your fault, you never knew."

He looked up at me, seeking reassurance, but I didn't know what to say.

Sometimes now, when I felt especially broken, I would think about Peter. And, if I did it hard enough, I felt like he was there with me.

"How long were you two together?" I asked.

"Two and a half weeks," he muttered, quiet again now that his story was done.

Wow, I thought. And *I* imagined I had it hard, only being with those I loved for a little over a month.

"Was there something you really liked to do togeth-"

"I don't want to talk about it," he said, louder, cutting me off.

"Sorry," I whispered, my voice now small.

We fell back into silence until he finally spoke again, feeling bad. "She always said that I was really good at chess. Explained that I got it from her. She was pretty bad, though." He smiled a bit, for the second time all afternoon.

"Um, she gave me a little wooden set. I carry it around-" he cut himself off this time, reddening slightly.

Pretending I hadn't heard, I sat back down, not even realizing I had stood up until now. "I've never played, you'll have to teach me."

"What? Well, come on, I'll show you."

And he did.

And I was terrible. But I think it made it even more fun.

He seemed to think so too, for we were in fits of laughter by the time he won for the sixth time in a row (the quickest time yet, below seven minutes).

"Wow, I think you're even worse than she was!"

I grinned. "You should try this against the twins, they'd have loved it!"

"The twins?" he asked.

I blushed. "Never mind." He must have noticed the wording I used, including "lov*ed*", and "they*'d*".

For the hundredth time in a row, we stopped, and just looked at each other.

Dean somehow made silence very beautiful.

Then, a big, fat drop of rain hit me on my nose.

He started to laugh. "What?!" I demanded.

"You just made the most priceless face," he said, still chuckling. He scrunched up his nose and made a confused expression.

And then, a second later he made the same face, but for real. A raindrop had hit his eye.

"See!" I cried. But just as I started teasing him back, thunder rumbled from above, and more, many more, drops came pouring down, wettening my cheeks, darkening my hair and gushing into my ears.

I screamed as the rain quickly soaked me through.

"Come on!" Dean called, shoving our stuff into the basket, then getting up and wrapping the picnic blanket around both of our shoulders.

Using the checkered cloth as an umbrella, I started running towards the house, but he pulled me the other way.

"Over here!" he called.

Laughing, wet and muddy, we tumbled towards a large dark mass, which soon turned into a small, worn down shed. He led me inside and lit an old, dusty lamp in the corner.

"This is where we hid my mum from my father when she came. That is, until we had no choice but to take her to the hospital. We can use it as a shelter for now, for my house always seems much too big, and much too lonely."

I looked at him, eyes wide. "My goodness, I've always thought the same! But, I just thought I was being greedy or something…" We looked at each other, and I finally admitted that I liked it.

And then I felt something, like a small tugging. And he must have felt it, too. Because he started leaning towards me, and without meaning to, I started leaning towards him, and then I couldn't stop. I was much too close, and I felt his breath brush my cheeks, and chin, and lips; I couldn't stop myself, for it felt different than when I kissed Peter - Edmund-

No, Peter. A tear sprung from my eye as I realized what I had been doing all along. Calling him Edmund, forcing myself to recognize him as a whole different being, just because - because I was afraid I may never see him again. Because I didn't want to give myself that false hope. But the truth was, being so close to Dean, so close to the gateway to complete and utter denial, I remembered. What it felt like when I first kissed Peter, how my heart soared. Home. It felt like home.

And this - this was only the refutation of that. And yet I was close, so close, and I couldn't stop myself. I couldn't, I couldn't, I - and suddenly he was kissing me. I closed my eyes and stopped for a second, not allowing myself to think logically. And when I opened my eyes, it wasn't Dean any longer.

It was Peter.

"No!"

I pulled away, suddenly aware how wet my cheeks were, more than rain could make. It was Dean that stumbled back, a finger to his lips and hurt in his eyes.

"I - Dean, I'm sorry, it's just that… that I…"

He shook his head soberly. "No, I get it. I'm the one that should be sorry."

But even though I waited a second, he never officially apologized.

"It's not you, it's…" I took a deep breath. "The truth is, well, that's the thing… it's not you. It can't be you, because… because it's - it's… him."

He looked up at me, but his expression was blank. "Oh."

"I… I'm so, so sorry."

He looked at me for a second, and then said, "Why did you almost kiss me then, if you were in love with someone else?"

Were. That hurt.

"Dean, I think I like you. You're a great person and all, and there's so much more to you than what meets the eye. But just because I kiss you doesn't mean I still don't feel him. And I realize that now. I'm sorry… I just can't explain. It's complicated. And anyway, you're better off. I'm not special or anything, I'm just… me. I'm sure you'll find plenty of better girls."

He smiled sadly. "Remember when you asked what makes me think like your the same as other people?"

"Yes."

"Well... I don't. You're not like other people, and this place... I don't bring many people here, to be completely honest. But you - you're different. That's why this date, it was the only one my father didn't choose for me. I asked for it. Because you are." He shrugged solemnly. "You're beautiful and special."

I looked at him for a second, speechless. There was nothing special about me, nothing the least bit interesting. I wasn't particularly beautiful, smart, talented...

I opened my mouth to say something. I'm not sure exactly what - to tell him I'm not all that he said, to argue... to apologize.

But he spoke before I was able to.

"Oh, look, the rain went away!" His cheeriness was terribly fake. "Let's go to my house, and we can see if your chauffeur is here yet."

I wanted to say something, but I could only imagine making the situation worse, so, instead, I followed him outside. He was right, the rain had stopped. But the clouds were still dark and angry.

The walk back was silent; even the birds stopped their singing. Soon, the sun disappeared behind the trees, making me ache subconsciously for home. But I pushed that aside and focused on the time. It was far into the evening, for sure. Which surprised me. I didn't even realize how much time Dean and I spent together; it flew by so quickly.

Finally, after an incredibly long and awkward forever, we stopped right before his front porch.

Someone in the car was waiting for me, the back car door propped open as they awaited my arrival. I noticed it wasn't Sofia, but this didn't phase me at the time, as I had more pressing matters.

I turned to Dean, but he refused to meet my gaze.

"Dean," I said, my voice sounding awfully weak.

"Goodbye, Ever."

"Just wait! Won't... couldn't we still be, you know, at least-"

"Ever, listen-"

I had just about had it. "No, please! I'm sick of people telling me to listen! You listen to me! This is just as hard for me, too, you know. I like you, I really do, so why can't we just be friends? Maybe I might never be able to see Peter again, maybe he's gone forever. But it would be an insult to his memory if I found love so quickly afterward; and even so, I just can't bring myself to. You have no idea what I went through, Dean. That doesn't mean I don't want to be friends, or that I'm trying to make you mad. I just... I just can't, okay? And if you really loved me, even though you only met me this afternoon, well...

then you should be okay with that." I took my first breath. "So can you please, just *please,* try to understand?"

He looked at me for a second, before saying, "You know, your mother might kill you if you say you didn't have a good time. So if you want to, I don't know, come over and pretend that we really, as the Americans say, 'hit it off', your... um, you're free to." He blushed three shades of rose. "If you want to."

I recognized it as an apology, so I nodded. "I think that would be really ice."

We stared at each other for a few moments in awkward silence, and then he said, "Well, maybe I'll see you then, Ever."

"Yeah, maybe then."

And then I walked towards the waiting car.

And as I was getting in the seat, Dean called after me.

"Oh, and Ever? I'm supposed to tell you to trust the stars. Especially the second one on the right."

I froze.

"What?" I whispered, turning back to look at him.

He was walking towards his house.

"Wait! Wait - what did you just say?!"

But we were already pulling out of the driveway.

...

I looked out in the starry night, wondering who relied that message upon Dean. Whoever did, they must know me well.

Will? Albie?

Peter…?

I found the Milky Way; it hadn't moved from when Will showed me. I also saw the Little Bear and the Big Bear.

What I would always tell Albie and Peter were the two of them.

I soon found Ursa Major and Ursa Minor; those two always reminded me of cards thrown about, like when Thomas or Oliver lost a game against their other half.

Then, for Elli, there was the big dipper, which was always, in my perspective, the most beautiful. But quiet. Quietly shining bright.

I don't know what could be more like such an amazing boy.

And then, lastly, the star on the right. What Peter always claimed was me. Because I had led him to Neverland. I was his Wendy.

And he was my beloved.

And now he was gone.

"*Second star to the right, and straight on till morning,*" I sighed, wondering once again why Dean told me this. Why him, why now?

Inhaling a deep and sharp breath, I closed my eyes.

"Stars, Neverland... oh, where are you? Please, I want to - to trust you. But I'm finding it difficult. Show me, please. Help me find him." I leaned my forehead against the cold window, not daring to open my eyes, not daring to break this hope.

"Help me find my Peter Pan."

Chapter Twenty Seven

Albie

Will rubbed his head with a sweet look, and I was scared. Elli was sick, not only sick - said the twins - but dying. They had told me to be grown up about it, that I needed to not act like a little kid with Peter gone and Will trying to take over, but I didn't understand that either. They said not to "act my age", but whatever that was, I felt like doing it.

I felt like crying.

"Will," I said meekly and ran over to him, big wet tears soaking my cheeks. "Will I'm scared."

I tried to hug him, and he hugged me back, but only quickly before pushing me off with a "not now" and walking fast to get to Thomas and Oliver. I sniffled, watching him go with big eyes, still not understanding.

Not understanding why no one wanted to comfort me like Peter had in bad times. Not understanding why Elli coughed up blood when he wheezed, or why the twins weren't pulling pranks on anyone anymore.

Not understanding why Peter and Wendy weren't here any longer.

Pushing aside my confusion, I listened to the conversation the other boys were having and looked back at Elli, who was still sleeping every time I checked.

"-you need to find out what is wrong," said Will with a serious face. "Mention all the symptoms and get someone to tell you the cure. Then take it."

I didn't know what "symptoms" meant, but they seemed to because they just nodded.

"And *don't* get caught."

Again, they shook their heads at the same time, about to leave, when Will pulled Thomas back, giving me a look. "Take Albie with you."

With a grumble and a pout, Thomas went in my direction, frowning at me all the while. I pretended I didn't know why, but I don't think I am a very good liar, because he seemed to know I knew.

"Come on," he spat, pulling me along when I didn't move. Oliver was already waiting by the trees, and with a nod to Will and a look at Elli, we were gone.

"Will Elli be okay?" I asked after moments of silence.

"Not if we don't get the medicine," Oliver replied shortly, and it was quiet once again. I didn't like the silence and was curious to know more.

"How do we get it?"

They both sighed at the same time, which hurt a little. Peter was always patient with me. Nevertheless, Thomas explained, his words fast and confusing. "We go into town and figure out what sickness is and then find the medicine that fits the symptoms. Then we steal it, just like we steal everything else."

I didn't know why he was being so rude about it, but I didn't care, because I still wanted to know more. "So what does *siptoms* mean?" I asked and ignored their know-it-all looks. They were only ten, which was three years older than me, I think. What made them so special?

"*Symptoms,*" Thomas repeated and made me more confused.

"That's what I said."

"No, you said *sip* - whatever. It's like what's happening that makes us know he's not feeling well."

"Like the blood?" I asked, and he nodded. I smiled a little, not because of the blood, but because I had gotten it right and that meant they couldn't be mad at me. They had been mad at me a lot; mad at me when I started to cry, and when I wanted to be read a bedtime story, or get kissed on the head goodnight like Wendy had done, or played Peter Pan like we used to. I tried to read the book to myself at night, but I just couldn't do it. Peter had said that I had to get older, but I knew he was wrong about that, because I was older than I was last year and it *still* didn't make any sense.

It just wasn't the same anymore. It wasn't fun.

I stopped talking and walked behind them for a while longer, but my legs got tired after what seemed like the first hour. "Thomas?" I squeaked, running up to be beside him.

"Yeah," he said and didn't look down.

"Can you carry me?"

And with another sigh, he knelt down and I hopped on his back, yawning widely. I wanted to feel happy and relieved that I didn't have to walk anymore, but his annoyed looks to his twin were bugging me.

"Why don't you like me?" I pouted and slid off his back. Oliver's eyes became kind, and he grabbed my hand as my eyes filled with tears.

"Aw, bud, we don't 'not like you', we just don't have time to baby you right now. Make sense?"

It didn't, but I wanted to sound grown up, so I nodded and kept walking, not complaining that my legs hurt and stomach cramped for food.

I guess I could walk for a little while longer. I remembered what Peter had said to me, before we left for the village, before he got on the big train and went away. *I know this is going to be hard for you Albie, but you have to be strong. For all of us.*

I remembered how I felt when he told me that. How I stood tall and acted brave. And I felt brave. I wanted to feel that way again, but with Peter gone, I just couldn't.

Not for the miles we were walking.

Thomas did end up picking me up a little later, and then Oliver did, so it was okay. But when we got into the village, I froze. I had never stolen anything before.

"Albie," Oliver bent down to look at my eyes. "Albie what you need to do it very important, okay?"

I nodded.

"You need to *not say anything*, and look sweet and innocent. Got it?"

Again, I nodded. I felt better that I didn't have to talk because I didn't know what to say, or who to say it to. I squeezed Oliver's hand as we walked through the town, not as many people in the streets as there were last time. I didn't know where we would get medicine, or even what it looked like. I imagined some kind of dust that was sprinkled over the sick person and made them better right away.

Oliver pulled me along, and we went into this small shop. Inside was a lot of weird things on tall stands. Some were in bottles, there were some foods, and other things I didn't know about. There was a man at the counter, holding a brown smoking... what was the name of it? I didn't know, but I watched in awe as he put it in his mouth and sucked in, then breathed out smoke.

"Um, sir?" Thomas said quietly, and the man looked closer at him.

"How can I help you, son?"

"We-we're looking for medicine f-for my... my brother. We don't know what he's got, but he's been coughing, and up at night, and he's cold, then he's hot, and he's always tired. And - and his chest hurts." The man was scary looking, so I didn't blame Thomas for stuttering.

The big scary man sighed, setting down his smoking stick. "Does he cough up blood?"

Oliver shook his head yes. The man continued. "The poor boy's got TB," he mumbled and when Oliver asked what that was, he said, "Tuberculosis. Awful disease, really. But a year or so ago we stocked this new drug that seems to do the trick, for some people at least. It's over here."

He left from behind the counter and walked over to the shelves of bottles, pulling one out. It was tinted brown, but inside I could see little white pills that looked like stretched out circles. "It's called isoniazid," He said. "If he's around your age and already has the sickness I'd have him take one a day, or maybe one and a half if the side effects aren't too bad." He put the bottle in Oliver's hands, and nodded to him, then went back to his place behind the counter.

We all stared at it for a little while, before Thomas pulled us to the back of the store. "Albie, you need to keep this hidden under your jacket, alright? We'll all walk out casually in about five minutes." I took the bottle from him in tender hands and tried to hide that they were shaking. I slipped it under the fold of my coat with a guiding hand from Oliver, and we waited.

And waited.

And waited.

Those five small minutes seemed as long as our hike down. But they passed, even if they went by really slowly, and soon I was walking out beside the twins, hiding my red cheeks.

"You boys find what you were looking for?" the man asked as we passed by. I froze, turned to him and nodded. Thomas nearly cursed and lowered his head. "Okay then bring it here, I'll tell you how much," he waved his hand for me to come, and all I felt was panic. I looked to Thomas, and then to Oliver, who didn't look at my eyes, and then I saw the man frown.

"You there, yes you. Take your hands out of your pockets." I didn't do anything. "Out of your pockets. I'm only going to say it once."

Trembling, I took out the bottle and felt tears coat my eyes, making everything blurry. The man walked over and took it from me, moaning as he looked at my quivering lip. "You don't have any money, do you?"

I shook my head.

"Is it bad?"

"Yeah."

Again, he sighed, but put the medicine bottle back in my hands and turned away. "Don't worry about it. I'll take care of it."

Oliver's eyes lit up, and he thanked the man, then pulled me out of the store. I still didn't really understand until halfway down the street when Thomas explained that he had paid the cost for us.

"Really? He did that?" I asked, not believing an adult could be so nice.

Thomas rubbed my head. "Yep. And all because you were so cute."

...

We went as fast as we could all the way back home. And this time, it didn't matter one bit that my legs hurt, or that I was tired or hungry, because now Elli was going to be okay.

And because the twins snuck some vegetables and crackers from the food store and said the faster I got home, the more I could have.

We got home fast.

And so I munched on the treat as Will helped Elli swallow the pill with some water. I felt good. I felt like Peter would be proud of me. I didn't steal, I didn't do anything wrong, *and* I helped save Elli. All in one day.

I only hoped Peter and Wendy were okay. I hoped Peter would find her and be home soon. Because I missed them, both of them.

I think, if they could come back, I would let them kiss all they wanted. If it meant they could come back.

Just not in front of me.

Chapter Twenty Eight

Peter

Over a week went by, and terribly slow in that manner. My father spent most of it periodically away, which was fine by me, but it did seem odd that he had so many places to go and seemingly no life to live. I spent the entirety of the time in my room when he was present in the house, trying to distract myself by reading books and writing down my thoughts.

I missed talking to Ever, and the boys for that matter. I found myself whispering to them on some occasions, probably sounding like a madman. I had never been without conversation for so long; therefore, it was easier to pretend I was asking Elli about his day or discussing something with Will then to sit and ponder alone. There was another letter that I wrote to Ever, which I would give to her if I ever got the chance, but for the time being, it was hidden underneath my bed in case my father came scouring through my room.

And of course, with the long pauses of silence, came the constant pang of heart reminding me how awfully homesick I was. I missed Will's encouragement, the twin's pranks, Elliot's smile, and Albie's hugs. I wanted to see all so much again, and I came to realize just how selfish I had been.

I had left them, not knowing if or when I would ever return, to find *my* love, *my* happiness. And I didn't think twice about theirs. I kept telling myself that this was what they would've wanted me to do, but it didn't satisfy my guilt. Nothing seemed to be able to that at this point, as I had nothing left to focus on.

My father found that focusing point very quickly by the end of the week, Friday. He commenced to tell me that it had been almost a fortnight since he had seen his beloved *date*, and that he had invited her over for dinner that night. His five o'clock shadow and soiled clothes made it hard for me to believe a word of it. Regardless, it wasn't smart to cross that line.

"Okay, so what does this have to do with me," I scoffed, crossing my arms as I tried to get the image of them kissing out of my head.

He stared through my skull.

"Yeah, I'll stay in my room during the time." And I began to walk away. Icy fingers froze me in my steps, and I turned around, whipping his hand off my shoulder.

"I'm going to be gone most of the day, and I'll be back with dinner," he continued. "This place needs to be cleaned. All of it."

I looked around in disbelief. "You want me to…"

He nodded.

Anger rose in my throat. Why should I clean up the mess he made?

"Why should I?" I shot back like a pouting child. He rolled his eyes like it was stupid he had to go through the trouble of explaining.

"Oh, I don't know. Probably because you want this date to go well." He paused, like that should be enough, and when I shot him a mixture of confused anger, he pressed on smugly. "Because that means there will be more to come, and eventually the little brat will have to tag along. I highly doubt she'll be coming tonight, but regardless I expect you in your Sunday best and this place to be spotless. You have an outfit waiting for you in your closet."

"You have to be kidding me," I sighed, and watched as he grabbed his coat and walked out, locking the door behind him as if to tell me that I couldn't get out.

But truthfully, Ever was reason enough. I missed her so, and the thought of leaving without her safe in my arms was too much to bear.

I looked around the filthy room, pillows overturned, dust on every corner, beer bottles and spills. It all reeked. But it was about to be the cleanest home London had ever seen.

I was going to beat Miss Kingsley at her own game.

...

It turns out he did have cleaning products, though there was only a few to offer. I set to work immediately, starting with the family room. I dusted every corner, pulled the rug out and beat that along with the pillows, then swept and washed the floors. I wiped down every surface, removed the sleeves from the couch cushions and washed those, then set them out to dry. By the time I was done, an hour and a half had passed, nineteen beer and liquor bottles had been set out in the recycle bins, and the place looked better than it had ever been before.

The kitchen took longer than I thought it would. It was far too dusty, most of the food rotted, and I even chased a mouse out. A mouse! It was like someone disgusting had lived in this place, and one day just got up and left, leaving everything as it was. How could he manage to keep it all so filthy?!

Anyways, I spent a good amount of time cleaning the floors, countertops, the stove, and the refrigerator. I organized the pantry, set out little knick-knacks my father had kept around the house on the edges of the counters to make it look nice, washed all the dishes and put them away, and then started on the table. The white tablecloth was washed with bleach and turned from a fading yellow to a bright crisp white. I then went out the back door that my father had forgotten to lock and picked some wildflowers from the backyard.

The outside breezes on my face gave me that little lick of freedom. I looked past the decaying gate, knowing I could leave.

No. There was no way Ever's mother had taken an eye off her. I couldn't plan this ill. No doubt if I just strolled away, my father would demand his trading pawn back. Make her life miserable even if he failed at his attempt. And besides, I had come this far, I wasn't about to leave without my Wendy. Without *our* Wendy.

I put the flowers in a little glass jar with some water and set it on the table, along with a table setting of clean plates, napkins, bowls, forks, knives, spoons, and glasses. I didn't really know why I was going above and beyond to do something in favor of someone I hated, but something told me it would help me see Ever sooner.

And this time, it didn't hurt to trust my gut. I mean, what was the worst that could happen, my father says something nice to me? I laughed wryly at the idea and moved onto cleaning the bathroom.

I'm not even going to get into how disgusting that was. Yet I managed. Afterward, it felt like a miraculous change. Like seriously, the before and after was just incredible.

Then I went into cleaning his bedroom, and washed both of our bedding together, then picked up, and neatened the place. I figured, with a revolting thought, that if they were to get to this room, Ever's mother would be less worried with the outcome of the room and more of what was happening inside.

So I neatened the knick-knacks scattered around, cleaned up a couple of bottles, and dusted off the lamp. The strangest thing happened as I pushed it back to its rightful place on the nightstand. Something hard fell to the floor, and I heard with a painful cringe, the shattering of glass.

Hastily, I pushed the nightstand aside and tried to pick up the bigger pieces of glass that had come from a little picture frame. Collecting them all carelessly, I sliced my hand and drew a small amount blood, an action that had me rinsing my hand in the bathroom sink before going to get a broom.

When I came back, I noticed the little paper that had been the picture in the frame and picked it up gingerly.

It was a beaten, crinkled, black and white photo of a little boy. He was smiling in the photo, holding his small toy ball that he was about to throw. I recalled it as one of the last happy moments I had before leaving my home.

But why did he have this picture?

People keep pictures of those they cared about, those they wanted to remember and see every day. But my father didn't care about me, no, he couldn't. You don't do things like that to someone you care about. Or do you? Did he really have control of himself at the time? Frustrated, I crumpled up the photo in my hands and threw it in the garbage along with all the other broken glass and the frame.

Now that the house was clean I didn't really know what to do with myself. Most of the day had been killed, but not all. I figured it would be about another hour before my father came home, and I wasn't ready to put on whatever clothes he had waiting for me upstairs, so I went back up to my bedroom and gnawed on my lip.

Looking across the room, I stared at the picture of my mother and father. I got up, taking it gently in my hands, and flopped down on my bed, staring at it. I imagined I could make out my mother's face from the dream, but between the blurry picture and my made up envisionment of her, I truthfully had no idea what she looked like.

"I bet you were beautiful," I whispered. My mind began to trail off, and I wondered what it would look like had she never died.

I could see myself snuggling up against my parents as they read to me, and myself in school, having all sorts of nice things, friends, extended family, people that cared for me - I would lead a normal life. It would be wonderful.

But I quickly came to realize that in my picture, the friends I had were that of Will, and Albie, and Elliot, and the twins. The girlfriend I spent my time with was Ever, and we spent many nights venturing out in the woods. And more quickly did I come to understand that wouldn't be in the picture.

They wouldn't be in the picture.

Count your blessings. All things work together for good. We don't see it all at first. All these things we've heard since we were children and could hardly believe at the time are true. They're so true.

So maybe, in some weird way, this would work out for good. And if there wasn't some bigger force helping that along, I would do it myself.

Or I would die trying.

I put my mother's photo back up on the dresser, a new determination arousing within me. I pulled back out my letter to Ever and readjusted it in some ways.

Let's just say I added a bit of pixie dust.

And then, with an outward sigh, I took a shower, neatened my hair, and approached my closet. Ready for me inside was nice black dress pants, dress shoes, a crisp white button down and a deep green tie.

I had memories of seeing my father put on a tie from my youth, memories of him going to work, still angry and full of hate, but not as messed up at the time. So, as it did take me a couple of tries, I got the tie down pretty quickly.

At my father's return home I was actually a little bit excited at walking down the stairs to face him, the entire house clean, myself included. I wasn't in the least bit excited to see him, no, but rather his reaction was what intrigued me.

And it was intriguing. I heard the door unlock and swing open, and with a hand on the railing, I marched down the stairs and looked him in the eyes. I could've sworn he did a double take. I nodded to him, like we needn't discuss this, and I went forward to show him around the house.

At the end he looked at me, with some sense of pride in his eyes, mixed with disbelief that I went above and beyond his orders. "You've done well, son."

I recoiled at his words and shook my head, my glare stone cold. "I'm not your son."

He sighed, licked his lips, and rolled his head downward. "We'll get there."

"You want to?" I asked, with a hint of mocking. He nodded, just barely, like it was instinct he hadn't yet thought through. "Then have her come."

"She will, eventually."

"No," I said, my chest swelling with pride that I was actually standing up to him. "Today. I want her here today."

He actually, most definitely, nodded. And then, he went over to the landline, dialed the number, and sat on the phone.

I stood, watching in disbelief, and listened to the buzz of the phone, then could hear the faintness of it being picked up. Another step closer and I could hear both ends.

"Hello?"

My father heaved a sigh. "Elvira, dearest, seems we have a double date."

Elvira. I could see where the name Ever sprang from. She seemed to hope it would be like mother like daughter. But it was far from different.

"Am I to be disappointed, Rufus?"

"No, just bring the girl."

The next words she said were spoken to fast to comprehend, but I could imagine what was said based on my father's reaction. He seemed almost… hurt. Like he actually cared.

And yet again there was another reminder that there was a soul behind the beast.

Another reminder that I absolutely hated.

Chapter Twenty Nine

$Peter$

I waited at the window like a puppy for its people. Excitement coursed through me at the thought of seeing Ever again, excitement like I had never felt before. My father told me multiple times to step back, that it was rude to wait and drool on them, but I didn't care. Because the moment the light blue car pulled into the driveway, the moment I saw the back door swing open and Ever step out gracefully, I tore through the front door and ran to her, my feet carrying me as fast as they could run.

Her face lit up in the brightest smile, as I ran and scooped her up in a bear hug, lifting her off her feet and twirling her around with a child's joy. Her dainty feet met the ground again, and we embraced one another happily. "I've missed you so much," I whispered in her ear. She replied with a comforted sigh, her warm hands wrapped around my neck, and she leaned in and kissed me on the side of the cheek. We could barely hear the voice of Ever's mother, who was yelling at my father to rip us apart. He obliged, but when he went to lift a finger to Ever's shoulder, I smacked him away and backed off.

I stood a pace away from her now, but still, I couldn't help the smile we both exchanged on either end. I watched from the corner of my eye as my father took Elvira's hand, and the two of them walked inside, and then my focus freed to Wendy.

She was dressed in a solid colored, faint blue dress, that had a thick waist high ribbon that synched her torso, a spaghetti strap top with a little white sweater, and the bottom was her usual fit and flare style. Her flats were pearly white, along with the choker that laced her neck, and her hair was done up in a curled high ponytail.

"Did I ever tell you how stunning you are?" I looked into her ocean blue eyes, still seeing the girl dressed in a t-shirt and Will's old pants. She rolled her eyes, oddly looking a bit uneasy, and grabbed my hand, pulling me along inside.

"Come on. My mother wants me in the house. We can talk once we're upstairs."

And we did go upstairs, all the way to my room, and I shut the door behind me. Ever sat down on the bed, poised, with a smile, and folded the pleats of her dress. I couldn't help but notice right away that something was off, and my presumptions turned to be true when she looked to me with a sugar-coated smile and told me she'd missed me once again. It had all of the sudden turned different, like she had had a second to process the situation and put her feelings aside.

"Ever what's wrong?"

"Whatever do you mean?" Her hands crossed and stretched into her lap.

"You're acting... off." I strode over and took my place on the bed beside her. She turned her head away from me, but I pulled it back to face me. "What's wrong?"

She broke the act almost instantly, her lip quivering under the pressure, and her cheeks flushing red with heat. She inhaled sharply like she was going to cry, but didn't, and started talking in a soft, low whisper. "Peter I've missed you so much. This whole thing, I-I don't even have the words to explain it. Then I got your letter and I wished upon the star and now you're here - now *I'm* here - and I don't even know, it's almost like a dream that can't be real -"

I drew her in and kissed her, something I had dreamt of doing since the train to London. She kissed me back, but only for a brief sad moment, and even I knew this wasn't the lasting image I wanted to treasure. "I know," I said, pulling away with my thumb resting on her chin, "I know."

Tears slipped off her cheeks and her head fell on my shoulder, wetting my clothes with her cries. I slipped my arms around her and held onto her as she sobbed, feeling with the deepest part of me her pain and mine intertwined. I didn't understand it, nor could I, how her broken soul had held up this long, or how mine had done the same. How we had gotten everything all at once, and then in the same fast manner it was ripped away. The forest felt like a daydream to a far off land, and suddenly I was being whipped back into reality.

She lifted herself off of me and wiped her tears, sitting taller with a burdened sigh. I slid off the bed and knelt before her, meeting her dropped gaze. "Look at me," I said, and she met my eyes. "You are so strong -"

"Ah-" She tried to interject, but I wouldn't have it.

"No, listen. *Listen.* You are the most beautiful, bravest individual I know. Ever Kingsley, you are so so strong. I know you think that this is all too much, but you've gotten this far, right?" I took a breath from my tacky speech, not caring anymore if it sounded fake. Because I meant every word. "And you can do anything if you just *believe you can.* Don't doubt yourself for a second Ever, because I believe in you. I see the girl you really are, that strong, fearless girl, and you just need to let her shine, okay? Can you do that?"

She nodded with a sniffle and hugged me. "Thank you." And then I pulled loose, only halfway so that her arms still linked around my neck, and mine still around her.

The moment I saw her smile I knew I needed to kiss her. Laughing between breaths, we fell back onto the bed and my heart flew. I could've stayed there in that moment, our lips locked and spirits alive, for the rest of time.

But our parents made sure that that didn't happen. Their screeching voices rung out and pierced our ears in seconds, and soon we were both scrambling downstairs, hand in hand.

They were sitting rather close on the couch, and I could already tell the start to the night had been a success. Although there was some emotion on my father's face I couldn't quite read... agitation, maybe? Ever's mother cut right to the chase with her speech.

"Peter, dear, as you may not have heard, Ever already has a boyfriend, so you may as well drop her hand now -"

"Mother it was one date!" Ever interjected when my grip on her palm loosened in confusion. She looked to me desperately, faultless guilt in her eyes.

"Ah - ah - ah, darling. I think it has already been decided that I, and *only* I, really know what is best for you and your romantic life - and this boy," she surveyed me up and down with filth in her eyes, "will certainly not do." She spoke with a pause after each word, declaring every sound like a drunken hag. This presumption was proven when she shakily brought a bottle to her lips.

"What are you saying, mum?" Ever wondered slowly with a dawning fear.

"I've already talked to Rufus, dear, you aren't to see him again. I wouldn't want your innocent mind filled with more rubbish about running off to some unsanitary forest, now would I?" I looked to my father with a desperate plea.

He only smiled. It seemed whatever kindness he had slipped in before had been taken over by his corrupted date. Or maybe there was just none at all. Maybe I had only imagined it.

"So run along, say your last words, whatever you have to get in before the night ends. Go on now," she shooed us away with the wave of her hand, and we trampled up back the stairs, confused and in a daze. The conversation had been so abrupt and beyond the purpose of the night, I couldn't fathom the reason for it. And here I thought things were going well. Here I thought this may have actually had a chance of working out. But of course, leave it to the two of them to abolish any hope left in our "innocent" heads.

I closed the door behind me once again as Ever paced the room, her anxiety rising. I watched her circle the area time after time before I finally said what we were both thinking.

"Let's do it. Let's run away."

She stopped and turned to me with sad eyes. "Peter, he'll hurt you terribly if we get caught -"

"*If* we get caught. Besides, what chance do we have except now? I need to go back, Ever. The boys need me."

She nodded and sat cross-legged on the floor, which was very unladylike but very much Ever. I loved it. "Then wait until this all dies down. Your father won't be stepping on your heels and you can slip away."

I shook my head. "I'm not leaving without you."

"It's me or them, Peter."

"No," I pulled her back up to her feet, "Why should I choose one when I can have both. Come with me. Tonight. We can do this. We've gotten this far."

She clasped my hands in hers, lifted and dropped them, sighing. "How?"

...

A plan had been formed, and now came the agonizing wait. I sat with Ever, watching the clock until we were ready to make our move. We listened in downstairs, pleasantly surprised by how well things seemed to be going, and estimated, around nine o'clock, we would have the freedom to leave without being noticed.

It was 7:54.

I stared at the clock, just then remembering I had something for her. "Ever," I alerted her, seeing her gaze lift. I pulled out the note from my drawer, which was folded up neatly, and handed it to her. She immediately began to unfold it, but I stopped her.

"No, wait. It's for - it's for if this doesn't work out. If I can't be there for you. It's for that day when you feel like you just can't do it any longer," she looked up with widened eyes, looking as if I had figured her out. I nodded. "It's okay. I have them too. This will help." I closed her hand around the note and she looked down into it. "Keep it safe. That way I can be there for you even when I really can't."

Again, she nodded and held tightly to the note. I didn't even realize the tears threatening to come until I found myself fighting them. None slipped, but she definitely noticed. She placed a hand on mine, and with a small smile said, "we're going to beat this."

And then we waited. For what seemed like hours more.

...

"Peter," Ever wondered aloud, and I perked up in interest. "What happens when we go back? I mean even if we make it back they'll never stop fighting for us. How are we supposed to live this way?"

I answered with a calm confidence. "We'll pack up camp and move again. We won't have the couch, but the hammocks break down, and everything else we can move. The forest is huge, Ever, they won't know where to look." She looked distressed so I pressed on. "What is it, Wendy? What's on your mind?"

"Peter you know this has been everything to me, my whole world just flipped around brighter because of you. You showed me life, and life to the fullest - in a forest," she laughed wryly, "and I loved it. I love all of you."

"But?"

"But it seems like a dream I'm snatching that I'm not supposed to have." She took a shaky breath. "Can I be honest with you?"

"Yeah, of course."

"I love the thrill of it all, I love what it has given me and what it's promising - I just don't know if I'm ready. I mean, I want to be - with all my heart and soul I want to be - I just don't know if I can."

I smiled, knowing if there was a right time, now was the time. I pulled her in closer so that I could feel her breath on my face, and met her solemn stormy eyes.

"I know what it feels like to not be ready. I mean, spending an uncertain amount of time in the woods is one thing, but devoting your life to it and being able to call it home - that's something totally different. But I want you to know that I am here for you, I care about you, and no matter what you decide, I just want you to be happy. God, all I want is to see that smile of yours." She dipped her head with flushed cheeks and beamed. "No, listen," I told her, "I know between the being tied up, adjusting, our first kiss, and the kidnapping I haven't been able to say this: Wendy, I really don't know much about our future at this point, but what I do know is that I care about you and I want to spend the rest of my life with you -"

A nervous tension filled the room as she cut me off with a quiet laugh. "You do know I'm only turning sixteen. I'm not old enough to..."

"No! No," I realized and joined her in laughter. "Ever, I'm not asking you to marry me, I want you to be my girlfriend! I don't know how long what we have will last, or what obstacles will stand between us, but I want to make every second we do have count. So…" I finished sheepishly, "what do you say?"

"Yes!" She threw her arms around my neck and kissed my cheek. "Yes, of course!"

And in that moment, my heart proved that you don't need wings to fly.

In our hug, I felt the joy turn to sticky tears on my back, and soon we were both crying. But the difference was that they were good tears. Accomplished tears. Tears that said *we've gotten through it so far, and we can get to the other end.* Tears that spoke of recovery.

Joy.

There was no more reason to feel like we couldn't make it through, because in each other we had been comforted.

For a second I thought that maybe, just maybe, if my father had this again, he would change. *Elvira* would change. And all would be well again. Because I couldn't imagine anyone who felt this special kind of connection that wasn't fixed for the better. Ever didn't complete me, she wasn't my other half, or my same being, because she didn't need to be.

She was herself, and I was myself. And that was enough.

I looked to the door for a second, expecting the parents to come bombarding in and ruining our one good moment. But it wasn't them this time. For when I turned around, a solemn, pale face had replaced Ever's.

"What's wrong?" I asked, seeing her eyes glaze over with non-existent tears. She wrung her hands, her fingertips red and raw.

"I kissed him. Well, more like he kissed me - but I pulled away, and - and I hated it, I swear I did Peter! I -"

"Wait, hold on," I threw up my hands, cutting her off in her rambling. "You kissed who?"

"Dean!" she exclaimed, tossing her head to stare at the floor, and pulled at the strands of the carpet below her. "My mother forced us on a date, and he's actually not - not half bad. But I didn't mean to kiss him, he just got so close and I-I froze. I didn't want to move. But the moment he kissed me, I pulled away. I'm telling you the truth."

She looked to me with desperate eyes, and I sat down slowly next to her, my face a blank slate. "Oh, won't you just slap me or something! Tell me you're angry and threaten that if I ever do it again you'll-"

"*Slap you?*" I reached for her hand, but she didn't take mine. "Ever I'm not going to *slap* you. Not in a million lifetimes will I ever hit you."

She looked up with eyes round as moons. "So... you're not mad?"

"Of course I'm not mad! I may be a little hurt, that's all, but I can't even decide that until I know -"

"Know what?" she piped up eagerly, hoping to ease any hurt I may have been feeling.

"Why you didn't move."

She stared me down with honest eyes, sighing. "Because I wanted it to be you. But it wasn't."

I nodded. "Let's just forget about this, okay?" And with a shake of her head, it was forgotten. Well, nothing is ever really forgotten. But once I decided on that very fact, I thought back to the time when Albie and I were reading.

"But it says 'no one except Peter'! Does that mean you can forget it? Like what your father did to you? Can you forgive him and forget?"

Maybe I wasn't ready to forget the wrongs of my father, but I could certainly forget this. I owed it to Wendy.

And so we sat there, and I let my mind wander. I thought about what had brought me to this beautiful, beautiful girl. What twisted path of fate that I had hated for so long had brought a precious rose from all the thorns? We had both been so damaged, and yet, if it weren't for that, we wouldn't be together. So maybe it was true. Maybe all things really do work together for good. For happiness.

It wasn't the only thought that occurred to me while we sat there together in silence. I realized that, as damaged as we may have been, our souls were not broken. Because broken souls are like criminals in a crime that is yet to be committed. They keep their shoes by their bedside, and one eye open while they sleep; they are prepared to flee.

But I wasn't ready to run, and neither was Ever. We trusted each other and were able to do so because, despite what we had been through, despite how many tricks and tears our minds played at us, our hearts came out pumping lion's blood.

And roaring a lion's roar.

"I love you," I whispered. "I just want you to know that, okay? I love you."

She laid her head on my shoulder and stared at the wall. "I do."

I did notice that she didn't say it back, but this didn't phase me, because, with a smile in her eyes and a squeeze of her hand, I knew she meant it too. I knew she felt it too. And just because she wasn't ready to say it, didn't make the feelings not true, it just showed that she still wasn't ready to admit it in the heat of all this. Because she was still afraid of heights.

And that was *okay*.

And it was okay that it was okay.

A bird doesn't doubt it's ability to fly, as then it will fall. And it doesn't doubt its friend's ability to fly, because it only has two wings to support itself. It must fly on its own, and trust the other can fly on it's own as well.

And that way it will not fall.

It will soar.

But I did hope that one day, her fear of never flying would overtake her fear of heights.

Chapter Thirty

Wendy

I hated the moment my fingertips slipped from his. We had a plan, we knew a plan. Yet still, when our hands stopped touching, all of a sudden this plan seemed impossible.

I wasn't allowed to look at him. That was our plan. I wasn't allowed to smile, or act like this separation was killing me. Instead, I had one line. But, at this exact time, my mouth started to feel like a paste.

Still, I had to play my part.

Taking a deep breath, I started. "Mother!" I said, grabbing her attention immediately. "I'm done. I'm sick of him. I want to go home."

Peter's father raised an eyebrow at his son, as if asking Peter if this was really the best he could do. I would need to be more convincing.

"Mother, he says that I shouldn't have gone out with Dean. He says that *he* should be the only boy for me to meet." I glared at Peter, and immediately saw he was brilliant at this. He was staring at me with such loathing hate, I almost believed it.

"He did, did he?" my mother inquired, trying, with a terrible effort, to hold back her pleasure.

Now it was Peter's turn. "Yes! Yes, I did. She *shouldn't* have seen anyone else, not if she truly loved m-"

"Well, maybe I don't!" I cried. "Maybe I don't really love you! It was all a thrill in the woods, yes, but when I got back I realized how much more I love it here! And I'm not in love with you, maybe - maybe I'm in love with... with... with Dean!"

This was another part of our plan. Our backup plan. Because if this didn't work, then at least I would be able to still see Dean afterward. Peter wanted that, because he knew that it would give me comfort. He didn't want me alone. Plus, if we said that my mother was right, she would be much easier to deal with.

His father, on the other hand...

To be honest, I wasn't worried what Peter's father would do. I assumed that he would be made of the same mold as my mother. But he wasn't. Not at all. He didn't seem to believe us; you could tell by his expression. But his next words surprised me.

"Well, maybe you should stay here, just a bit longer, Elvira. So they can... I don't know, *mend* this relationship that was so much better earlier." Through the sneer and side eyes, we could tell that he was saying that it would cause more pain if my mother and I stayed, drive the separation even further, thinking that we wouldn't see right through him. But we did. Of course we did.

It was all a part of our plan. To make them want to let us stay longer, or at least not detest the idea, so we would have more time to run away. But if Peter's father didn't believe us, why would he be helping us? I risked another look at Peter, but he didn't look confused at all by his father's words.

Regaining my part, I quickly started pretending to be mad again.

"Mother, that's actually a great idea. Let me, let me! I want to show Peter that he really isn't the only boy in my life!" I whined, in my best voice that sounded like the little brat she always hoped me to be.

She looked at me pitifully, and I could see the wheel turning.

Peter's turn. "No, don't stay. I don't want to see you again, *Ever*. You're a liar and -"

But I was already sitting at the table. "What's to eat?" I asked Rufus politely, getting startled looks from him, my mother, and then, a bit delayed, Peter.

And so, with my mother making the decision, we all sat down to eat, with Rufus raising an eyebrow, but still playing along, and Peter exaggerating his anger and annoyance.

It was a quiet meal, awkward, yet neither I nor Peter could barely withhold our excitement. Finally, I asked, "May I please be excused to go to the bathroom?"

My mother waited for Rufus to say something, for, of course, he was the *gentlemen* in the room. But, after a second of silence, she shot him a nasty look and said, "Why, of course, my Ever dear."

"Thank you, mother," I replied, trying to mimic her angry stare at Peter's father. Briskly, I got up to go to the loo.

Restrooms were most often in the back of the house, and thankfully this house followed that layout, so they shouldn't have heard me. With one big window, too. It was just perfect. And now, now this plan was going to work!

It had to...

I couldn't bear giving fake joy, no, not anymore. I sighed. *There's no point in pretending.* I couldn't pretend to think this plan was going to work. Even though I had to.

Because, most of all, I couldn't bear the thought of having my hopes up, of living happily ever after, only for them once again to be broken.

Like glass.

Like me.

...

I took the jackknife that was recently bestowed upon me and drilled it into the window. The outer edge, the inner edge, all the way around. It was just the screen, not the full window, but enough to get me out. Finally, after minutes of prying, hoping against hope that my mother wouldn't suspect anything, the window popped open.

I was just winding the crank to open up the glass part when she called my voice. "Ever! Ever, are you okay in there?" The fright she caused me made me jump, and the knife slipped, the blood of my cut finger splattering on the floor.

Rubbish, I thought angrily, throwing the knife in the tin can by my feet.

But it was no use; she had heard the loud noise it had made when the knife had fallen.

"Ever, sweetie, what was that?" Her voice didn't sound sweet at all, though.

I ignored her, and instead, kept shoving the old and cranky window.

"Ever, I'm coming in. You better not be-" And then the realization hit her.

I didn't care to be secretive anymore. "Get... OPEN!" I grunted, pushing and shoving and then, BAM!

I yelped as the window opened, just a bit, but that bit was all I needed. Unfortunately, it was all my mother needed, too.

"Rufus! Rufus, they're running away. Quick, where does this rotten bathroom lead to?!"

I heard him leap up, immediately, prepared for action, and soon the sound of a slamming door came.

I had no doubt that Peter's part of the plan had succeeded. And with that hope fresh in my mind, I was shoving all my weight (though not much) against the window, so much so that I finally fell out. Literally fell. Hard. Wincing slightly, I shook my head - I had no time for pain. Peter was already pulling me to my feet.

"They - my mother heard me, I - oh, Peter..."

"I know, I know," he replied, hurriedly. "I heard. We've got to go." He was suddenly strong, firm, all action. He reminded me of someone, but for a second I couldn't place it. And then I remembered.

His father. Ten seconds ago.

We were halfway across the yard when I heard his father. And the yard was small.

"No! No, Peter!" He was panting, and when I risked a look, he was clutching his side, but his eyes were wild and mad. "I gave her to you, this is how you think to-" pant, pant, "repay me?!"

Peter pulled me faster, harder, but I couldn't do it. I was too delicate anyway, without him pulling me like a madman.

And then I was being yanked one way, and then the other, and Peter's father was, of course, going to win, for he didn't care if I got hurt or not. And indeed, he did win. He pulled me so harshly one way, a cry of pain escaped my throat, and Peter, out of worry for me, let go. I tumbled on the ground and looked up, meeting his bright green eyes, full of compassion and sorry.

I shook my head at Peter, telling him that it wasn't his fault. No matter if he had hurt me, it would have been worth running away.

Meanwhile, Rufus was fed up to the brim, and all of a sudden I wished I had just stayed home. His eyes burned a dark, raged grey, and the sound coming from his throat seemed like he wished death.

He grabbed me by the shoulders and hauled me to my feet, giving no condolence, no matter Peter's desperate cries.

"Stop! No, don't hurt her! You wouldn't dare - are you really as weak as that? To hurt someone else because you can't help your anger at me?!"

His breath smelt of liquor - and I knew of what he had been drinking throughout the day a thousand times over. There was this look in his eyes, the fierceness of a pride, and suddenly I understood. Why he had to hurt. He had pushed down so much pain - again and again, until he felt as if the only way to release himself from that pain was to push it on someone else.

And I was that someone else. Not because Peter loved me, not to hurt him, but because I loved him back. He hated that so many people were loved, were cared for, when he seemingly had no one. And he hated himself the most because he had caused this horrible fate to be put upon himself in the first place.

And suddenly, not anger, not loathing rage, but... but sympathy was the emotion that washed over me. How peculiar.

But if you think about it, it really wasn't peculiar at all. No, not for someone that hated love, only because he didn't have any of it... not peculiar indeed.

Just sad.

It was impossible for me to think that he wasn't loved, though. There must be or have been someone, something greater than we are, who still has the heart to love the unloved, no matter the horrible things they've done. There must be someone who loves all of us.

Because someone found that we were worth creating. For if that higher being didn't love you, and they knew they weren't going to, why would they create you?

But that, that right there, confused me. Because that meant that even if I lose Peter, someone still loves me.

Do they?

...

Peter's father's quick and stony hand broke me free from my thoughts as it met my cheek. I was going to try to show no signs of weakness, no signs of hurt to make him pity me. I knew those signs would only frighten Peter more. I had told myself that I needed to stay strong for him.

But that sharp, burning pain reddening my cheek had surprised me so much - I couldn't help but gasp and clutch my face in my hands.

"Wendy!" I heard Peter scream, and he was on top of his father now, who easily threw him off in seconds.

Another person was halfway up the yard, screeching at the top of her lungs. I thought it might be someone to help me, when I realized, with a look of dissatisfaction, it was only my mother, someone who wouldn't think to break a fingernail was worth as much as her daughter.

Meanwhile, as Rufus prepared his next hit, and I tried to get ready for it this time, Peter spoke magic words.

"Stop!" Breath. "*Father*, stop this!"

And he did. Because that word, that phrase, that name, it meant love. That someone loves you.

And that made me feel even worse for Rufus. Because his son didn't really love him. He just loved me. And he was prepared to lie for me. He was prepared to use his father's longing for love for the thing he really loved. Me.

But wasn't deceit and lies exactly what our parents lived on?

...

Sometime later, my mum and I were driving home, her being much too angry to speak to me. For Peter and I had tricked her. But I have to admit, it was quite obvious. If she really knew us, she should've known that it would take more than another boy to draw us apart.

But knowing my mother, it was no question that she would cling on to any lie, no matter how obviously unreal, if it meant that I was turning into her.

And then I realized something else. If I followed in her footsteps, that would mean I looked up to her. Which would mean that I loved her, or at least admired her. So really, today, Peter and I both manipulated our parent's lack of love and want for that very feeling to be felt for our real love.

Wow. Were we really that different from our parents at all?

I looked out the window and saw our house getting closer and closer. As soon as we were inside, my mother would probably waste no time and start yelling at me, not even trying to understand why I felt like I needed to run in the first place. Not even caring.

I wanted that to make me feel saddened, hurt or even for a bit of me to take it personally, but all I felt was anger. At her. She may not have a love for herself, but nevertheless, she's supposed to love *me*. Her *daughter*.

I breathed a sigh of confusion.

How messed up was this world?

Chapter Thirty One

Will

"Mama!" I screamed at the top of my lungs, tears streaming down my hot and sticky cheeks. I clung to the stair railing, too frightened to make my way all the way downstairs. In the living room, my father had my mother against the wall, and even through the dim light of the room, I could make out the bruises on her face and arms. I yelled out to her again as she rambled on defiantly to my father, who cut her off with a startling shout.

"Shut up!" he howled, whipping his coarse hand over her face. I cringed, shivering in my place, fright taking over my will to stand up against him.

But I wasn't going to let that happen any longer. I had only just turned seven, but it was enough for me. "Stop!" I screamed, trampling down the stairs and into the living room. My father turned around with a huff, glowering at me. He muttered something angrily and started to approach me, and I took a shaky step backward.

"Phillip!" I heard my mother exclaim, glued to her place on the wall with a hand to her sore cheek. "I swear to God, leave him out of this!" At her cry, he stopped and turned around, then swore and pushed past me, heading out the door.

"Mama," I cried in a hushed tone, wiping my tears and running to her with open arms. I tried to hug her, but she only pushed me away, impassiveness clouding her expression. She crouched down and held my chin, and I stood there confused. This was usually the time where she would hug me, kiss my forehead and tell me everything was going to be alright.

But she only stared into my weeping eyes with no endearment, no love, nothing. "Listen to me," she spoke sharply. "No more of this. You can't come running into the scene every time your father tries to hurt me. He hurts you to hurt me. Stay away. Stay far away."

I didn't understand. Where was the love? Why was the only person who loved me now pushing me away? I nodded solemnly and turned away from her, wiping my nose and running back up to my room. My father was at the top of the stairs, and I noticed tears also stung his eyes.

"Will, I'm sorry -" he started, but I had heard enough. Every day I heard it.

"No, you're not! You're a bully! I hate you, I hate you!" I stormed into my room and slammed the door shut, collapsing onto my bed in sobs.

...

I woke up in a sweat, anger flooding my blood as I rolled over in the hammock, hating that I had to live through that dream yet again. I didn't usually dream, but when I did, it was always that. Every night I would relive the scene, the loneliness and pain it brought back to the surface.

And then I would push it all back down.

I never told anyone about the dream; I thought it pointless to worry Peter when he thought I was better.

Better. What a trivial term. In my earlier years, Peter had tried to diagnose me with some sort of "depression", as if he were a doctor. He said I wasn't the same after the first few weeks of running away, that I had changed. He told me, later of course, that he had been scared to leave me alone at times, how sullen my face looked, and how skinny I had become.

But we had both become thin, right? I mean, we were living in the woods.

I sighed. As much as I tried to deny it, I knew he had been right. But not for those reasons. See, when he did leave me alone, I wouldn't hurt myself. I knew that's what he thought. I wouldn't though; I would only sit and cry.

For as long as he was gone. And that's what I felt like doing. The thing was, Peter always assumed, after Albie came at least, that I *had* gotten better. I guess he just had more important things to focus on. But that thing was, whatever feeling he "diagnosed" me with, I still had it. And now it had only gotten worse.

But I had to focus on the others, on Elli. *They* were more important, *they* were what mattered. They had been since the day the twins came. Thomas and Oliver first, then, because we were on the lookout, Elli came only months later. And then little sweet Albie.

And lastly Ever. Our beloved Wendy.

They always came first. Because I could handle myself. Because I was older. Because I was used to this life. Because, because, because - that's all it was.

It's okay, don't get me wrong - I agreed. But that didn't stop the feeling of rejection, missing how it was when it was just Peter and I. When I was more important.

And maybe it was that I was afraid. Maybe I knew that I was, in truth, still that little boy scared of being alone and that I couldn't do all this. Regardless, the feeling was there. And it wasn't going away.

It felt like a broken wind-up toy; no matter how much you winded it up, it wouldn't release. You could wind, and wind, and wind, and spin the little clicking wheel as many times as possible, and all that pressure would keep adding on, just waiting to be released.

This, with Peter gone and Elliot sick, was one of those times when the winding went on for hours. And I feared, because there was no way of release, that soon that toy was going to snap.

All at once. Out of control.

"Will," a small voice tore me from my thoughts. I turned over in my hammock to see Albie, standing there with shining wet eyes.

"What is it bud?" I yawned, and he inched a little closer to me.

"I had a bad dream," he mewed in a small voice. I leaned out of my bottom row swinging bed to scoop him up into it.

"You and me both." I let him snuggle in next to me, wrapping the blanket over the both of us. He obliged to my request, and pulled the blanket up to his chin, leaving my feet bare to the cold night air. But I didn't mind. "Tell me, what was it about?"

He lowered his thumb from his mouth, trying to recall the nightmare. "M-my parents. They wanted to take me back, and they kept running after me, but I didn't want to go with them. I wanted to stay with you."

"Kinda like Peter's dad?" I asked, watching him realize the connection between both situations. He nodded and sunk down closer to me.

"Are they going to be home soon?"

I sighed, ruffling his hair and peering into the stars, finding the big dipper. "I hope so buddy, I really do." I stopped looking at the stars, knowing it was only going to make me wish they were here more, and turned back to Albie, who had just yawned. His little mouth stretched wide and he moaned as it closed, exhausted.

"I have this feeling in my stomach," he said, and instantly panic rose within me that he had what Elli had. But it lessened as he continued. "It's not just in my stomach really, but that's just where I imagine it comes from. It feels like - like weird and itchy almost. It makes me feel kinda tired and… sad."

I shook my head in agreement, thinking I knew what he was talking about, if anyone can really understand what a six-year-old talks about. "Does it hurt?"

"No. I just don't like it. I think it's a - a *siptom*."

"A symptom," I guessed, holding back a laugh.

"Yeah, that's what I said."

I nodded so he wouldn't be offended, and put my serious face back on. "Why would you call it that?"

He shrugged awkwardly and shifted his position. "Well, Thomas and Oliver said that a siptom is part of what happens when you are sick or not feeling well. I'm not sick like Elli, but I thought it was kinda the same way."

I poked him in the stomach and watched him cringe with a smile, then unfold like a little potato bug. "I think I know what it is you're feeling."

"What?" He sat up, curiosity getting the best of him.

"You're homesick."

To his six-year-old self, this made no sense. "No." He decided plainly. "I can't be homesick if I am home."

He half started to laugh, like I was tricking him, but I shook my head. "Does home feel the same to you with Peter and Wendy gone?"

"No."

"So it's not the same. And you miss the old home."

Still confused, he looked around in the dim light of the stars. "But this place hasn't changed just because they're gone. There are still the same trees and leaves and -"

"Home isn't a place," I corrected kindly.

"Is it a person?" he asked, baffled.

"No."

"Then what?"

I smiled, knowing exactly what to say. "Home isn't a place," I said again. "Or a person, for that matter. It's a feeling." He looked at me, muddled, but I told him with my eyes that I was yet to continue. "It's the feeling you get when Wendy kisses your head goodnight, or when the twins choose you to be on their team in a game. When you get something right, when someone compliments you, or you bite into a juicy delicious apple. It's when you feel good inside, when you're able to wake up and smile and know that the people you are with are going to be there for you you're whole life. It's when you know where you are right there and then is a place you never want to leave. It's an indescribable feeling."

"So is this my home?"

"I don't know, do you think it is?"

"Yeah," he decided with a cute smile. "What about you. Are you at home here?"

I looked into his expecting eyes and nodded. "Yeah, buddy, I am."

Although, to be honest, I didn't really know.

...

"There you go," I eased him on, helping him swallow the pill in the lukewarm water. He coughed, spluttering up some of the water, and the pill, that fell onto his shirt. The poor kid, however better since a couple of days of treatments, still couldn't figure out how to swallow a pill. He said he had only had one or two before this in his life, so I couldn't blame him.

"Sorry," he muttered as I picked up the pill and wiped his wet shirt with a wrinkled nose.

"No matter," I replied, and took it over to the pantry. I dug through and pulled out a cracker. Crushing the pill and mixing it with water to create a form of paste, I spread it onto the cracker and carried it back over to him. "Fair warning, this isn't going to taste very good." I handed him the cracker and saw his lip turn in. "But I'll have water right here you can down when you're done."

He looked to me with tired, weak eyes. "Do I have to?"

"You want to be better, right?"

"Yeah," He nodded solemnly, and without a second thought popped the food in his mouth. His face contorted as he chewed, and I most certainly didn't envy him. He reached for the water bottle, and I handed it to him, watching him pour it in his mouth and gulp it down.

When the water was gone, he handed me back the empty bottle and sunk back down on the couch, closing his eyes. I patted his shoulder and left him be, thanking whatever force that was up there for saving him. He was going to make it, I was sure of it now - although exhausted and weakened from fighting off such a bad illness, he was back to his usual self, and pretty soon his playful spirit and light eyes would be there too.

I had promised the twins I would play a round of cards with them, so I put down the bottle and made my way over to where they were already laying out the cards.

"What are we playing?" I asked, forcing a smile. They didn't come too easily anymore with the little sleep I was receiving each night.

"Slap," Thomas offered, arranging the last card on the ground. They were spread out and figured like a box, in neat rows and columns. They had made up this game, and this one I liked. Since we didn't know the rules to any real cards games, the twins would come up with them and named them differently. In the game, one person would take their turn flipping over five cards. If any of the two matched, the other players would have to slap their hands down on the matches before the others to collect their cards. Then, the task of flipping would go to the next person and so on. The person with the most matches at the end of the game won.

We played three rounds, on the fourth, and for a while, I actually forgot about all that was happening. I forgot that Elli was sick, that Peter was gone chasing after some girl, that I was in charge. All the troubles I had seemed to drift away when I focused on the boys and our time together.

Maybe that's what Peter's secret was. Maybe all he really did was focus on being with them.

But was it really that easy?

Chapter Thirty Two

Peter

I sat slumped down on my bed, licking dry lips. It felt good to relieve them from their parched and cracked state, even though I knew it was only going to make it worse later on. Yet I couldn't help myself, as long as they weren't hurting now.

I would keep licking them until I could find a better solution.

But for now, I just couldn't. Not with the door locked and me behind it. It may as well have been bolted shut, for even if I could get out, there would be no use. My father would be waiting for me downstairs with a forceful hand. I sighed for what seemed like the thousandth time as my stomach rolled and groaned, reminding me yet again of how hungry I was. I knew I was relatively okay when compared to the number of harsh winters I had survived through with the other boys with little to no resources of nourishment for some periods of time, but it didn't change the fact that my raw stomach ached for something to satisfy its hunger and thirst. Anything.

Throwing myself back down on my bed in defeat, I stared glumly out the window and thought once again of Wendy. Of what had brought me here.

...

I forced myself up groggily, and cleared my vision, seeing distinctly now the image of my father approaching Ever with a hateful snarl. Her mother ran up behind her, looking wildly to me with a desperate plea in her eyes that I had never seen before.

For the first time ever, she needed something from me. For the first time ever, we wanted the same thing. She didn't have to speak; I could see it in her eyes what she was yelling out to me: *Please, Peter I'm begging you!*

I nodded to her, inhaling sharply before calling out to my father. I braced myself for a hit and stood my ground. "Stop!" Nothing. "*Father, stop this!*" My word choice, however untrue, alerted him. He whipped around to face me, some of the anger leaving his eyes. Just the tiniest bit, but it was enough. "Please," I lowered my voice, "leave them alone."

He turned back to Wendy, who stared at me, fright still lingering in her sad eyes.

"Leave them alone," I said again, and signaled for Miss Kingsley to take Ever and leave. She did so, fierceness already returning to her person as she grabbed her daughter by the arm with a willful grip and dragged her to the car. Ever winced and went along with her mother, her head still thrown over her shoulder to look at me. I tried for a smile, tried to tell her everything was going to be okay, even when I knew it wasn't. We couldn't come back from this. I knew that, sadly, as my father came after me, also taking me by the arm, with a seize strong enough to leave a bruise.

He marched me back down the mud-covered streets, not saying a word. That was fine by me, only that he didn't release my arm from his fist the entire way down. The escape leading up to this had seemed so little in distance, and yet the walk back felt like miles.

When we reached the house, he led me up the front porch and threw me through the front door. I caught myself before falling, nursed my arm, and wheeled around on my heel to face him. His face was scarily sober, so... real. For a second he seemed almost hurt, but that appeal was shaken off the instant I frowned.

"Father," he repeated in a low, scratched voice. "You called me father. Did you... mean it?"

I shook my head, too vexed to speak. He sucked in, not allowing himself to be disappointed. My stomach grew sick of his look, and my head hurt with hate. I pressed on. "I didn't mean it, and I never will. It was all for her. Nothing you *ever* say or do can make up for what you did to me. I hate you," I decided, the very statement so real and full of passion it scared me. But at the same time, it was... comforting. "With every bone in my body *I hate you*." I let my words sink in, not caring that his face was growing red with every second, not caring that I knew what he was going to do next.

And what surprised me most was that he didn't. Years ago, surely I would have had bruises coating my arms for that very statement, but now he only took me by the arm yet again and dragged me upstairs. I fought, but he didn't fight back. He didn't need to, given his grip was stronger than ten men, but he could've easily. He let me thrash, spit, and hit him, never fighting back. I felt like a child having a tantrum as he dragged me up the stairs, threw me down on the floor of my room and slam the door shut behind him.

I picked myself up off the floor, glaring at the locked door with a detestation that sent fire through my veins.

And then I thought of Ever, and how she was alright, and a cool blue wave came crashing over the fire.

...

That was two days ago. My foot kicked the wall, lightly, but enough to make a sound. Again and again, it thudded against the paint-chipped enclosement as if in some lazy attempt to kick it down. Enclosement. That's exactly how I pictured it. Walls were just a way to trap you in, to tell you that there's always something you can't get past. Especially these walls.

In the woods there were no walls, no barriers; there was nothing to confine us. And here, here was the most confining place I had ever spent any time in at all. The door locked, the window bolted down - I hated all of it. I wanted the door to open, just to have that little option of freedom. As if it were an option.

And then suddenly it was open, and just as suddenly, I wanted it shut and sealed. My father clicked the lock free and shouldered his way through the cracked doorway. I watched him, averting his eyes, close the door behind him.

Yet again I was trapped.

"Edmund - uh, Peter. Is that what they call you now?"

I shot him an agitated glare. "Don't call me that."

He said nothing and bit down on his lip. *Don't feel bad. Don't feel bad. Remember what he did to you.* I let myself fill to the brim with awful memories, how he treated me as a child, the hurt I felt from my distance from the others, what he did to Wendy and everything else that made me shake. I was allowing such anger to fill me, needing it to hate the person in front of me. I kept telling myself that I needed it, that everything would crumble without it, and it wasn't until the soft whisper of a woman in a faraway dream spoke to me that I realized what I was doing.

Just let it all go.

Could I? Could I when he was standing right in front of me? All the nightmares, visions, beatings, all right in front of me?

I decided to let that depend on him, on what he said. Yet still, I folded my arms, waiting for him to speak, but at the same time displaying that I wouldn't hear it. It was hard to refrain.

"Edmund, I just wanted to say that I'm -"

"No," I cut him off sharply, his next words scaring me more than I thought. "Don't even -"

His anger boiled to the surface along with mine, and he lost control, cursing loudly and throwing his hands up. "JUST LET ME SAY IT!"

"NO!" I met his fire with my own. "No, I won't!"

He looked desperately to me, and to my surprise inquired as to why. I bit my lip, holding back tears. "Because for every day for the past sixteen years I've had nightmares about you. That you will come and rip me from the life I worked so hard to build, and give back to me the one I ran so far from. And you did, you did! I was broken, because of *you,* and I will NOT let you do that to me again! You can't apologize, *father,* because I won't let you have the satisfaction of feeling better about your pitiful self. You need to live with the person you were, because it's the person you always will be!" I didn't care how loud I was shouting, that the neighbors could probably hear, or that angry, hot tears were rolling down my cheeks. I continued, in the heat of the moment, all of the pushed down emotion coming to the surface. "You ruined my life, all because what, mother died in pregnancy? HOW IS THAT MY FAULT! *HOW IS THAT MY FAULT?!* You made me feel, for so long, that I was worthless, that I had sinned in some way and caused her death. I actually believed that!" I choked down saliva with a sneer and pressed further before he could even open his mouth. "You were wrong. I know that now. You say we could've been a happy family if she just lived; well I ask you, why couldn't *we* have been a family?! What did I ever do to you that made you hate me so much?!"

He didn't say a word, and my blood was boiling. "WHAT DID I EVER DO TO YOU?!"

There was a long, empty pause before he spoke. "You killed the woman I loved. Whether you meant it or not it was you who caused her death." He rubbed tired, wet eyes, and said in a low growl, "you want to know why we could never be a family? Because every time I look in your eyes I see her. And it kills me."

I shook my head, expecting better. "Mother would be disappointed. Can you honestly think she is able to look down and feel comforted in her death? How did she even *love* you, you cruel, son of a _"

"No! Don't you see, I'm trying to be better!" His words struck me like a slap to the face, and the more I looked at him, the more I realized he was serious. A wry laugh came to my lips, and I let it take me over in disbelief.

"This is you *trying* to be better? What do you think, that after you nearly struck Ever, have torn me from the only ones I love, and starved me for the past two days, that I'm just going to hold your hand, call you papa, and we'll go play catch? What is wrong with you?!"

How could he be so vain?!

He answered my sneering retort with a rather calm manner, asking me only one question. "What is it that you want?"

I didn't even have to think of my response. "I want to see Wen - Ever again."

He shook his head with a sigh, rubbing his temples. "Peter, Elvira isn't going to let her keep seeing you. She wants to build back the mother-daughter relationship just like I want to -"

"Well, sorry -"

"Edmund!" he snapped, the both of us taken aback. "What I'm trying to say is, that it's only going to hurt your girlfriend more if you keep trying to see her. What are you hoping to accomplish?"

"I want to say goodbye." My voice was so pained, so low and unlike me, stripped of its defiance. He nodded again with a sigh, and waited.

He wanted something in return. Why, I had actually believed for a second he had changed. Not a bit.

"What is it?"

"After that," he squirmed, "You are going to stay here. Believe me, I can make you *want* to stay here."

I was about to shake my head when it occurred to me that that was exactly what I had said to Wendy when I had tied her to the tree. *No, it was completely different,* I told myself.

Was it, though?

I found nothing in trying to argue, at least he was giving me what I wanted, so I shook my head in agreement. He turned to leave, tossing his head over his shoulder before opening the door. "What do you want me to call you?"

"Peter is fine," I spoke before thinking, but, surprisingly, I didn't want to take it back. I was okay with what I had said.

Then he left. And the first thing I noticed was that the door was left open.

But it may have as well been closed.

Chapter Thirty Three

$Peter$

"No, I absolutely will not!" I could hear Miss Kingsley's raging voice through the phone, making me shiver.

"Elvira, dear, this will be the last time. Believe me, I will not let the boy see her again. Make a deal with her, get her on your side by doing this. Please."

Anger boiled my skin, but I pushed it down. Miss Kingsley was bound to be cruel to Ever regardless; at least this way I could see her one more time.

One more time. Sadness pricked my skin as the thought came, its reality setting in. I had only known her so long, but now it was like I couldn't fathom my life without her.

And the boys. They were what made the tears come at night. I had known them for years, loved them for years. They were like brothers to me, but even more than that. I missed them with everything I had, and knowing the only option was to trust that Will would take over honestly scared me.

The thought had crossed my mind at one point that I could go back, run away in the middle of the night. But getting Wendy was another thing. Could I leave her? Could I go back to my old life and push away the remorse of knowing where she was?

Of knowing that my father would take it out on her.

Either way, my heart would ache for home. Either way, I would be lost.

...

"She's coming in half an hour. Her mother agreed to your meeting for only an hour. That's it." I nodded, unable to argue, and began to walk away, when he stopped me with a hand to my shoulder. "Peter?"

"Yeah."

"I swear if you mess this up -"

"I won't." I shouldered him off and marched back upstairs, knowing that the hour would pass as seconds. The entire day my father had made it seem like I owed him for some reason, like the favor he was paying me was huge. As if he had forgotten all that he had done to me! And for it only to be an hour!

My father was up in my room in moments, an agitated expression washed over his face. He had a small piece of ripped paper in his hand, a number penned in ink on it. I didn't turn to look at him; staying at my place beside the window, I only asked what he needed.

The rain dripped down silently before he spoke, and I wondered how long a pause it would be before he found the words.

It was quite long.

"Um, son - I mean, nevermind. Listen, I know about those boys in the woods you had with you -"

I whipped around to face him. "What boys?"

"Come on Peter, I know it wasn't just you. The thing is, I thought you would like it if I called social securities, if they got them to safety -"

"No!" I cut him off hastily. "No, please don't!"

"Peter, they'll -"

"I said *don't!*"

He nodded, more so aggressively than not, as he wasn't familiar with not getting his way. He had never known what it was like to lose the battle. And so he walked away. And once again it was peaceful. As peaceful as it could be in his home.

...

Ever got out of the car, her mother following her. She pulled her to the side, whispering harshly to her as they approached the front door. I couldn't help but notice Ever wasn't as dressed up for this occasion, only wearing a casual light pink dress with a button up front and flats along with that. I assumed her mother let her pick her outfit as she didn't care much for this 'exchange'.

And I couldn't help but notice how beautiful she was.

I inhaled sharply as she stepped up to the front door, opening it with a small, sad smile. It was hard to be excited for such a painful goodbye. She returned the gaze as her mother clicked her tongue.

"You have one hour. You may go outside, but Ever you *know* what happens if you get out of sight."

"Yes, mother," she dipped her head, grabbing my hand and pulling me out of the house. We were going to make the most of the time we had together.

We said nothing until we were a couple of houses down, and I took her hand in mine, intertwining our fingers.

"Peter," she spoke in barely a whisper at the touch, tears stinging her eyes.

"I know." I needn't say anything more; we understood each other completely. We walked a couple paces more in silence, the clouds seeming to darken around us.

"Peter," she said again in the same manner, now wiping the tears the that kept coming. "I don't think I can do this without you." Her lip quivered, making me shake. Never before had I seen her this heartbroken.

"Yes you can," I tried for a smile. "You're incredible, Ever, you're _"

"Go back to them," she silenced me, not allowing herself comfort. I then understood what she really meant. It wasn't that she couldn't do this, knowing that I was only miles away, knowing there was still that small chance of seeing me again; it was that she knew I *had* to go back, and didn't know whether or not she could cope when I was gone.

"Ever, I can't..." I trailed off, unsure of how to continue. A little part of me wanted to, the selfish part that wanted to be away from my father and back home with the boys again. But more of me knew what would happen, and how I had to do everything in my power to prevent that. I shook my head, my decision final. "I can't leave you here to pick up the pieces."

She squeezed my hand reassuringly, but I felt no comfort in the gesture. If I went home, I surely would feel the remorse of leaving for the rest of my life. So as much as I couldn't do that to her, I couldn't do that to myself. "I'll be fine," she tried to press, "besides, I would feel better if you were with them." Her tears once again lined her cheeks, and I knew there was more to it than that. I kissed her forehead as she sank into me, finding contentment in our closeness.

"What is it?" I asked, despondence edging my tone.

"I can't," she whimpered yet again. The cold wind blew her hair over her face, turning our cheeks and noses a shade of rose-red. "I can't move on. Not when you're still here." She broke down in sobs, wrapping her arms around my neck and burying her face in my shoulder. I hugged her back with pursed lips.

I had nothing left to give her.

She sighed into my sleeve, breathing in the scent of the forest that still lingered on me. "I don't want to move on."

"But it's okay if you do," I pulled away slightly and locked eyes with her, our foreheads now touching and hands linked. "Because I won't. Ever Kingsley, *you* have left your mark, and I won't ever let that go."

She nodded, wiping her nose on her sleeve with a sniffle. "Can we just not talk about this now?"

I gave her a sly, sideways smile. She laughed slightly and her eyes twinkled, a bit of our sorrow leaving the air. "There's the smile I miss so much."

"And you won't ever have to miss it again." I gave a playful, sweeping bow and held her hand. "How about dinner, tomorrow?"

"I would like that, sir," she beamed, enjoying our game of pretend. As long as we pretended, all was gleeful, all was happy.

"We will have a grand ball! And I shall *surely* sweep you off your feet, madame," I simpered, offering her my hand. She wiped the last trickling tear away and took it with the most animated acceptance.

"Oh, but you are mistaken sir, for I am not a madame, but rather a mademoiselle." Her beam was brighter than a hundred suns.

"All the better!" I noted with a wink. "In that case, you must allow me to escort you home afterward."

She nodded eagerly, carried away with playing along. Breaking from my grip and flouncing forwards, she stared into the sky that held her envisionment. "And we will have a grand time, you and I, run away into the great unknown, swim in glittering lakes and laugh and talk for hours. Oh, and we shall dance underneath the stars, most certainly! We will spend all the nights away, and come back as the sun kisses the trees, with breakfast waiting and the boys -"

Her voice, almost instantly, became sad, and she twirled around on her heel to face me, completely taken away from her fantasy. "And the boys…" She tried for a lightened tone, to keep the momentum going, but she could only falter.

I strode over to her, taking her hand up in mine by our faces and kissing in gently. "And the boys will be free."

She bit down on her lip hard, her eyes watering as she nodded her head vigorously, trying ever so hard not to break down in tears again. "The boys," I said again, "*most certainly,* will dance underneath the stars."

She averted my eyes, her own glossed over and red, and squeezed my hand with an unconscious force. "Peter, I *can't* do this."

"*Yes* you can," I tried to tell her, tucking a wild strand of hair behind her ear. She shook her head.

"No, you don't understand. Peter, I tried to - I tried to… there was glass on the floor, and it was sharp and…" She was gnawing on her lip now, wringing her hands in fear.

"Oh, Ever," I enveloped her in a hug, my eyes wetting with hers. It then struck me - I couldn't leave this girl alone. She was broken, more so than I had ever thought of her to be, and there was no way I could let her go free. She was a bird with a broken wing, a bird that hadn't healed right, and my job wasn't to release her to fly. It was to heal the wing and slowly show her the sky again.

I wiped the tears from her eyes and held her chin in my hands, much like I would hold Albie's. "We're going to fix this, okay? We're going back to the forest."

She let her head dip off my hands, sincerity masking her emotion. "Peter, we can't."

"Yes, we can. I'm going to march back in there and tell my father we're leaving. They've forced us into so many decisions that weren't even ours, it's time we show them. If it's a fight he wants, then it's a fight he'll get." A hint of a smile appeared on her face, even through the doubt.

And as I pulled her back from the way we came, I thought about how ridiculously stupid this whole ordeal was. Could I do this? Could I fight my father and win?

But this thought was only brief. For now, I had a new set of mind to focus on. All this time it has been a matter of if I could, when really it was about if I would.

And I would.

I would fight my father, free my darling dove, and see the boys again if it was the last thing I did. Because I had the option to try. And if I failed, at least I hadn't given up so soon.

At least I had allowed myself a chance of happiness.

A chance of freedom.

Chapter Thirty Four

Wendy

I wish the walk back would have been longer, for it seemed much too fast by the time we got to the door. My hands were trembling terribly, and I reached out for Peter's, feeling comfort in the warmth of his fingertips.

It felt steady, though, when we walked inside, as if everything was in slow motion. I saw Peter and his father exchange a look, his father's face reading, *I gave you time, why didn't you take it? Why are you bringing this upon yourself?*

But we were. Because the worse that might happen is that we would fail, and together, we're weren't going to. We were going to get through this, and it was going to be alright.

My mother, on the other hand, was looking at me with a bit of pride. As if she was thinking, *good job, Ever. End the… little reunion now, it will make it easier in the long run.*

How wrong she was.

Peter and I exchanged a look, too, different from both our parents. Our look said we could do it. We *would* do it.

We squeezed hands, reassuringly, and I felt a bit better.

But nothing, absolutely nothing, would have prepared me for what our act of defiance was going to turn out to be.

...

When he slapped me, I wasn't prepared for it.

Peter had told him what was to be, and they had both stared at us for a long second, my mother surprised and disappointed, and his father...

His father gave him the longest look, as if asking Peter why he himself had even tried to get on his son's good side. And then, all of a sudden, he raised a hand and prepared to strike.

And I winced, and screamed because I thought that he was going to hurt Peter.

But then his rough, calloused hand collided with my cheek, and my shout got lost in my throat, for I wasn't prepared for him to channel his anger at me. I was caught by such surprise, and such force, that I fell to my knees, clutching my fiery cheek.

Pain shot up through my legs as I fell on the hard tiled floor, and I realized it was the same as last time. If Peter was the one he wanted to hurt, I was the one he was going to target.

And indeed, as I held my red, burning cheek, Peter shouted. "No! No, stop, stop hurting her!"

He threw himself in front of me, and I thought his father was going to stop, like last time, but he didn't. Instead, he threw an arm out and Peter slammed into the cupboards underneath the sink.

Rufus sent an angry heel barreling into my knee, and I doubled over with the loud popping sound it gave. I rolled over in distress, my vision blurry, barely making out that Peter had taken the next blow for me.

"Father, don't do this!" he yelled in protest. "She's done nothing to you. Remember, it's *me*! It's me who killed mum! It's me who ruined your life!"

The broken man snarled, standing over me, and looked to his son. "That's not going to work again, Edmund."

Peter rose shakily, defeated, buying me time as I tried desperately to stand. But before I was even halfway up, a fist slammed into my jaw.

I gasped for breath, with no victory, the wind being knocked out of me. Finally, I found it, and then reached for my aching jaw. My fingertips barely brushed it, but even that hurt like nothing before.

A second later, I realized that Peter was once again on the ground, and his father was getting ready for my fourth hit.

Meanwhile, my mother was screaming. "Get up, you foolish boy, and save my daughter!"

Both boys ignored her.

I ducked as Peter's father reached for my hair, but Peter, with surprising strength and resilience that I so deeply admired, threw himself on top of me once again.

Gently, of course.

"NO!" he cried. "Father, you asked why I couldn't forgive you. This is why! Because you are still the same person that beat his five-year-old son, you're still the same person that ruined a little boy's childhood - all because what, a drink?! The same person that didn't find all of that, not even *that*, enough! How many lives do you have to go through before you'll find yours finally complete?! YOU WILL NEVER CHANGE!"

He was now sobbing, and I would have been too, if I had enough strength left. But the thing is, I needed to find that strength. With how Peter acted, giving his life to save me, protecting me over all else.

I have never loved or admired someone so much. I didn't know what I would do without him. I wouldn't have anything without him. I wouldn't *be* anyone without him.

The madman was now talking in a quiet, deadly voice. "Well, you know what? I think you are the one who needs to change. You are the one who needs to learn when it is right to stop. You need to stop now, boy, you need to *stop*. You need to give up. Because no matter how hard you try, you will never, *never* beat me. So work on living with it."

"You're right. I don't give up. You know why?"

Silence.

"Because I have found someone worth fighting for, and right now, that is enough for me."

And then he lunged towards his father, and they met, but I didn't really see what happened, because just then my mother was dragging me up on my feet.

"What - what are you-" I gasped in confusion.

"Come on," she said hurriedly. I got up, addled, and stumbled after her for a second.

And then it clicked. "Wait, no!" I said, tugging back on her firm grip. My voice sounded distant, and every movement hurt my jaw terribly.

"We can't just leave them, Mum!" I looked at her desperately, knowing I wouldn't be strong enough to fight back and go save Peter.

But he had tried. He had still tried, so I would too.

Just as my mother told me firmly that we *were* going to leave them, and that, like usual, I would understand when I'm older, someone slammed into her, and she fell backward onto the corner of the counter. Her lips widened for a second, her grip faltered, and then her eyes rolled back into her selfish, greedy head, and she slumped forward.

At first, I thought it was Peter that had fallen into her, and fear for him washed over me.

But then Peter was behind me, pulling me out the door, and I realized it was his father.

Unfortunately, Rufus was already getting up, unlike my mother, and I knew that both of us, crippled and tired and bloody, weren't going to make it far.

But both of us agreed that we still had to try. We had to.

We ran like the wind, flying down streets, past houses, through alleyways. We ran and ran, panting and tripping and stumbling, and still, not giving up. Because we were going to make it.

Even though we were the hurt ones, I could hear Rufus's ragged breath behind us growing more and more distant. Finally, I couldn't hear it at all.

Peter had the same idea.

"I think we lost him," he gasped, looking for the ghost behind us, but seeing no one.

"Yes," I agreed, and we stumbled into a dark alley between two townhouses, knowing that hiding would be the safest for now.

We sat, catching our breath for a few moments, before Peter stood up again.

"Okay," he said. "We should keep going. We could catch a train, and go back to the forest, and-"

"No," I pleaded, searching his eyes hopelessly. He looked at me in surprise.

"No? Why, what's wrong?"

I sighed. "I'm just sick of running. Please, I'm exhausted. We can go soon, just... let's just stay here for a little longer. It's not like we are going to miss anything. Plus, how would your father even find us-" I cut myself off, knowing that staying a few more minutes might actually mean discovery or not.

But nevertheless, Peter nodded. "Okay," he whispered.

We stayed there, close together, for a long, quiet moment. And then Peter tucked a stray dirty blonde strand behind my ear, and slipped his hand through my clean, neat bed of hair, ruffling it.

I didn't mind.

My eyes flickered to his lips, without meaning too, but he seemed to be thinking the same thing. We stood still for a second, and then our lips met.

And it was incredible. There was more passion in that one kiss than ever before, and after all we had been through that day, it only seemed right.

His lips locked right into mine, perfectly, and his hand slipped around my waist, pulling me closer. I buried one hand in his hair, drawing him nearer to me. The other hand I wrapped around his back, feeling my way gently down his spine, feeling and knowing his strength, no matter all things that had weighed him down. He was the strongest person I knew, and every time a second passed by, he only felt stronger. A second later, our quiet moment was done, and he was lifting me off my feet. A laugh, a true laugh, the first one in a while, bubbled in my throat, and I let it out. His breath felt warm against my raw cheeks, and I barely had time to sigh my happiness before our lips were meeting again. But this time the kiss felt different. As if we were back in the woods, not down a dark alleyway, and he was simply spinning and twirling me around. This time I grabbed the front of his shirt, pulling him even closer. After all the time we had lost together, I wanted to more. I needed more.

A bit later, we were breaking apart, my hands still resting gently on his chest, his hands still sturdy around my waist. Our foreheads gently touched, our breath felt warm as they intermixed. And I totally understood why I didn't want to continue; we both understood. We had spent so much time running away, not enough just being together. But now we were together.

And suddenly, I felt free. I felt like I was finally the bird that flew away.

"Peter," I breathed, so happy that I was able to brave my fear of heights.

"Wendy," he whispered back, his breath tickling my lips.

"I'm going to tell you something I think is long overdue." I smiled, and he did too.

"And what would that be?" he asked innocently. I opened my mouth, feeling that these words would finally free me, when his face fell.

"What?" I asked, confused by the sudden change. "Wh-"

But I was too late. He didn't even have time to call out my name; instead, he instinctively threw me to the ground, leaping in front of me. I rolled to my side, confused and in a daze, and picked myself up, wiping dirt from my eyes.

Peter's father was before me, holding his son up by the shoulder in one hand, and in the other a... it took me too long to register the image. A large, crimson stained kitchen knife had just been forced through his chest. Flustered and in a rage, his father tore it back out, tossing the weapon aside with tears of confusement blurring his vision. "I-I'm sorry," he mumbled in an instant, his voice cracked with age and pain.

He lowered the boy to the ground as I screamed, running to his side in an instant, the seconds passing as years. I cradled his head in my lap, frozen with the bewilderment of what had just happened. A second later, my hands were desperately trying to stop the waterfall of blood that was pooling from his shirt.

"No, no, no, no, no! Make it stop, Peter! Make it stop!" Tears of mine met with his blood, creating a terrible stream. "Peter, why would you do that?! Wh-why would you... why would you..." I started to feel the warmth leaving his fingertips as I clung to them, in desperate need for reassurance.

"Wendy," he whispered.

"Oh, oh Peter!" I cried. "It's okay, you are going to be okay." I threw my head up to face his father, who was staring back, in the shock of what he had just done. "THIS IS WHY HE COULD NEVER FORGIVE YOU!" I screamed, spitting out my words in rage. "ALL YOU'LL EVER DO IS HURT!" I wanted to yell more as the man stumbled into the darkness, but Peter squeezed my hand with a gasping breath and I knew I couldn't leave him be. He started shaking, his eyes glossing over with pain, but when he looked up at me, he was smiling.

"I never imagined it so beautiful," he said, his voice choked with hurt.

"What?" I breathed, rocking him closer to me.

"Dying for someone you love so much."

I paused for a second, his words sinking in. "No, Peter," I said. "NO! No, you're not dying... I - oh Peter, I never even got to tell you that I... love you." I sniffed. "I love you, Peter. So very, *very* much."

He gave a weak smile. "I know, Wendy. I knew it all along."

I felt his grip loosen on my hands, the light leaving his eyes, his whole body growing cold. Panic aroused within me. Panic that I didn't have enough time. "Stop! Stop, don't leave me!" But he was, he was leaving me.

"Ever, you gave me everything I ever wanted." I choked down sobs as he grew limp in my arms, his eyes closing with a last ragged breath. "The stars... look at how they dance."

I did. I breathed in their beauty, blurred from tears.

The Neverland star grew brighter with his presence, and I knew he was finally home.

"Oh, Peter," I whispered, and then laid my head down on his still shoulder, letting the world turn to nothing. Because without him, I was nothing.

"I love you."

Chapter Thirty Five

Will

The fire danced and grew, flickering brighter with a certain joy. Elli had healed. And not only that, but he was dancing and hollering with all the other boys, like a fearsome warrior whom death could not claim, no matter how hard he tried. I could tell he was still hurting, and by his tired eyes that he still longed for sleep, but it had only been a little over a week of treatment. We still had more nights of it to come.

Regardless, he had healed.

There were so many laughs, smiles, shouts and praises that night. Peter and Ever were sure to come home to a healthy, happy group of lost boys. "Alright everyone!" I yelled, grabbing *Peter & Wendy* and preparing to read. I opened the text to the bookmarked page; we were at the end of the story.

"'She is my mother,' Peter explained; and Jane descended and stood by his side, with the look on her face that he liked to see on ladies when they gazed at him.

'He does so need a mother,' Jane said.

'Yes, I know,' Wendy admitted rather forlornly; 'no one knows it so well as I.'

'Good-bye,' said Peter to Wendy"-

And all of the sudden I could read no further. The boys looked to me in distress, but it didn't matter. For this cold feeling had washed over me, covering me in a terrifying sorrow and taking all the other joys away. I trembled, tears wanting to coat my dry eyes as I shook, suddenly understanding why I felt this way.

I didn't know how, but somehow I knew.

Peter wasn't coming back.

My hands went numb, and without my control, the delicate book slipped from my fingers and fell, all too soon, into the burning flames. And as the fire licked the pages to ash, I felt all of its hope and promise leave the air.

For our beloved Peter was gone.

Acknowledgements

This book has been an amazing journey for the both of us, and we cannot even begin to express the beauty and inspiration it has revealed in the past couple of months. There have been countless people that have helped to make this fairytale come true, and we would like to thank some of those who have especially touched our hearts.

Above all, from the stars He created to the hands He made to write, the Lord has set so many inspiring people, places, and experiences before us to which we owe this book, and we cannot thank Him enough for that. Because He loved us, we can now love others and are able to share out our works in glorifying him.

We would also like to thank our family and friends, who have been so encouraging and optimistic. Our friends, who have supported and motivated us since the very start to the very end of this book; who were all eager to be the first ones to read it.

We would like to give a shout out to all teachers, for the prodigious help you give, and especially to Mrs. Farrance, who set us on the path that led to this story being published. Mrs. Farrance, you have touched so many lives in incredible ways, and we cannot thank you enough for the love that you pour into your students.

And to our families, who have always been there for us, writing or not, and have inspired us profoundly to write this book. All these people gave us constant reminders that we can be authors, no matter the age. How undeserving and immensely grateful we are for you all! And, we could never forget, our first readers: Jackson Ormond, Lilly Benfante and Samantha Fallone who gave us amazing and constructive feedback... thank you! For all of you were some of the most helpful people - our editors in disguise! All of you, friends and family, thank you, you who helped to spread that little bit of pixie dust the book needed to soar.

aLastly, we owe this to you dear readers, who have taken a little leap of faith and made our dreams of becoming authors so much closer. We hope that this is proof enough that age doesn't matter. Because if you want something that badly, no matter who you are, where you come from, no matter how afraid, how terrified you are at making that jump, you need to do it. Time won't wait for you, it will only slip away.

Kathryn Rider & Emerson Ormond